BUFFALO RUN

Bryce grabbed at the sweat-matted hair, twisting his face up. Then his gun slashed down in short chopping blows and Stephen's nose flattened, spurting blood. His scream was choked off as Bryce's gun smashed into his teeth. Bryce shoved the battered, bloody face into the dirt and stood up.

He had put one killer out of commission. But another one waited for him somewhere in the night . . .

VIOLENT MAVERICK

He breathed and shut his eyes against the orange-red glow of the branding iron. Boudry's big hands ripped off his shirt. Two of the outlaws held him down while Boudry pulled the red-burning iron from the fire.

"Talk!" Boudry roared.

He clamped his lips shut, and the sizzling iron arched down and bit into the skin of his chest.

"*Talk!*" Boudry shouted again. And when there was no answer, the iron plunged again into tender flesh.

And again. . . .

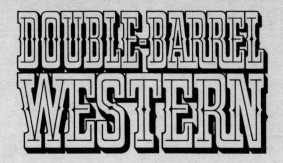

BUFFALO RUN
and
VIOLENT MAVERICK

WALT COBURN

LEISURE BOOKS ▬ NEW YORK CITY

A LEISURE BOOK

July 1989

Published by

Dorchester Publishing Co., Inc.
276 Fifth Avenue
New York, NY 10001

Printed in the United States of America.

BUFFALO RUN

CHAPTER ONE

Bryce Bradford had ridden a long way. He was seeing the little cow town of Buffalo Run, Montana, for the first time after a heavy rain when the clouds had cleared and the sky was a sapphire blue and the muddy ground steaming.

The hitchracks along the street were lined with saddled horses and teams hitched to buckboards or wagons. Most of the buildings were saloons, except for a trading store, an assay office and a two-storied hotel. There was a large warehouse at the end of the street.

Bryce had taken off his fringed chaps and they hung from his saddle-horn in front of his long legs. His California pants were new, with an Indian-tanned white buckskin seat sewn into the heavy wool. He wore a six-shooter in a holster tied to his thigh. He was clean-shaven, his features clear and strong. His hair was heavy and black.

As he sat his horse deciding whether to dismount or take his horse to the feed barn and corrals at the edge of town, he heard a woman's voice cry out, in anger rather than fear. Bryce spurred his horse towards the boardwalk when he saw the girl struggling to free herself from the manhandling of a flashily dressed man whom Bryce spotted for a gambler. He was trying to drag the protesting girl into the El Dorado Saloon.

Bryce quit his saddle with a quick, easy swing. He

jerked the man around by his coat collar, then landed a hard, open-handed slap to the face.

The man jerked free. His hand slid under his coat and came out with a snub-barrelled gun, the type carried by gamblers and known as a belly-gun.

Bryce's six-shooter was in his hand with an unbroken movement, spewing a streak of flame. The gambler's gun roared but the shot went wild as his knees buckled and he crumpled in a heap.

Bryce picked the girl up and swung her into the saddle, then vaulted up behind her, spurring his horse to a run. 'Whichaway, ma'am?' he asked.

'Past the barn, then turn right. You killed him, didn't you?'

'I didn't shoot to miss, ma'am.' Bryce's voice was tense, unsteady. The girl's thick copper-colored hair was in his face and when she turned her head he saw that her grey eyes were dark with fear and her tanned cheeks pale.

They were headed across a strip of land covered with tall buffalo grass, following a trail that led to a sod-roofed log cabin. As they approached, a gaunt man in a white shirt and baggy trousers came out. His mop of iron-grey hair was untidy and he was swaying a little unsteadily.

'Well, well, daughter, who is this gallant blade? Judge Plato Morgan welcomes you, sir. . . .'

'Please, father! We're . . . he's in trouble . . . he told me his name was Bryce Bradford, a stranger in town. He just shot Charlie Decker, the gambler!'

'In that case, my hospitality increases a hundredfold. My legal advice is at your service, sir.'

Bryce slid to the ground and lifted the girl down. Her smile was strained. Obviously her father was a little drunk. Her sunbonnet hung from her throat and the top of her head came below the level of Bryce's shoulder, so that she had to tilt her face up to look at him.

6

There was a strange fear, almost loathing, in her eyes as she backed away from him. Her hands were clenched into small fists as she spoke, 'You just killed a man. Take my advice and leave Buffalo Run right now. And never come back!'

Her face was drained of color, her eyes glazed with horror. It was as if she were accusing herself of having taken part in the killing. She kept staring at him as if he were a vicious animal that killed wantonly.

Bryce felt the slow anger and resentment chilling his insides. Instead of thanking him, this girl was blaming him for shooting a man in self-defense, accusing him of rank murder. She had gotten him into it and now she wanted him to run off like a coyote.

He had just killed a man, just missed sudden death by inches. He had undone all his careful planning to lose himself and his identity in Montana. He was in a tight and there was no chance to run, even if he wanted to. Buffalo Run was a prairie town. For miles in every direction the country was flat, with rolling hills and distant high benchlands. The nearest rough country that would afford a hideout were the distant blue Highwood Mountains and the badlands along the Missouri river, a long hard day's ride on a fresh horse.

The girl's father said he'd bring a jug and some glasses from the cabin, but Bryce didn't wait for him to come out again. He stepped up on his horse and rode away without a backward glance.

The sun had gone down and the shadows of dusk were covering the prairie, grey and threatening as the danger that lay in wait for him at Buffalo Run.

As he approached the town he could tell that a posse was being organized. Men on horseback were waiting in front of the El Dorado where the gambler still lay sprawled on the boardwalk where he had died.

7

Bryce Bradford was a stranger in a strange land. So far as he knew he hadn't a single acquaintance or friend to take his part.

A dozen or more men had been eye witness to the killing in self-defense. They had seen the whole play from start to finish. Bryce kept telling himself to bolster his courage, but the chill of dread was pinching his belly when he rode at a walk up the main street, noticing that the men on horseback sat their saddles with hands on their guns and that three men stood apart from the milling crowd to block his approach.

Bryce halted in front of them. A hush had fallen over the crowd, a tense, dangerous silence. Bryce's two hands rested on the saddle-horn and he met their cold scrutiny with steady eyes. The tall, black clad man, Bryce thought, would be the one most likely to make a gun play so he kept his eyes on him, ready to pull his gun and play it out to a swift deadly finish. He tried not to let them see that he was quivering inside as they measured him with cold appraisal.

'Get off your horse, Stranger,' the tall dangerous looking one said.

Bryce dismounted. Someone took his horse.

Bryce followed the three men into the saloon and down a narrow hallway to a room that was perhaps fifteen-feet square, furnished with a large round green-covered cardtable and half a dozen heavy chairs. A bartender wearing a soiled white apron followed them in with a whisky bottle and glasses which he set on the table, then departed.

One of the men closed and bolted the door. They all sat down.

Bryce could hear the clumping of boots in the hall and figured the room must be guarded. The one window was painted with layers of blackish green to make it opaque.

The only light was a swinging lamp over the card-table.

Bryce told them his name when they asked him. The tall black-clad man identified himself and his two companions, saying, 'I'm Jack Quensel. I own the El Dorado Saloon. Tim Fogarty here owns some freight outfits and operates the Wells Fargo Express from Buffalo Run to Fort Benton. Pete Kaster is a mining and cattle man.'

The whisky bottle was passed but Bryce noticed that Quensel did not take a drink. He had a sallow face that did not change expression and a drooping black moustache concealed the barest smile of contempt for his two companions. His opaque black eyes kept sizing Bryce up.

Tim Fogarty was a large man, all hard muscle and big bone. His fiery red hair was tossed around his roughly hewn face, his green eyes blazed. Bryce figured he'd be a hard man to whip in a fight.

Pete Kaster was short and barrel chested, with bowed legs. He wore the rough clothes of a cowman and his greying black hair and beard needed trimming. Bryce didn't like what he saw in the man.

It was Jack Quensel who said, 'As a committee of three representing the Stranglers of Buffalo Run, we find you guilty of the murder of Charlie Decker. Witnesses have been questioned who agree that you first struck Decker, then when he drew his gun, you shot him. Have you anything to say for yourself, Bryce Bradford?'

But before Bryce could answer in his own defense, the raised voice of Judge Plato Morgan could be heard out in the hall. He was demanding entrance.

'Let the old rascal in', chuckled Tim Fogarty. 'I'll get him to recite "Osler Joe" or the one about Casey at the Bat. Get him likkered and he's better'n your stage shows, Quensel.'

Before Quensel could offer protest, Pete Kaster had pulled back the bolt and opened the door.

9

Judge Morgan had on a black coat, a black Confederate army hat and a hastily tied black string tie. He carried a gold-headed ebony cane like a sabre.

He strode in, his gait steadier than it had been at the cabin. Pete Kaster closed and bolted the door.

'Drink, Judge?' suggested Tim Fogarty.

The judge declined. He said, 'I am here to demand justice for this young man. His was an honorable deed in defense of my daughter's honor. He shot that blackleg tinhorn only after Decker pulled his gun first.'

'Bryce Bradford has just been tried by a committee of three representing the Stranglers', Quensel spoke up quickly. 'We found him guilty!'

'Have a drink, Judge,' interrupted Tim Fogarty, 'then give us "The Face on the Bar-room Floor"!'

'Hah! You mock a man who stands before you in the name of justice. You, Fogarty, a foul tongued bull-whacker, and your illiterate partner, Pete Kaster, who jumps the mining claims of honest prospectors, and you, Quensel, a man who fills his coffers with the ill-gotten gains derived from this den of iniquity.

'Who among you is fit to condemn this man who within the hour has rid the earth of as unmitigated a villain as ever tainted the clear air with foul breath?

'I demand that my client be set free!' Judge Plato Morgan paused, out of breath.

'In that case,' Jack Quensel's flat voice fell across the last echoes of Morgan's speech, 'I think the case should be dismissed.'

'Hah! By God. . . . !'

'Just one minute Morgan', said Quensel. 'Bryce Bradford will not be allowed to leave town until his case is dismissed by a two-thirds vote of the Stranglers, at their next meeting.'

Jack Quensel's cold black eyes were fixed on Bryce

10

now. He said, 'Give us your word that you'll not try to leave town, it won't be necessary to lock you up, Bradford.'

'I give you my word', Bryce answered quickly.

'Where did you come from, Bradford?' Quensel shot the question.

'My past history is my own business.' Bryce was suddenly on guard.

'Right as hell!' chuckled Tim Fogarty. He filled a glass and shoved it into the judge's hand. 'A fine speech, Judge,' he said, 'even if you did call us names. Now if you'll give us that one about Lasca, we'll call 'er a day.'

Judge Morgan twirled his glass of whisky and smiled. It was good whisky.

'To Bryce Bradford,' he bowed stiffly, 'Gentlemen!' He swallowed his drink thirstily. Before he could set down the empty glass, Fogarty had it filled again.

Judge Plato Morgan was reciting poems at the long well-patronized bar when Bryce went out through the swinging half doors.

A cowpuncher's first thought concerns the welfare of the horse that packs him. Bryce headed for the feed and livery barn at the end of the street. Blobs of yellow light from the row of saloons fell across the plank sidewalk and reflected on the puddles of muddy water on the wide, wheel-rutted deserted street.

A cold white half moon rode through the stars. The men were all inside the saloons, gathered for the most part at the El Dorado where a sort of wake for the dead gambler and part owner of the place was in progress.

The clump of Bryce's boot-heels made a mocking echo in his ears. Then he stepped off the sidewalk into the sticky gumbo. He stopped just inside the lantern lit barn to scrape the mud from his boots with a manure-fork.

He found his horse in a stall, the manger filled with

11

fresh wild hay cut on the prairie. He began reading the
brand on each horse in the barn. He paused at a double
stall that held a bay and a sorrel, and his jaw muscles
tightened as he read the identical brands on the left thigh
of each saddle-horse. His hand instinctively dropped to
the butt of his gun and he looked around almost furtively.

He wondered how many men in Montana knew that
Square and Compass brand that belonged down in Utah.
It branded some of the world's finest horses, bred to
mount that grim and secret band of men known as the
Avenging Angels of the Mormon Church.

The door of the saddle and harness room was kicked
open. The grizzled barnman came limping out on saddle-
warped rheumatic legs. Bryce stepped out from between
the two Square and Compass horses. He asked the
barnman who owned the two mounts.

'One was a big rawboned feller with grey hair and a
spade beard,' the barnman told him as he hooked up his
suspenders. 'The younger one was the spittin' image of his
old man except that he was cross-eyed. They paid two
weeks' feed bill in advance. Bought two of the best
grain fed saddle-horses Tim Fogarty had and pulled out.
That was a week ago.'

'They say what fetched them to Buffalo Run?'

'Neither one of 'em said a word. When the spade beard
feller looked at you, you plumb forgot whatever it was you
were going to ask him. If ever I seen a pair of killers, and
I've seen plenty tough men in my day, that old man and
his son had the brand on their hides.'

The old man's puckered eyes squinted. He took a
gnawed plug of tobacco from his pocket and bit off a
piece, tonguing it into his cheek before he spoke. 'If you
need a fresh horse, son, Old Dad Jones will go back to bed
and know nothin' if one of them Square and Compass
geldings is missin'.'

12

Bryce Bradford shook his head and grinned his thanks. 'I have to stand a Strangler trial for the murder of Charlie Decker. Judge Morgan is my lawyer. I gave Quensel my word not to leave Buffalo Run.'

'Listen, son,' Dad Jones lowered his voice in a confidential whisper, 'Quensel is the law here. A group of his followers known as the Stranglers are a disgrace to the Montana Vigilantes such as you'll find at Virginia City and Fort Benton. They're a pack of murderers.'

'What about Judge Plato Morgan?' Bryce inquired.

'The Judge likes his likker along with a little game of cards. He likes to spout poems. He had considerable money when he stopped overnight here about a year ago; got drunk and gambled it all away. Quensel gave him the position of Justice of the Peace. The job turned out to be judge of a kangaroo court.'

'He lives with his proud daughter Virginia in a sod roofed log cabin. Sometimes they don't have enough to eat.' Dad Jones spat tobacco juice on the dirt floor.

'I'll be around about then', Dad Jones told him. 'I ain't so old but what I can still handle that ol' hawglaig I got in my warsack.'

'No need in you getting messed up in a gun ruckus, Dad.'

The old man chuckled. 'That Virginia Morgan is worth fightin' for.'

'She backs away from me like I had smallpox,' Bryce said.

'Like as not she never saw a man shot down. You can't blame her for shyin' off from a man she's just watched kill another man. Give her time to get over the shock. One of these days she'll realize you killed Decker on her account and she'll come runnin' to thank you.'

'One of these days I won't be here, Dad. If my luck holds out I'll be driftin' yonderly. There's no place for a

13

girl like Virginia Morgan along the trail I'll be travellin'.'

'On account of those two Square and Compass killers?'

'That's right, Dad,' Bryce answered, his heavy brows pulled into a thoughtful scowl. 'I better show back at the El Dorado before they send for me.'

'Watch your step, son. I'll be around if I'm needed.'

CHAPTER TWO

Jack Quensel, Big Tim Fogarty and Pete Kaster were holding a meeting behind a bolted, guarded door.

'He's our man,' said Quensel. 'Bryce Bradford is made to order for the job.'

'What makes you think he'll string along with us?' growled Fogarty.

'We'll vote him in as sheriff and we'll elect that old rum-soaked Plato Morgan as judge. Buffalo Run will have law and order.'

'We've been getting along so far,' protested Pete Kaster, 'without much trouble. What's the sense of electing a sheriff and a judge?'

'We've gotten along so far,' said Quensel flatly, 'by wiping out any man that looked like he might give us trouble. If you think we're not skating on thin ice, just study the letter that would have gone to the Wells Fargo Express headquarters at Fort Benton if Decker hadn't shot that man I spotted for a detective yesterday.

'I got the letter out of Decker's pocket. It's got his blood on it. Decker, unless I'm badly mistaken, was holding it with some idea of double-crossing us.' Quensel reached into his pocket and produced the letter. 'I'll read it aloud,' he told them. 'Listen carefully.'

To the Wells Fargo Agent, Fort Benton, Montana
Confidential.

My investigation here has proven beyond all doubt that the frequent holding up of the stage and robbing the mail and Wells Fargo Express shipments of gold, etc., has been the work of one man. His name is Charlie Decker. Decker is simply a tool in the hands of more dangerous men who have hired him to do the actual road-agent work. The stage driver is in the employ of Big Tim Fogarty and is paid to keep his mouth shut. The shotgun messengers you have hired were either intimidated or bought off by Fogarty, Jack Quensel and Peter Kaster. One or two who couldn't be bribed or scared off were murdered.

Fogarty, Quensel and Kaster are the organizers of the Stranglers here at Buffalo Run. Even Decker is a member of that secret organization supposed to uphold law and order. Few, if any, of the Stranglers are aware that they are being hoodwinked by the three leaders. When any man begins to suspect the truth, that man is murdered. I will be fortunate if I am allowed to leave here alive. Decker suspects me. He has tried to get me drunk in order to loosen my tongue. He has made me a secret proposition to double-cross Quensel, Fogarty and Kaster. I am leading him on cautiously, in hopes of obtaining definite proof we need.

This letter is to keep you informed as to my activities. It may be my own death warrant I am writing. In case I am killed, these three men will have hired Decker to do the actual job.

I will mail this at the first opportunity or send it by some messenger I can trust. Though it is hard to find a man in Buffalo Run. . . .

'The letter,' smiled Quensel, 'was never finished. Decker walked into the detective's room and shot him. He

16

didn't hand over the letter for some reason. I think he had some plan to sell us down the river. Bryce Bradford did us one hell of a big favor when he killed Decker.'

Quensel folded the letter and put it in his inside coat pocket. The face of each man showed that they were badly disturbed.

'So,' Quensel said, his eyes watching his two companions closely, 'we need to change tactics. What that long-nosed detective learned before I paid Decker five hundred dollars to rub him out, other men must suspect. We'll be strung up by our own Stranglers unless we act right now. And our surest, safest bet is to do an about face.

'A dozen or more men saw Bryce Bradford kill Decker. Most of them distrusted Decker. They saw the stranger play the big hero. Nominate him for sheriff and they'll yell three cheers till they're hoarse as a flock of crows. Sheriff Bryce Bradford is a cinch bet.'

'Supposin' he's honest?' Fogarty's red brows knit in a scowl. 'He don't look easy to handle, Quensel.'

'I've got an ace in the hole, my friend. I'm keeping it buried till I need to play it. I don't back losers.'

'Bryce Bradford,' growled Pete Kaster, 'is as safe as a black powder keg next to a red-hot stove. If we got to have a sheriff here at Buffalo Run, let's put in a man we can handle.'

'And be in no better fix than we are now. We've got to put in a man who can't be bought or scared off. Buffalo Run is going to have an honest sheriff. When the time comes, I'll handle Bradford. I'm calling a meeting of the Stranglers tonight at midnight.'

'All right, Quensel,' agreed Fogarty reluctantly. 'But what about this electing Morgan for judge? Ain't he cussed the three of us out? For all his drunken poetry spoutin', that old coot has more fire an' brimstone in him than a camp meetin' preacher. If ever we get up before

17

him, he'll have us swingin' from a cottonwood limb!'

'Sure,' smiled Quensel, 'Morgan is going to take his job seriously but don't forget that he's the biggest drunkard in Buffalo Run. He gambled away every dollar he had when he came a year ago. He's a bar-room bum. He and his daughter are practically living on charity right now. She was on her way to keep an appointment with me regarding a job when Decker made that clumsy play that sent him to hell. I'll handle the Judge and his daughter, gentlemen. I may even marry the girl.'

Tim Fogarty's big hairy hand clenched, showing a gold ring mounted with the biggest diamond in Montana, his bloodshot eyes glared at the suave, handsome gambler. He said, 'Stick to your honkeytonk wenches, Quensel. Bother Virginia Morgan and I'll twist your head off your neck.'

'Since when, my bullwhacker friend, did you become a champion of womanhood? You, with a squaw on every reservation between Fort Apache, Arizona, and the Flathead. The last man who wanted to wrestle, Fogarty, had his guts ripped open before he got a strangle hold.' Quensel's upper lip lifted like an animal's showing his white teeth.

'Quit it, you two,' growled Pete Kaster. 'This ain't no time to be wranglin' over a female. Let's get down to business.'

'United we stand,' said Quensel. 'Divided we fall. Hang together or we might hang separately. Kaster's right. I'll pass the word that the Stranglers will meet at midnight at Fogarty's warehouse.'

The gambler's hand came from beneath his coat where he carried a pearl handled dagger. He was faster with that weapon than most men were with a gun. He could, with a flip of his hand, hit a card at fifteen paces.

Quensel quit his chair with a smooth, catlike grace and left the room.

18

Bryce Bradford smiled grimly at the thought of being trapped here at Buffalo Run, held prisoner until those two men from Utah returned from a fruitless hunt for him across the Canadian border. The Avenging Angels were thorough in their methods. They were more deadly than any Vigilante gun-toters or the hired killers of Buffalo Run. Men stared at him curiously as he walked into the El Dorado. He saw Judge Plato Morgan at the bar reciting some ballad, with Fogarty and Kaster and a group of half drunken men an appreciative audience. Bryce was not certain whether Big Tim Fogarty really enjoyed hearing the recitations or whether he was baiting the white-maned old judge.

Men moved back from the bar to give him a place, but they were not making any friendly overtures that might displease Jack Quensel.

Bryce turned to find the gambler at his elbow. His hand dropped to his gun. Quensel smiled thinly and shook his head.

'I'm not playing Decker's hand out, Bradford,' Quensel said.

The bar-tender shoved a glass and small bottle of mineral water across the bar. Quensel filled his glass. The men who lined the long bar watched, diverting their attention from Plato Morgan to the owner of the El Dorado.

'Welcome to Buffalo Run, Bradford,' said Jack Quensel. He lifted his glass and drank.

The crowd relaxed. Quensel was accepting the stranger who had killed Decker.

But Bryce was not quite sure of the gambler's sincerity. There was something about Quensel's eyes and the faint twist of his mouth that belied this friendly gesture. Bryce wasn't trusting Jack Quensel for a minute.

He was about to turn and leave the saloon when a woman's throaty voice said in his ear, 'I'd like to shake the hand that held the gun that shot Charlie Decker.'

He was vaguely aware of the sudden hush of voices in the saloon. The eyes of the tall slender girl were almost on a level with his. Amber eyes matched the mass of tawny hair and the golden texture of her skin. There was no trace of face powder or rouge on her cheeks or natural scarlet lips. She wore a golden yellow evening gown, low cut to show the swell of firm rounded breasts. Her faint smile put a strange warmth in her eyes that were shadowed by soot-black fringed eyelashes.

She was by far the most exotically beautiful woman that Bryce had ever looked at. He felt the dull red flush of embarrassment as he tried to look away.

'Women aren't allowed at the bar,' she said, linking her bare arm through his with a meaning pressure. 'The stage show is just starting, we'll watch it together from my box.' Her eyes met Quensel's and slid away. Her throaty laugh had a challenge in it.

Bryce was painfully aware of the hard stares of every man lined up at the bar as she led him away. His feet felt awkward in mud caked boots. He could feel the brush of the girl's long thigh against his.

Her free hand shoved aside the dark red drapes as she ushered him into the last box. Bryce pulled aside the curtain at the front of the box and saw the stage and entire floor below. Then he let the curtain drop.

When he turned around, the girl twisted against him and her lips fastened on his and held with a bruising force. He felt the hard thrust of her breasts as her slim length moved with a sensuous slowness that quickened his pulse. The blood pounded in his throat and temples. His senses reeled. Never before had he felt anything like this intoxication. The musky odor of her hair and body cloyed in his nostrils as the girl clung to him with a primitive, savage fervor.

Bryce was dizzy headed, taut and quivering inside with strange aroused emotions, when her hands pushed him away with provocative slowness. Her pale eyes were filmed over with a thin glaze under lowered eyelids. Her wide red lips were curled back from strong white teeth. Her quick breath was hot, feverish against his face as she pushed him into one of the chairs. Then she straightened up with an unsteady shaky laugh.

Bryce sat tensely in his chair as she twisted the cork of a champagne bottle in a bucket of chopped ice. When the cork popped she filled two glasses and handed one to Bryce.

There was a strange unreality about the whole thing, like a mixed-up dream. The nearness of the beautiful girl, the lithe movements of her sensuous body, the musk of her tawny hair, the husky voice. All of it had a strange power that left him helpless, and because there was an element of danger it added spice to his desire for her.

There was a faint smile on her lips as she stood just beyond his reach.

'It's my job, Bryce Bradford,' she said in a voice vibrant with emotion, 'to soften you up. Get you drunk enough on wine and kisses to loosen your tongue. I'm to find out who Bryce Bradford is. Where he came from.

What brings him to Buffalo Run.'

'Why?' Bryce asked, the words harsh in his tight throat.

'Strangers who are fast with a gun are not welcome here. Your number is up, Bryce.' She reached for the wine bottle and filled her glass and drank slowly.

'Why are you telling me all this?' Bryce asked.

'Since I can remember I've had to fight for an existence. I was tossed with a child's body into a man's world. I learned to fight with a man's weapons and a woman's treachery and deceit. I made my body into a beautiful weapon and used it in my hatred for all men.' Her laugh had an ugly sound as she leaned across the table.

'Here at Buffalo Run I'm known as Quensel's woman. But Nile belongs to no man on earth.' There was a strange mixture of provocative mockery in her smile. She bent over and pulled up the hem of her skirt to show a webbed black silk stocking such as worn by can-can dancers, encasing a beautiful slender leg. There was the smooth ivory length of shapely thigh showing. From a yellow silk garter that held the high stocking in place she took a long thin blade with a pearl handle from the sheath.

'I was going to kill Charlie Decker with this tonight,' she held the knife palmed in her hand, then twisted the blade to catch the lamplight. 'You saved me that trouble when you shot him.' Her lips twisted in a smile that held no warmth. 'Decker used narcotics. One night when he was snowed under I got him to make out and sign a paper that gave me his half-interest in the El Dorado if he should die or get killed. I have the paper safely hidden. Last night Decker tried to get it back with a threat. He pushed me around and I knew he'd kill me if I didn't kill him first.'

She leaned across the table, lowering her voice. 'How would you like to own Jack Quensel's half-interest in the El Dorado? Be my partner in the business?' she asked.

Bryce shook his head, puzzled, the forced grin on his face twisted out of shape.

'I'm a cowpuncher, lady. Not a gambler or saloon man,' he said.

'I'll handle the gambling and the rest of it,' Nile told him. 'I need a man I can trust all the way down the line.'

'You mean a killer?' Bryce said bluntly.

'If it becomes necessary, yes.'

'You better get another man. Gunslingers hire out cheap.'

'I want a man named Bryce Bradford. And I usually get what I go after.'

'You don't mean this man, lady. I'm drifting directly Plato Morgan gets things shaped around to the law and order he wants.'

The thin stem of the wine glass snapped in her fingers. The wine spilled across the table. The glass rolled off and smashed on the floor. Her short laugh was as brittle as the shattered glass.

'Quensel will cut Morgan into the discard when he's out-lived his purpose. His big mouth has declared his own death warrant. And yours. Tomorrow or next week or next month, whenever the time is right Judge Plato Morgan will be dead. Murdered, to put it bluntly. And if you choose to accept that tin badge, you too will be dead. And that will leave Buffalo Run without a man to protect Virginia Morgan against Jack Quensel who aims to get her, even if he has to marry her.

'I know this mudhole of Buffalo Run and every man who hangs out here. Jack Quensel owns the town and runs every damn man who jumps around when he cracks the whip.' Her hand reached out and closed tight over his. 'A pack of mongrels trained to lay down and roll over, sit up and beg for drinks.'

The heavy red drapes at the entrance of the box moved

agitatedly. Bryce's gun was in his hand, his thumb on the hammer when a waiter called out.

'Miss Nile! They're hollerin' for Bryce Bradford downstairs!'

'If that drunken mob wants him, let them come after him,' Nile told the waiter.

'You got it all wrong, Miss Nile. They just voted Bryce Bradford into the sheriff's office and Plato Morgan in as judge. Every man in town has voted them in. Quensel said for me to come up with the news.'

'Tell Quensel that Bryce Bradford got his message,' Nile said.

When the waiter had gone the girl looked at Bryce, her eyes clouded with suspicion.

'Quensel has checked the bet to you, Bryce. But don't forget to remember he has the deal. Every card is marked. Think it over before you buy chips in their game.'

Bryce nodded and shoved his gun back into its holster. 'Looks like it's up to me to play my hand out, regardless,' he said grimly.

'It's on account of Plato Morgan,' Nile said tonelessly as her eyes met his. 'On account of his daughter, the virgin of Buffalo Run.' Her upper lip curled back.

'I reckon that's about the size of it, Nile,' Bryce forced a grin.

'I'm glad you didn't try to lie out of it, Bryce.'

'I'm a hell of a poor liar,' he kept grinning.

'And I'd be lying behind my teeth if I told you I wished you luck with Virginia Morgan.'

Bryce shook his head. 'I told you before that I'm drifting. When I leave Buffalo Run I'm traveling alone.'

'What are you running away from?' The question came abruptly.

'Trouble,' Bryce admitted. 'Gun trouble. Whenever it catches up with me I got to face it alone.' He looked at her gravely. 'There is no place in my life for a woman. That's hard for you to understand, because you're a woman.' Bryce's words sounded inadequate in his own ears.

'On the contrary, Bryce. I know what you're talking about. And I know what you're up against here in Buffalo Run far better than you do, mister man.' Her eyes were cold, calculating.

'I'll lay it on the line. The girl who got you into this dangerous fix couldn't get you out of the mess even if she knew how.' Her lips curled contemptuously. 'You need a diagram, Bryce?'

'No.'

'When are you going to quit running and make a stand, Bryce?'

'Hard to tell, Nile.'

'Buffalo Run could be as good a place as any.' Her eyes held his.

'I was thinking the same thing,' Bryce said. 'The way things are shaping up I'm caught in the broad middle.'

'That's about the size of it, if you're fool enough to let Quensel pin a phony tin law badge on your shirt.' She reached out and gripped his hand. 'I don't know who's on your trail or why, but I can arrange it for your quick getaway between now and daybreak. You can travel alone or take me with you. I can ride and I can take my own part. I know a hideout where we can hole up and nobody can get to us without being shot down.'

Nile was standing close to him now. There was a strange look in her eyes. A reckless, dangerous glint that backed up her every word. There was a set to the line of her wide mouth and she was breathing fast.

Bryce had heard tell of women who led an outlaw life and shared whatever dangers and hardships there were to endure without complaint. Content with a few reckless hours of pleasure that balanced the scales. This girl was offering to share his hunted life, without questioning the why or wherefore or the cause behind it.

No man worthy of the name could discount or ignore the sheer magnetism of her nearness. Somehow Bryce knew that Nile was offering him something that she had never before offered to any man. Her closeness was as heady as strong wine and far more potent and lasting.

Bryce's every nerve was pulled tight as a keyed-up fiddle string as they stood close to each other. Split seconds became eternity, time lost value as they stood close without touching.

Then from below on the stage came the tipsy voice of Judge Plato Morgan. In a maudlin voice he shouted, 'The men who have held this election are clamouring for the presence of Bryce Bradford! Release yourself, Sheriff, from the sinful embrace of that jezebel. Descend and take a man's place among men! Accept the high honour the citizens of Buffalo Run have bestowed upon you!'

Angered beyond all reason Bryce pulled the front curtains apart. His hard cold stare flicked the white-maned judge as he stood in the center of the stage, his handsome face flushed with liquor and the excitement within him. Then Bryce saw Big Tim Fogarty and Pete Kaster standing together, a little apart from the milling drunken crowd. Jack Quensel stood alone at the far end of the bar, a tall glass in his hand. His eyes were fixed on the box above and Bryce felt the triumphant cold enmity of the gambler's pale eyes. A sardonic grin twisted the thin lipped mouth.

Then the swinging half-doors were flung back on their hinges. Virginia Morgan took a quick step inside and stood there for a long moment in the smoke filled lamplight of the El Dorado. She had changed to a somewhat worn and shabby divided skirt made of

26

buckskin, and a silk blouse. Her burnished coppery hair hung down behind her back and her grey eyes were shadowed, her face chalk white. Her tan boots were covered with mud. She held a riding crop gripped in her hand.

When she caught sight of her father, her hurt cry broke across the silence that had fallen over the room at her entrance. She crossed to the stage quickly to stand beside the bewildered man, cold fury and humiliation choking the words in her throat as she trembled in a pent up wrath that could find no outlet.

For once Judge Morgan was at a loss for words. The effects of the whisky quickly soured and died within him as he stood with his daughter in the merciless glare of the footlights, facing a crowd of drunken men and their staring eyes.

'God help us!' The words that came from Virginia Morgan's throat were torn loose from some hidden depth. Then the girl collapsed and lay at her father's feet as motionless as a grey dove shot down by a hunter.

Bryce swung both legs over the edge of the box, hung for a few seconds by his hands then dropped twenty feet to the stage. He had the unconscious girl picked up and in his arms when Nile came down the stairway and motioned him towards the small side door she was holding open.

Bryce moved fast across the stage, the judge at his heels. They followed Nile outside and along a dark alleyway behind the El Dorado, then across a vacant clearing about a hundred yards to a whitewashed log cabin with a white picket fence. Thick morning glory vines climbed wooden trellises on the wide veranda. The yard was planted in flowers of every description. Sweetpea vines grew along the picket fence to make a hedge and the wide plank walk from the gate to the porch was shaded by purple lilac bushes. The windowsills and shutters were painted a soft blue, in contrast to the red brick fireplace

27

chimney. A stone's throw behind the cabin flowed the creek with giant cottonwood trees and thickets of wild rose bushes.

There was a light behind the curtained front windows and as they approached the veranda steps the door opened. A fat squaw in a voluminous calico dress and scrubbed moon face blocked the doorway. The squaw had a formidable look as she stood there, the lamplight behind her and a double-barreled sawed-off shotgun gripped in her hands.

The levered shotgun slowly lowered as she recognized Nile when she spoke. 'Get the bed ready, Rose. I have brought a sick girl who needs our attention.'

The squaw turned and padded back on mocassined feet, putting the gun on a rack in the hall near the door.

'Rose is my guardian angel,' smiled Nile. 'A shotgun chaperone.'

When Bryce had laid the girl on the bed Nile told him to take Judge Morgan into the front room while she and Rose put Virginia to bed.

Books lined the shelves of the front room that was furnished in heavy polished mahogany. A big silver tip grizzly bear rug was on the floor in front of the fireplace. A spinet piano occupied one corner of the room. The heavy silver and cut glass on the sideboard were in good taste, as were the rest of the furnishings throughout the house.

Judge Morgan poured whisky from a decanter into a whisky glass, and held it in his hand, staring into nothingness. When he spoke it was with contrition and a little sadness.

'I have maligned the reputation of a good woman,' he said, a film of unshed tears in his eyes. 'I've befouled the air with maudlin mouthings in the presence of a motley gathering of drunken companions. A spendthrift of tongue. Let shame lower my head to receive the heaping

28

coals, red from the fires of hell.' The judge mopped the moisture of mingled sweat and tears from his face with a silk handkerchief.

Bryce knew that in spite of his flowery speech, the man was wholly sincere in his self-condemnation.

Nile came into the room. She had changed to a house dress of bleached linen that brought out the golden color of her skin and eyes.

'Your daughter is running a high fever, Mr. Morgan,' she told the judge. 'I have sent an Indian boy to Fort Benton with an urgent note to the doctor. Until he gets here Rose and I will do the best we can.' She looked at the judge with troubled eyes and asked, 'How long has it been since Virginia has had a decent meal?'

A dark flush came into the judge's face. His hands went out in a flat gesture. 'Our credit is no longer good at the store. The larder is bare. Quensel offered to renew our credit but my daughter refused his charity. Would be to God we had never left the State of Virginia,' he spoke fervently, the bitterness of regret in his voice.

Nile forestalled any speech that might be forthcoming by crossing the room with a lithe stride to put a drink in the judge's reluctant eager hand.

'Drink it down,' she said gently. 'There's times when a man needs a drink. More than he needs absolution for his past sins.'

She poured pale sherry from the other decanter into a glass for herself. She quirked an eyebrow at Bryce. 'That goes for you, too,' she said with a smile.

Bryce poured about two fingers of whisky into a glass and held it until Nile lifted her glass and said, 'Let me be the first to congratulate both of you when you take your oath of office.'

Bryce saw the challenge in her eyes. It was both a challenge and a promise of her support and something else

29

beyond his comprehension. With it came a strange clarity of thought and final decision. It showed in his eyes and every line that etched his face as he drank.

Judge Morgan's futile words were choked down with the emotion that rendered him voiceless.

Nile took him by the arm and led him to the bedroom where his daughter lay propped up on pillows drinking the strong beef broth Rose was feeding her.

A dozen wax candles in a tall heavy silver candelabra lighted the table with its white linen and polished silver and cut glass as they sat down to dinner.

The judge carved the roast beef. Mashed potatoes, sourdough biscuits, corn on the cob and greens fresh from the garden were on the table. Home-made butter and thick cream and strong black coffee, with strawberry shortcake for dessert.

It was the finest meal Bryce Bradford had ever sat down to and he said so. It was an hour until midnight by the high old-fashioned clock that chimed the half-hour and hour. Nile was a gracious hostess in every way.

No mention was made of the danger that the hour of midnight might bring. The table conversation had the tang of the wine that was served with the meal. The judge's anecdotes matched Nile's gay banter. Even Bryce had shaken off the burden of dread. There was a recklessness to his grin and it showed in the glint of his eyes.

When the hands of the big clock pointed a quarter of an hour before midnight it was time for the men to depart.

The judge tiptoed into the bedroom to take a last look at his daughter. Nile and Bryce were in the shadowed way in an awkward silence as they stood apart like strangers. Then Bryce reached out and pulled her into his arms and their lips met and clung for a long time.

When they heard Judge Morgan coming they pulled apart. Bryce took his cartridge belt and holstered six-shooter from the hall rack. The judge's voice choked with emotion as he gripped Nile's hand and thanked her warmly for all she had done.

When they were outside the white picket gate and plodding across the moonlit stretch of drying ground, Bryce halted, his hand on his gun. He had caught sight of two horsebackers skylighted on the high bluff that gave the town of Buffalo its name. There was something familiar about the pair of night riders, the way they sat their horses as they rode the skyline. As remembrance came, his lips spread in a flat grin. The hard, brooding look came back into his eyes as his grip on his gun tightened.

They were the Avenging Angels who had been hounding his trail north, from the badlands of Bryce Canyon in Utah. As he watched them out of sight a cold chill wired down his spine. He stood for a minute in mud that was ankle deep before he took his hand from his gun.

'What's wrong?' The judge spoke in a whisper.

Bryce shrugged off the dread fear and shoved the Colt back into its holster. 'Some horsebackers rode across my grave,' he said with a forced grin as he walked on towards the lights of Buffalo Run ahead of the older man.

A crowd of men lined the plank walks. As the hour of midnight approached they had come out from the dozen saloons to await the coming of Judge Morgan and Bryce Bradford.

The El Dorado was in total darkness. Quensel had closed the saloon until after the funeral of Charlie Decker.

Bryce sensed the tension that held the men gripped in a grim hand as he and the judge walked down the middle of the street toward Tim Fogarty's warehouse at the end of town as the midnight hour approached.

Those same men who had so readily shouted their unanimous vote for Judge Morgan and Bryce Bradford, had been outwitted, outmaneuvered. Even as they toasted

31

an overwhelming victory in crowded bars, the Stranglers, bound by secret oath, had, one by one, come into the warehouse by way of a back door. Now they were barricaded behind locked doors and shuttered windows, heavily armed and masked.

It was only when the two men neared the warehouse door that they found their way blocked by the crowd that now milled the street. Bryce recognized old Dad Jones, the barnman.

'Tell it to the Judge, Dad, lay it on the line like we told you!' came a voice from the crowd.

'The boys got it figured,' Dad Jones blurted out the words, 'that you two might be bulldozed into takin' the Stranglers' oath, once you get inside and the doors locked. There's some got the notion it was a put up job from the start. They think you are in cahoots with the big three.' The grizzled barnman's eyes narrowed. 'There's twenty-five Stranglers inside and we had it made to set fire to the buildin' and smoke 'em out. We was just waitin' till you showed up.'

'Violence begets violence,' Judge Morgan said with sober dignity. 'In the name of law and order I ask that you men disperse.'

Bryce took a step forward and the crowd that blocked the doorway backed away. Then the door of the warehouse opened and the two men walked inside. The wooden bar made an audible rasping sound as it locked the door behind them.

A raised platform about six-feet square made a raw scraping noise as it was pushed from a corner into the center of the room by a couple of masked men. A long rope with a hangman's knot was lowered slowly from the ridge log of the high beamed ceiling until the noose hung limply a few feet above the platform.

32

'Are you ready to take the oath of office of judge, Morgan?' Quensel asked from the shadows.

'I came prepared to take that oath,' came the firm reply, 'but not under the intimidation of such trappings. Masked men and a hangman's rope.'

A tall man with a black silk handkerchief covering the lower part of his face came into the yellow glow of the overhead lamp. He carried a large black leather bound Bible in both hands.

Quensel ignored Judge Morgan's remark. He told the masked man to swear the judge into office. When the words of the solemn oath had been repeated by Plato Morgan, Quensel called Bryce Bradford to the platform.

'Are you ready and willing to be sworn in as sheriff?' Quensel asked Bryce.

'I'm ready,' Bryce answered, his eyes fixed on the gambler's.

Even as Bryce Bradford repeated the oath he felt the trap closing in on him. It was like the cold clammy hand of death as he watched the noose with the knot hanging limp and empty and ready. It was only a matter of time until it would be fitted around his neck.

By some trick of lighting the shadow of the rope hung between Quensel and Bryce Bradford. It fell across the Bible like a wide black ribbon, a sinister marker, as Bryce slowly repeated the final words of his oath of office.

A loud pounding on the door interrupted the proceedings. Every man's hand dropped to his gun.

The guard at the door was told to see who it was.

The mud-smeared man who staggered in, cursing thickly, was Jerry O'Toole, Tim Fogarty's stagedriver.

'I was set afoot fifteen miles back on Cottonwood Creek,' he told Fogarty who had asked him what had happened. 'I hoofed it in. The hold-up gent made me unhook the horses and turn 'em loose. He killed the shotgun guard and shot the lock off the strong-box. He sent me on my way with Winchester bullets singing around me like hornets.'

Big Tim Fogarty looked at Quensel. 'The stage was held up. What do you make of it, Quensel?' he said.

'I'd say,' said the gambler, his voice sharp, 'that the new sheriff has his first job cut out for him. He can pick his posse from these Stranglers and take the trail before it gets cold. I was expecting sixty-thousand dollars in currency in that strong-box from the Fort Benton Bank.'

'I don't need a posse,' Bryce spoke up quickly. 'How many hold-up men were there?' he turned and asked the stagedriver.

'I saw only one man but there might have been another feller hid out in the thick brush. When the hold-up feller told the shotgun guard to lift his hands, I kicked my brake on and quit my seat and lay in the mud playin' possum. I'm drawin' stagedrivers's pay and don't get paid to referee a gun fight.

'When the Wells Fargo shotgun messenger falls over dead, a tall feller in a yellow slicker with a black handkerchief across his face kicked me in the ribs and told me to unhook the four horses and pull the harness off. Then he told me to start walking for Buffalo Run and not to look back. "Lot's wife," he said, "looked back and was turned into a pillar of salt. I'll turn you into something just as dead if you don't keep movin".'

'What did he look like?' Bryce asked. 'The one you saw.'

'He'd stand six feet and he was neither skinny nor porky. He moved quick and talks as quiet as if he was passin' the time of day.'

'I'll need a good horse,' Bryce turned to Fogarty.

'You don't know the country,' said Big Tim. 'Better take a posse.'

'The ground should be soft enough for trackin'. There's only one hold-up man for sure. A posse would get in one another's way.'

CHAPTER FOUR

Bryce Bradford shoved past Quensel and Fogarty and Kaster who were close grouped around the luckless stagedriver. He slid the heavy bar back and pulled the door open, motioning to the judge to follow him.

The crowd of men who still filled the street were eyeing Bryce and the judge uncertainly. Curiosity mingled with suspicion was written in their eyes and their wordless questioning.

Old Dad Jones limped forward, his eyes cold and bright. 'How'd you make out?' he asked.

'I'm the Sheriff of Buffalo Run,' Bryce grinned twistedly, 'if that means anything. Plato Morgan has taken his oath as judge.'

The grizzled barn man jerked a thumb towards the building. 'How about the Stranglers? Them sonsabitches still run the town?'

'Judge Morgan will fetch you up to date, Dad. The stage has been held up. I'm going out after the road-agents. I'll need a stout grain fed horse.'

'I can still handle a gun and travel the route, Bryce,' Old Dad said.

Bryce grinned faintly and shook his head. 'I'm going alone, Dad.'

Old Dad snorted. He opened his mouth to say some-

37

thing, then changed his mind. 'Come along, Sheriff,' he said. 'I'll mount you on the best damned hoss you ever throwed a leg over.' He shoved through the crowd. 'Open up a lane for the Sheriff of Buffalo Run,' he said waspishly.

When they were beyond earshot, he said, 'You're a damned fool, boy. High time somebody told you what you're up against. Hell's fire! Them road-agents is in cahoots with Quensel. They're hired hands drawin' down fightin' pay. Fogarty owns the stage line and works in with Quensel and Pete Kaster, Decker when he was alive.

'When I stake you to this ridge-runner, Bryce, you drift and keep on going till you're plumb outa the country. Don't try to pick up the trail of those road-agents or you'll run slap-dab into the bushwhacker trap they got set for you.'

Dad led the way into the lantern light of the barn. He limped down between the rows of stalls. 'Gawdamighty, they're gone!' Dad Jones fouled the air with profanity. 'Either some hoss thief got away with them or those two Square and Compass killers came back.'

Bryce grinned mirthlessly as he walked on. He went into a stall that held a big brown gelding wearing Pete Kaster's brand. He led the horse out.

'That's Pete Kaster's private,' Dad told him. 'Best damn hoss in the barn. Pete will blow up like a powder keg.'

'Let his friends pick up the chunks.' Bryce saddled the big brown. He shoved his Winchester carbine into its saddle scabbard and mounted. 'Take good care of my horse till I get back, Dad,' he said as he rode away.

He tied the horse to the hitchrack in front of Nile's log cabin. He crossed the porch and rapped on the door. When nobody came he opened it and walked in. There was nobody at home except Virginia Morgan who called, 'Come in, please,' from the bedroom.

38

Bryce walked into the bedroom. Virginia was still in bed, propped up by pillows. She said the doctor had come from Fort Benton and he'd told her to stay in bed until she regained her strength from malnutrition. She said Nile had gone out on an errand and that Rose had gone home for the day.

'I'm glad you came, Bryce,' she said, forcing a wan smile. 'I wanted to see and talk to you. Please sit down. I want to talk to you about my father. Where is he? Is he all right? I mean. . . .' Her hands clenched into tight fists. 'Are those men making a fool of him again?' Her eyes were darkened with worry, her lower lip clenched between small white teeth.

'The judge was cold sober,' Bryce sat down in the chair beside the bed. 'He'll be along directly. He was just sworn into office.'

'Then he wasn't lying. It wasn't just an excuse to get back to the El Dorado. I didn't believe him because he has been tricked so many times by those men with promises.'

Her head lifted proudly. 'Don't misunderstand me. My father is the finest man on earth. He was a Major in the Confederate Army, on General Robert E. Lee's private staff. After Lee's surrender and he came home, it was a terrible blow to find his plantation gone, his wife dead and his daughter living on the charity of friends in Richmond.' Her chin quivered as she fought back the tears.

'I didn't mean to pour out our troubles to a stranger,' she said. 'But I have to get my father out of this town. He has a few friends at Fort Benton and can go into law practice with a boyhood friend there. He lost all our money at poker here and was too proud, too ashamed to reach Fort Benton penniless. Decker and Quensel both offered us help, but there were conditions.'

Bryce took her small delicate hand in his and told her she had nothing more to worry about. He reached inside

39

his shirt and unbuckled the money belt he wore around his waist, and tossed it on the bed.

'I came to give this to the judge before I left town. There's five thousand dollars in it. It's all yours. I may not come back alive.'

Virginia looked at him, bewilderment in her eyes. Then she shoved the money belt away like it was a snake that had crawled up on her bed.

'Take it easy lady,' Bryce shoved back his chair. 'My horse is saddled. I'm pulling out in a few minutes. Chances are I'll never get back to Buffalo Run. There's no strings to that money. Your father has befriended me and I want him to have this money,' Bryce backed towards the door.

'You've no reason to treat me nice,' Virginia told him. 'I haven't even thanked you for all you've done. But before you leave I want you to know that I think you're a good man, Bryce Bradford. Take care of yourself in this town or they'll kill you,' she warned.

'I'll see what I can do to get your father to take you away from Buffalo Run,' Bryce promised her. He hung the money belt over the chair back. 'You need this money worse than I do. Use it,' he said, then left the house.

Quensel and Fogarty and Kaster were waiting for him when he rode into the alley.

'That's my private horse you got saddled,' Pete Kaster snarled.

'That road-agent has a two hour head start,' Big Tim Fogarty complained. 'Maybe this new sheriff is in cahoots with the hold-up man,' he suggested to his two companions.

Now that the brave lone-handed hero has kissed the gals a fond farewell,' Quensel leered, his hand inside his coat where he packed his knife, 'he's ready to pick up the cold trail. That road-agent got away with sixty thousand dollars of mine. Bring it and the road-agent back, Bradford. Or don't come back!'

Bryce had dismounted and was standing on spread legs, rolling a cigarette while his hot blooded temper had a chance to simmer down.

'Are you three jaspers talkin' to throw a scare into me?' Bryce asked. 'Or are you trying to prove something to one another?'

Bryce lit his cigarette. He thumbed the burning match into Quensel's eyes. As the gambler brushed the burning stick away, Bryce took a quick step. His hard fist sank into Quensel's belly, just under the lower ribs where the nerve centered in his solar plexus. It had all Bryce's hundred and eighty-five pounds behind it.

Quensel's knees buckled, his arms dropped as his eyes rolled back. Bryce slammed a vicious left hook under his lean jaw as the gambler went down to lie motionless on his back in a mud puddle.

The pistol in Bryce's hand moved in a short flat arc to cover the other two men.

'Any further orders you want to give the sheriff?' he asked.

'Only this,' Big Tim Fogarty said, his voice a husky whisper. 'You better finish the job on Quensel. That's advice, not an order.'

'Pick the knife-slinger up and bed him down beside his dead partner,' Bryce told them. 'When he comes alive give him a message. Tell him that if he ever lays a hand on Nile or Virginia Morgan I'll shove his tinhorn neck in that Stranglers' noose you had made up for me.'

Quensel moaned in agony as his legs doubled up. He rolled over on his side and commenced vomiting.

Bryce saw the folded piece of paper that had dropped from Quensel's pocket as he turned. As he picked it up, he saw Fogarty and Kaster exchange swift sidelong looks.

41

Both pair of eyes had the same panic in them.

'That letter you picked up,' Pete Kaster said harshly, 'belongs to Quensel. Dropped out of his pocket. Hand it over.'

'Hell,' Big Tim Fogarty forced a chuckle. 'It's from one of his women, one of them mushy love letters. Put it back in his pocket, Bradford.'

'I'll give it to him, personally,' Bryce eyed the pair narrowly, 'when I get back.' He put the folded paper carefully into his shirt pocket.

'What gave you the notion you was comin' back?' Pete Kaster bared his stained, discolored teeth in a snarl.

'Shut up, Pete,' Fogarty growled. 'Let's get Quensel back to the El Dorado before he pukes his guts out.'

'Send my horse back or I'll have you hung for a horse thief,' Kaster said as they picked Quensel up out of the mud puddle.

But Bryce had already ridden off into the night. He was headed for the high bluff where he had seen the pair of Avenging Angels. Long before the coming of the white man the Indians had used the cliff to spook herds of buffalo into stampeding, charging blindly over the fifty foot drop to pile up dead at the base. Then the squaws would gather and butcher the animals and hang the meat in strips to dry. There would be meat for the coming winter and tanned hides for robes and tepee coverings. The high bluffs were called buffalo runs.

Bryce picked up the tracks of two horses and followed them cautiously, leaning sideways from his saddle. As he rode at a running walk he tried to think things out, but thoughts of Virginia Morgan and Nile kept crowding in, and he finally gave it up as a bad job. He'd better keep his senses alert for a bushwhacker gun trap.

First things come first, he told himself. Before he cut sign for the road-agent, he wanted a showdown with the

42

two Avenging Angels. The horse tracks angled towards the wagon road, the same road, rutted deep by freight wagons, that was used by the stage. A crimson-streaked dawn showed on the skyline. When the light was sufficient Bryce took the folded sheet of paper from his pocket and read it. It was the unfinished letter the range detective had written before he was killed by Decker.

This was all the death warrant Bryce needed for Quensel and Fogarty and Kaster. He'd heard that Decker had killed a man named Henry Black the night before he got shot himself.

Bryce had all but convinced himself to turn back to town and have Judge Morgan issue bench warrants for the three men, but changed his mind when he came upon the stage-coach hub deep in mud where the stage road crossed a boggy creek. Horse collars and bridles and harness lay in the mud, the shotgun guard lay face down in an awkward sprawl, one leg twisted under the other, a gun still gripped in his lifeless hand. Drying blood from his bullet-torn body made a sticky red puddle under him. The lid of the strong-box was open. Horse tracks and the tracks of men's boots were all around.

Bryce rode in a slow circle around the empty, deserted coach, his Winchester carbine in the crook of his elbow, reading meaning in the sign.

The locked canvas mail sacks were intact in the leather boot under the driver's seat. The express strong-box only had been looted. Leaning down from his saddle, Bryce peered into the empty strong-box at a piece of white cardboard with crudely printed words on it.

He leaned over and picked the cardboard up. His eyes narrowed as he read the road-agent's cryptic message:

NOTICE AND WARNING! TO WHOM IT CON-
CERNS! TITHE HAS BEEN COLLECTED BY THE
AVENGING ANGELS. 7 & 11.

The cabalistic numbers that served as a signature had a
significance to Bryce Bradford. Every Avenging Angel
had his own number. A written name could be held as
damning evidence in a court of law, while numbers had no
value as evidence, proving no identity to anyone save to
those initiated into the secret order.

There was something grim and sinister here that puzzled Bryce. He wondered how and in what way, shape or
form Quensel and his dead partner were tied in with the
exiled, outcast Mormons who dwelt in the hidden settlement of Rainbow's End in the broken badlands of Bryce
Canyon in Utah.

Time had been when the Avenging Angels under the
leadership of the giant statured, curly maned and bearded
Porter Rockwell, had been the far reaching arm of the law
laid down by the Book of Mormon, when the Mormons of
Utah were under the stern rule of Apostle Joseph Smith.
Those were the blood-spattered final years of lawfully
practiced polygamy. The years when Rockwell organized
a band of men to mete out punishment to those who
disobeyed Mormon law.

The Mountain Meadow massacre of men, women and
children by the Mormons brought the United States Army
into Utah. The abandonment of the secret killers of the
church was ordered, together with the practice of
polygamy.

The foolhardy stubborn few Mormons who chose to
defy the United States Government were forced into exile,
both by our Government and by the Mormon Church.

Those few who fled with their plural wives and children,

travelled by wagon train, herding their livestock, migrating to the all but inaccessible, broken-timbered country of Bryce Canyon on the north side of the Colorado river. Their settlement of Rainbow's End looked down on the vast eternal beauty of the Grand Canyon of the Colorado.

A handful of people. Brave men and women who dared defy the mighty government of the United States in the practice of their belief as written in the Book of Mormon, pointing out that any man was free to practice his own religion without prosecution.

Rainbow's End became the last stand of the outcast Mormons who had been driven from their homeland. There they practiced their religion and their Avenging Angels took care of those who broke the laws.

Bryce Bradford's grandfather had been one of those exiles. An Apostle with only one wife, but nevertheless in sympathy with the self-exiled people. He had led the bitter trek to Bryce Canyon. He had been one of the founders of the forbidden settlement of Rainbow's End. When he and his wife died they left behind one son, Bryce's father, Robert Bradford, who had a streak of rebel in him. When he was chosen to take the secret oath of the Avenging Angels, he revolted.

Robert Bradford had taken his young wife and son and left the forbidden land in the night. He had taken with him only what belonged to him, his horses, his wife and five-year-old son who had been born in the log cabin overlooking the Grand Canyon of the Colorado.

He had broken one of the cardinal laws of Rainbow's End when he left. Because it had been decreed from the beginning that once a man or woman chose to live within the boundaries of the settlement, there they must dwell until they died.

A child born within the forbidden land was governed by

the same rule that held the parents confined within its boundaries. Therefore, Bryce Bradford came under the laws of the outcasts and within the far reach of the long riders who enforced the laws.

Bryce had always been aware of the futility of escape. Sooner or later those long riders would close the gap. If he showed fight now, those two Avenging Angels were bound by oath to shoot him down. If he surrendered, he would be taken back to Rainbow's End to stand trial before the Apostles of the Latter Day Saints as written in the Book of Mormon.

Since the exiles of Rainbow's End were guided by the Book of Mormon, they were duty bound to pay tithe to the Mormon Church at Salt Lake City in Utah.

Surely the gambler Quensel had no connection with the outcast Mormons, nor with the Mormon Church. No man abiding by the strict laws set down by the Book of Mormon was ever the owner of a saloon or gambling house. Both Quensel and his dead partner were far, far below the level of the moral standard of living of a decent Mormon, even those who drank and gambled and committed adultery, known derisively as Jack-Mormons.

Bryce scrutinized the wording of the message that puzzled him, for the last time. Then he leaned from his saddle and replaced the cardboard.

It was up to him now to pick up the trail left by the two Avenging Angels. He was remembering what Jerry O'-Toole had quoted the hold-up man as saying, 'Lot's wife looked back and was turned into a pillar of salt.' The two killers from Rainbow's End would be able to quote from the Bible.

Their trail was plain for Bryce Bradford to find and follow. Bryce stiffened at the thought. Those two men had a motive in setting the stagedriver afoot. They had been in Buffalo Run and knew that a stranger named Bryce Bradford had just been elected sheriff. They had gotten their horses out of the barn and ridden back to the stage-coach to leave the cryptic message and a plain trail for him to follow.

Bryce had a strong hunch where they were headed for.

CHAPTER FIVE

Jack Quensel gritted back a low moan of agony and opened his eyes. They had laid him beside Decker's open coffin. He rolled away from the black box and swung his legs to the floor. He was bent over a little as he took a couple of steps and dropped his sick weight into a chair. His sleek hair hung down in dank strands across his pale sweat beaded forehead.

'Sheriff Bryce Bradford,' Big Tim Fogarty mused aloud. 'When he hits a man, by hell, he stays hit. Like bein' kicked by an army mule, eh Quensel?' A grin spread his whiskered face but his eyes were cold.

Quensel lifted his head. 'What the hell were you sorry yellow bastards doing while he worked me over?'

'Lookin' into the round, black hole of his gun barrel,' Big Tim chuckled. 'I told you you'd got a bear by the tail, Quensel.'

'Fetch a pail of water, some towels and a bottle of whisky,' Quensel told them as he shrugged out of his coat.

'Why in hell didn't you burn that letter you took off Decker?' Big Tim growled. 'That new sheriff picked it up when it fell out of your pocket and rode away with it.'

'Why didn't you shoot him?' Quensel's voice was shrill. 'There were two of you.'

'Any time that Bradford feller pulls a gun,' Fogarty said, 'he figures on usin' it.'

'You had your hand on your knife when he hit you in the guts', Pete Kaster sneered. 'He had a gun in his other hand before you knew what hit you.'

Quensel slid from his chair, a deadly short-barrelled derringer in his hand. His thin lips twisted.

'While Charlie Decker was alive,' Quensel said, 'I paid him to do my killing. He was a natural killer who enjoyed his work. His death left me short-handed, and until I hire another killer to take Decker's place, I'll do my own gun chores.

'You two drunken bastards both know where you stand. The El Dorado holds heavy mortgages on the Diamond F freight outfit and stage line. The El Dorado holds controlling interest in Pete Kaster's mining claims and his K cow outfit. Any argument to the contrary?'

'You got us by the short hairs,' Big Tim shrugged massive shoulders. 'No doubt about it, Quensel.'

Quensel eyed both men coldly as he held the gun on them.

'The easiest way to foreclose those mortgages is with this gun. Can either of you give me one reason why I shouldn't gut shoot both of you before you do any more talking out of turn?'

Quensel had been fist whipped and these two men had witnessed the humiliation of Bryce Bradford's easy victory. It rankled like poison inside his bruised belly. Both men read murder in the gambler's eyes.

'Off-hand,' Fogarty grinned and shook his head, 'I can't think up a reason.' He chuckled. 'As the saying goes, if I was to die for it.'

There was a heavy pounding on the door, then Jerry O'-Toole's whisky voice was saying he'd just brought in the stage-coach and harness. The horses had come in by themselves.

'Did you see anything of the new sheriff?' Quensel asked.

'Nary a sign. But I found this message inside the strongbox. It makes no sense to me.' He read the message aloud before he handed the piece of cardboard to Quensel.

The blood had drained from the gambler's face, leaving it grey as death. The hand that gripped the snub-nosed gun was white-knuckled.

'What the hell,' Big Tim Fogarty's voice was heavy with suspicion and puzzlement, 'is a tithe?'

'A tithe,' volunteered Pete Kaster, 'is a Mormon tax assessment. Every Mormon pays his yearly tithe from his earnings to the Mormon Church. If he don't pay tithe, they send their Avenging Angels out to collect.'

'What the hell has a tithe tax got to do with holding up one of my stage-coaches?' asked Fogarty. 'I ain't no Mormon.'

'Old Dad Jones told me,' Jerry O'Toole spoke up, 'that those two Square and Compass geldings he had in the barn are gone. Two fellers came and got them during all the big election excitement. They left the two horses Fogarty sold them in the feed yard. That Square and Compass horse brand is used by the Avenging Angels of the Mormons.'

'Well, I'll be damned!' Fogarty said, puzzling it out. 'Then it was that goat-whiskered gent and his big, overgrown son that held up the stage.'

Quensel had been standing silent, his stare fixed, as if he hadn't heard a single word of what was being said.

'Shut up, all of you,' the gambler cut in like a knife

51

blade. 'Let Jerry out and shut the door, Pete.' The cold threat in Quensel's eyes was backed up by the gun in his hand.

When the stagedriver had gone, Quensel asked, 'Did either of those Square and Compass men talk to you, Tim?'

'The big one with the billy-goat whiskers did the talkin',' Fogarty said. 'But outside of the horse dicker, he didn't say a word that ties in with the hold-up. He never said where they came from or why they were here, just that they had a long ride to make. They paid two weeks' feed bill in advance and said they'd be back for their horses.'

'Wade Applegate whose ranch lies between the Bear Paws and the Little Rockies,' the gambler said, 'comes from the Mormon country in Utah. At one time he was a high ranking Apostle of the Church. I have a hunch those two held up the stage and are headed for Applegate's hidden ranch in the badlands, with sixty thousand dollars of my money. And I suspect our newly elected sheriff is close behind them.' Quensel's thin smile left his eyes cold as he picked up the cardboard and read the grim message.

He too, was remembering what Jerry O'Toole had quoted the hold-up man as saying about Lot's wife. The hold-up man knew his Bible

'I'm betting,' Fogarty snorted angrily, 'that you know more about this than you're sayin', Quensel. Better lay your cards face up so a man can read 'em.'

Quensel laughed in Fogarty's face. A short laugh, like splinters cracking. He got up and left the room without speaking.

Jack Quensel was one of that breed of man who should never touch whisky. One drink and he emptied the bottle, and before it was empty there was another ready.

Sober, Quensel was all that a high stake gambler should be. Cold nerved, cautious, deadly, he played his cards close to his belly and when the bets were down, it was Quensel who raked in the chips.

Drunk, Quensel was ugly, swaggering, quarrelsome, treacherous. He killed without a hint of warning, knifed or shot a man in the back.

Whisky warped his brain, twisted his mentality into grotesque, ugly shape. Brave men gave Quensel a wide berth when he was on one of his habitual drunks. Women, even the hardened percentage girls who danced the can-can at his El Dorado, were wont to vanish when Quensel took his first drink. All the veneer and polish of a gentleman of breeding and education dissolved by the alcohol that poisoned his brain cells and fired his unholy lusts.

No man on earth was more bitterly aware of this than Quensel himself as he sat slumped in a bar-room chair, the half-emptied whisky bottle in his hand, brooding thoughts of the past he had buried crowding his mind.

When Nile came into the room and stood with her back

53

against the door she had closed, the gambler's thin lips twisted. He picked up the cardboard from the table and motioned with his head for Nile to come over. He tipped the bottle to his lips while she read the message.

'You know where those cheerful tidings came from?' he asked.

'Jerry O'Toole brought me up to date,' Nile said.

Quensel smiled thinly as he lifted the bottle again and drank.

'Did you know that Decker signed a paper leaving his half interest in the El Dorado to me?' Nile asked.

Quensel nodded that he knew.

'I'm buying you out at your own price, Quensel. On one condition. That you leave Buffalo Run, quit Montana and never come back.'

'And if I choose not to sell out?' Quensel asked.

Nile's hand slipped into her jacket pocket, her fingers closing around the butt of a .38. 'I came here prepared to kill you,' she said, her voice deadly.

'All I have left,' Quensel spoke quietly, 'from a misspent life is my doubtful reputation as a high stake gambler, and a true gambler plays his hand out. Even if it's a losing hand.' He twisted the bottle in both hands as he held it between his wide-spread legs, eyeing it sightlessly as he spoke.

The spots of grey at his temples seeemd to have spread and Nile noticed the sprinkle of grey in his thick black hair that was uncombed, dishevelled. There were lines etched deeply on the man's face that she had never noticed before. It was as if he had aged overnight.

He lifted his head and looked at her searchingly. Something of the bitter hardness was gone from his eyes as he smiled. 'You are a remarkable woman, Nile. The most beautiful woman I have ever known, with a woman's courage that shames the bravest of men.' The smile faded. His eyes went black.

A slow flush came into her cheeks. She had her lower lip bitten between her teeth. 'Damn you,' she licked a drop of blood from her lip. 'Damn you, Quensel.' Her hand came from her pocket empty, ringless.

'Get out, Nile,' Quensel told her in a dead voice. 'Get away from me, before I cut your beautiful throat.'

Nile backed away from his eyes. She opened the door and went out, closing it on the gambler and his bottle.

Tonight when Jack Quensel had need of all that cold deadly calm gambler's mind, he had reached for the bottle. No man in Buffalo Run knew what had caused Quensel to take his first drink at the bar. No man alive knew. But a woman named Nile Carter knew the reason, even as she knew beforehand that he would get drunk before tomorrow came.

Charlie Decker, if he were alive, would know the cause. Tithe was only part payment on the balance due. Quensel and Decker had been drunk together that Christmas Eve a year ago when they had incurred a debt that would be paid off in full by the Avenging Angels from Rainbow's End.

Decker had gotten a tip-off that there was to be close to seventy-five thousand dollars on the stage they had held up that night. Too big a haul to trust to any hired road-agents or to share with Pete Kaster or Tim Fogarty. The memory of the hold-up came back now with startling clarity, as Quensel poured a drink and sat with brooding thoughts.

'There's a big fat Christmas cake in the Wells Fargo strong-box,' Decker had needled him. 'Too big a plum cake to cut more than two ways, Quensel.'

There had been four passengers inside the buckled-down canvas curtains of the stage-coach that night. The snow shone like Christmas tree decorations on the scrub pine thicket that had hidden Quensel and Decker in long fur coats and muskrat caps, black silk mufflers across their faces.

Quensel had drunk to drown the memories of other Christmas Eves that came to haunt him as he and Decker had waited. Poignant memories of gay parties and the perfume of a golden-haired girl with his engagement ring on her finger. A past that Quensel never spoke of and had left buried along his back trail.

He was remembering how Jerry O'Toole, the stage-driver, had sleighbells buckled between the hames of his six-horse team. He had shared his jug with the shotgun guard on the seat beside him. Both men a little drunk and singing off-key as the stage-coach rounded the bend, 'Jingle-bells, jingle-bells, jingle all the way. . . .'

A big man in a fur coat had been the first to step out into the snow, a man with a leathery face and drooping iron-grey moustache. Two other men came out, their hands in the air, then a tall girl in a mink coat and cap and fur boots stepped out, lifting her skirt to show a length of shapely leg. She had stood boot deep in the snow, a faint smile on her wide red lips that were the color of the holly berries pinned to her coat. There had been no trace of fear in her amber eyes.

Decker voiced some vulgar remark about the girl. Quensel slapped him, back handed, across the face hidden behind the muffler. Decker saw the glint of the knife in his hand and stepped back beyond reach.

'Get on with the deal, you foul-mouthed sewer rat,' Quensel had told Decker.

For a long moment their eyes had met and locked in a tight, tense grip of hate. Then Decker's eyes had slid away as he made the half turn. The gun in his hand spat a jet of flame, then a second flame spat through the gun smoke that wisped from his gun-barrel. Two of the men standing knee deep in the snowdrift had doubled up, falling slowly.

The tall man had dropped on one knee beside one of the dead men. His hand groped inside the pocket of the dead man's coat and came out holding a gun. Quensel shot him as he thumbed back the gun hammer.

The shotgun guard had thrown down his gun. His hands were high in the air when Quensel shot him. Quensel had told the girl to get back inside the coach.

Jerry O'Toole was sawing on the lines as the horses jack-knifed. When he had got them straightened out and under control, Quensel had stepped out from behind the ambush.

As he walked out into the cold pale moonlight, he had made a sinister figure in his beaver coat, a gun in his hand. He lifted the curtain to let the moonlight penetrate the dark interior of the coach. The shaft of light had caught the girl unawares.

She was bent over, lifting a black leather satchel from the floor on to the seat with her own luggage. She shoved it between a hatbox and a suitcase and was pulling the buffalo lap robe up over the bags when Quensel's low laugh came from behind the muffler across his face.

'Even a gentleman turned blackguard,' he said mockingly, 'never robs a woman's purse nor strips the rings from her fingers.'

'Thank you,' her husky voice was contemptuous.

'But the black satchel you were concealing does not belong to you, lady. Hand it over.'

When he saw the stubby derringer pistol palmed in her hand, the gun cocked and levelled at him with a steady hand, he had said, 'The lady has courage. The gentleman is mistaken.' The black muffler masked a sardonic grin. 'We may never meet again, lady. Would it be too much to beg the sprig of holly you wear? The red of the berries matches your lips.'

Her free hand unpinned the holly and handed it to him. Their eyes met and held for a long moment.

'Shove that tin cake box off,' Decker's voice crackled at the driver in the cold night. 'Drag the wench out. The stage goes off without her.'

Quensel had stiffened. 'Down on the floor, quick,' he whispered. 'Cover up with the lap robes.' He withdrew his head and pulled the curtain in place.

Quensel turned to face the masked Decker, whose gun was pointed at the belly of the stagedriver who was heaving the strong-box off into a snowdrift.

'Get going, driver,' Quensel ordered. He eyed Decker bleakly. 'The lady goes on to her destination,' he said, his voice deadly.

'You God damn fool,' Decker spat out. 'You're lettin' that wench put a rope around our necks.'

Jerry O'Toole's long buckskin lash popped like a pistol. The horses lunged and the coach rocked and swayed on its way.

When the stage had rolled out of sight, Quensel had told Decker to frisk the three dead men while he filled the canvas sack he had taken from his saddle, with the money in the strong-box.

There was an official brown envelope on top of the taped money. Quensel slit it open with a knife. There was enough moonlight to read the paper inside. 'For the Fort Benton Bank, consigned by Wade Applegate, to be deposited to the account of the Mormon's Church in Utah. Seventy-five thousand dollars.'

Quensel put the paper in his pocket. When Decker came over. Quensel looked up at him questioningly.

'No identification on any of them,' Decker reported. 'No wallets. No money. Two had guns, the older man was unarmed. Looked like he was a prisoner.'

'I gave the unarmed man a chance for his taw, Decker,' Quensel said. 'He had a gun in his hand when I shot him. Who knows, perhaps I saved the man from hanging.'

He put the last of the money in the sack and pulled the draw-string tight. 'Seventy-five grand here, Decker, to split two ways,' he said. He unscrewed the cap on a flask and proffered it to Decker.

'You know damn well I never touch whisky, Quensel.'

'You'll take a drink now, to bind the deal that seals our lips to secrecy.'

Decker took a swallow and handed back the flask. 'Secrecy, hell,' he had said. 'Jerry O'Toole knows better than to let out so much as a hint, but the only way to shut a woman's mouth is to kill her.'

'Have you ever killed a woman, Decker?'

'Two.' Decker's teeth showed as his lips skinned back. 'The common law wife I'd been living with. The tart I was shacking up with. Both for the same reason. They gossiped too much about the way I was earning the money I was giving them to spend.'

Decker took two capsules of morphine from a small box and swallowed them. 'I was killing men for the reward they brought. I was a bounty hunter and couldn't afford any loose talk. That's why I never drink. I'll settle for a couple of capsules.'

'You're welcome to the dope, Decker. But one thing; if you ever meet that girl and lay a finger on her, I'll rip your belly open.'

Quensel drank from the flask and walked over to where the three dead men lay in the crimson-stained snow. He stared down at each face, memorizing every feature, then walked to his horse.

'You know who Wade Applegate is, Decker?' he asked.

'Hell, yes. He has a horse ranch hidden in the badlands

59

below the Little Rockies. Raises the best horses in Montana.'

'Wade Applegate comes from the Mormon country in Utah. There's a rumor that he was a high-ranking Apostle of the Mormon Church.'

'What difference does it make, Quensel?'

'Seventy-five thousand dollars. He was sending it to the Mormon Church. That's a hell of a lot of horses to sell.'

'Then the Mormons have donated a Christmas present to you and me.' Decker grinned and swung into his saddle. He rode away, leaving Quensel to follow.

Quensel slid the Winchester from the saddle scabbard when he had mounted his horse. He lined the sights to the three hundred yard notch and held the gun on Decker's fur-coated back, with the hammer thumbed back and his finger on the trigger, until Charlie Decker had ridden out of sight.

He told himself he should kill the bounty hunter now, then decided to let it ride for the present.

*   *   *

A cold sweat beaded his forehead under the sweatband of his hat. His hands were unsteady as he lowered the gun and put it back in the scabbard. He rode along with the uncorked flask in his hand, deep in thought, drinking to get the sound of sleighbells from inside his brain.

A few hours later when Quensel came into the bar at the El Dorado, the bartender leaned across the polished mahogany and whispered, 'There's a swell lookin' gal waitin' to see you in your private office. I sent her a bottle of champagne to keep her company till you showed up. Some men are born lucky.'

It was the girl from the stage-coach. Her fur coat and

60

cap lay on a chair and she had a half-emptied wineglass in her hand. The black satchel was on the floor beside her chair.

'I'm Nile Carter,' she said with a smile. 'I came here to make a deal with you, Jack Quensel.' She rose from her chair and holding the gambler with her eyes, she adjusted the spray of holly in his lapel.

When Quensel took her in his arms, a movement like the quiver of a trapped animal swept the length of her body. His wide mouth fastened on hers.

'I play for keeps, Quensel,' the whispered words were in his mouth. 'I want a cut of the El Dorado, a half interest.'

'I have a partner, Charlie Decker. He owns a half interest in the El Dorado.' Quensel's voice was unsteady as he held her in his embrace.

'Deal Decker out', her voice cut like a whetted blade as she freed herself with a twist of her body.

Quensel suddenly reached for her again. Her throaty laugh sounded as he breathed hotly against her breasts.

CHAPTER SEVEN

Bryce Bradford pushed the big brown gelding to a long trot. It gave him no little satisfaction to know that he was forking a horse that would put the miles between him and the men who would be cold-trailing him.

Bryce picked up the trail of the two stage robbers and followed it slowly. He was badly handicapped because of his lack of knowledge of the country. So far, the trail led northward and a little to the west of the stage road to Fort Benton.

Then he lost the trail. Lost it in a bewildering maze of horse tracks. The two lone riders had used an old trick to blot out their sign. They had picked up a bunch of wild horses and had drifted for miles with the loose stock. They had been long-sighted enough to pull the shoes off their own horses.

Bryce slowed to a running walk and let the horse follow in the general direction of the unshod horses. He rode for perhaps fifteen minutes before he came to a decision. The moonlight gave him a fair idea of the topography of the country, hills, coulees, long draws, flats, a square table-topped mesa to the north. Following horse tracks now was a fool's game. The two men knew every trick and twist of the dangerous role they were playing. They'd probably split up ten miles from here and meet again at some hideout.

Bryce knew that the Little Rockies would be their ultimate destination because he was drawing upon his memory, remembering stories his father had told him before he was killed, about a man named Wade Applegate, a Mormon from Utah, who had come to eastern Montana and bought a ranch. He had described the country and shown Bryce a rough map of the exact location of the ranch.

Bryce's father had described Wade Applegate as being a just and stern man, slow to anger, never making a decisive move until he was absolutely certain he was in the right. A man past his prime of life who had married a full-blood Indian woman in Montana.

Applegate stood for justice towards all men. The two lone riders would find refuge at his ranch, even as the son of Bob Bradford would be welcome and safe under the same roof.

Bryce asked for nothing better than to meet the two Avenging Angels under the roof of Wade Applegate. Fate seemed to be shaping his destiny, pointing the trail out for him. He had been travelling north and west, now he swung eastward, taking his course from the stars.

Bryce's horse was shod. His trail would be easy to pick up. His aim now was to get a long head start. He made a rough guess that the distance he'd have to cover would be seventy or eighty miles and he rode his horse accordingly.

Bryce welcomed the sunrise. He rode all the next day, halting an hour or two during the middle of the day. He saw scattered bunches of cattle and an occasional rider in the distance. Luck favored him and he came no closer than a mile to the nearest rider. He rode out of his way to avoid cow camps and ranches.

It was difficult to tell if the pair of riders he sighted

behind him three or four times were cowboys after cattle or men trailing him. It didn't much matter because he was a long way ahead of them and he reckoned he would be reaching Applegate's ranch by dusk. He wondered if the pair of riders were the Avenging Angels, though he figured they'd be ahead of him and would be at the ranch with their loot when he got there.

Sundown found him in the broken country south of the Little Rockies. Long ridges spotted with scrub pines, long draws thick with brush. It was the fall of the year and the wild berries were ripe on the branches. He'd lean from his saddle and scoop a handful to satisfy the hunger that was beginning to bother him.

He topped a ridge and came on to a wagon trail. Five minutes later he was looking down on a small cluster of log buildings and corrals. He knew he had reached Wade Applegate's horse ranch.

No man challenged his approach, not even the barking of a dog. But he knew that he was being watched as he reined up in the slanting rays of sunset in front of a big log barn.

A tall, white-moustached man, with a six-shooter swinging low on his lean flank appeared in the doorway of the barn. His skin was leathery, seamed, stretched over a big boned, homely face. His deep-set eyes were dark brown, flecked with grey. He scrutinized Bryce closely.

'You are Bryce Bradford,' he said in a deep, soft-toned voice. 'You're the livin' image of your father. I've been expectin' you to show up here sooner or later. Get down and put up your horse.'

'There's two men here ahead of me?' questioned Bryce.

'Two men, yes. But keep your hand away from your gun. They've given their word. I want yours. This is not the time nor place for gun fightin'.'

Bryce dismounted. His hand was gripped so hard that

he almost winced. Wade Applegate was sixty or more but he was hard as rawhide and his joints were limber.

'One of Pete Kaster's horses,' he said, reading the K brand on the sweat-streaked brown. 'A good one, but I raise better.' The man spoke without bragging. He was simply stating a fact.

When Bryce had unsaddled, watered and fed his horse, they walked together towards the house. As they went in, Bryce saw the two men he was looking for standing in front of the open fireplace, facing him.

The larger, older man had a black-spade beard streaked with white. His eyes were as cold and hard as grey steel. The younger man's eyes were crossed but of the same color. His hair was straight and coarse and black. They were undoubtedly father and son.

'The older man is Matthew,' Wade Applegate introduced him to Bryce. 'The other is Stephen. Seven and Eleven!'

The Avenging Angels, according to the law at Rainbow's End, were allowed to keep their given names only. They were always referred to by number.

That they knew Bryce's identity was a foregone conclusion. They eyed him with cold enmity and he faced them with grim-lipped defiance. These were the two men who had been sent from Rainbow's End to track him down, but they had given their word to Wade Applegate that they would not stain his hospitality with bloodshed. Bryce was likewise bound.

Bryce had hung his hat on the elk antlers in the hall and had put his Winchester carbine in the gun rack that held a dozen rifles and carbines and two sawed-off double-barrelled shotguns. He had unbuckled his cartridge belt and hung it with his holstered six-shooter below his hat. He'd seen the two black hats and belts and guns on the rack that belonged to the two men.

'You two men,' Wade Applegate spoke to father and son, 'will use the attic room. The ladder is at the end of the hall. Supper will be on the table in an hour. That will give you ample time to wash up.'

Wade Applegate made no pretence about the broad hint. When they had left, Bryce turned to him and asked bluntly, 'What happened to my father, Bob Bradford? I've come a long ways to find out.'

'Bob Bradford is dead,' Applegate told him.

'Then he was murdered,' Bryce said tensely. 'Destroyed by the Avenging Angels of the Mormon Church.'

'Your father was shot down before he reached my place. The two Avenging Angels who had him prisoner, taking him to Fort Benson, were killed at the same time. All three men were on a stage-coach that was held up by road-agents on the night before Christmas one year ago. The stage was robbed and the three men murdered.'

Bryce sat stiffly, letting the truth sink in. Then he said, 'One thing I have to tell you now, sir.'

'If it concerns the stage hold-up and your being elected Sheriff of Buffalo Run, I am already aware of it,' Wade Applegate interrupted.

'Those two men told you?'

'No. They are bound by their oath to silence. I have other sources of information.'

'What crimes am I charged with, sir?' Bryce asked. 'These men have been sent to track me down.'

'You'll hear the charges at sunrise. Until then, there will be no discussion under my roof.'

Bryce glanced quickly around the big square room. Fur rugs covered the floor. Books lined the shelves along the wall. A glass humidor was filled with coarse tobacco and a dozen pipes were in the rack on the home-made table that was piled with newspapers and periodicals.

'Your room is across the hall from mine, Bryce. Would you care for a drink of good whisky before you wash up?'

'I'm not much of a drinker,' admitted Bryce, 'but I need one to get the taste out of my mouth.'

Bryce didn't hear the squaw come in on moccasined feet. Her guttural voice behind him startled him. The meaningless string of cuss words that came from the scrubbed moon face was even more startling.

'Leah has her likes and dislikes. She don't happen to like our other guests,' Wade Applegate explained.

'I hope I meet the test, sir,' Bryce said with a tentative smile.

'She knows something about you. Her sister works for Nile Carter at Buffalo Run.'

He showed Bryce his room and left him to wash up.

The squaw seemed to have outdone herself. Clean white sheets and pillow cases on the big bed. Wild roses in a glass jar on the dresser. A clean shirt, underwear and socks folded neatly on the bed. On the washstand there was a shaving mug and brush and open razor.

He was tucking in his clean shirt when he noticed a twice-folded envelope pinned inside the shirt pocket. There were two sheets of writing paper. One was the farewell letter from Bryce's father that he had forgotten to remove from the money belt he had left with Virginia Morgan. The other was a note from Nile Carter. It read:

Do not, under any circumstances, return to Buffalo Run, Bryce Bradford! The Stranglers here have tied your hangman's knot. Judge Plato Morgan and his daughter Virginia are leaving by stage for Fort Benton. I have persuaded Virginia to accept your generous gift.

Every man and woman in Buffalo Run has been commanded by Quensel to attend the funeral of Charlie

Decker, shot down by the stranger from nowhere.

As for me, Nile is still dealing at the El Dorado.

N.

Bryce put both letters in his pocket. The supper bell was ringing. His door opened and the younger one of the Avenging Angels stepped in and closed the door. 'We got a notion that Wade Applegate will clear you tomorrow,' he told Bryce. 'But we'll follow you to hell and bring you back to Rainbow's End, dead or alive.' He opened the door and walked out.

Bryce caught a glimpse of his own face in the mirror. He didn't like what he saw reflected there, a pair of cold eyes that held murder set in a greyish-green mask of bitter hatred.

'To hell with it,' he spoke aloud to the mirrored face, not knowing exactly what he meant.

He let himself out and walked down the hall. Wade Applegate and the two Avenging Angels were in the big room. Neither of the two men had changed clothes.

Applegate motioned them to their seats at a heavy plank table twenty feet long. Matthew sat at one end of the table, his son at his right. The host sat at the head with Bryce on his right.

Father and son commenced wolfing their food in a wordless, noisome exhibition of uncouth table manners. The food on platters and in bowls in front of them had been there for a long time, getting cold. The squaw brought in hot platters of steaming food and put them in front of Wade Applegate, then a big pot of hot black coffee.

Bryce had never tasted better food. The thick T bone steak covered the huge crockery plate, the mashed potatoes had a creamy color. The dutch-oven biscuits were hot to the touch, with wild strawberry syrup and home-made

69

butter, and cream so thick you had to spoon it into the cup.

All men were welcome here. But those who came took whatever they got. Wade Applegate's squaw did the separating.

The four men finished supper in silence. Supper over, Bryce walked in the moonlight with his host in the lead. They came to a grassy clearing fenced in by a white-washed rail fence. There were three grave mounds. One grave was marked by a large boulder on which was crudely chiselled the name ROBERT BRADFORD.

'I brought your father's body here for burial, together with the bodies of the two Avenging Angels who had him under guard. I knew your father but the two others still remain without identity.'

'I don't know how to thank you, sir.' Bryce said, his voice choked. 'I can't find the right words.'

'No need to thank me. Your father was my friend.' Applegate put a hand on Bryce's shoulder. 'I had seventy-five thousand dollars in the strong-box on that stage. It was tithe money I owed the Mormon Church, consigned to the Bank at Fort Benton. Two masked road-agents held up the stage, killed the shotgun guard, the two Avenging Angels, and shot down your father who was unarmed. Only the stagedriver and one woman passenger were spared. The tithe money was stolen.'

Wade Applegate's handsome weathered face looked like it had been chiselled from grey granite.

'I am still held responsible for every dollar of that stolen money.' He gripped Bryce's arm. 'Matthew and Stephen have been sent here to collect that tithe. Tomorrow morning they will demand payment. Both of them are killers.'

'There were sixty thousand dollars in the strong-box

they just robbed,' Bryce told him. 'They collected that tithe of yours in the same way your money was stolen. You don't owe them too much, sir.'

'They have not mentioned anything about robbing a strong-box,' said the older man.

Bryce told him about the cardboard signed by 7 and 11. 'They made it plain enough it was tithe collected. I followed their trail here,' Bryce told him.

'I'll bring up the matter of the robbery with them,' Applegate said grimly. 'Now concerning your trial tomorrow morning, Bryce, they will demand twenty-five years tithe owed by your father, and according to their rules, a son is held responsible for his father's debts.'

'My father held out tithe each year from his earnings,' Bryce said hotly, his temper rising. 'He kept it in a black satchel. He must have had it with him when he was killed. I have his letter to prove it.' Bryce took out the letter and handed it over.

'I was sent out as sheriff to fetch back the road-agents and the sixty thousand dollars they stole,' Bryce grinned twistedly. 'I aim to do just that.'

He shoved his hand into his pants pocket and crushed Nile's note into a crumpled ball and left it there.

Bryce told him about Stephen coming into his room and making the threat.

'I don't trust that unholy combination of father and son,' said Wade Applegate. 'They're an evil example of two generations of polygamous inbreeding. I was sent from Salt Lake City along with your father's father to guide those exiled outcasts to some isolated spot beyond the reach of the law of the United States. Those outcast Mormons set themselves apart as holy martyrs. I left them there and came to this place to lose my identity. So I have waited, even as your father waited, for the long arm of the

Avenging Angels to reach me.'

'Did you know who those men were when you offered them welcome?' Bryce asked.

'I recognized the Square and Compass brand on their horses.'

'Then why?' Bryce asked.

'The sign above the gate that reads, "All men are welcome here. Let no man violate that trust".' The tall white-haired man smiled tolerantly.

The blast of gunfire punctuated whatever Bryce was about to say. He reached instinctively for his gun but the gun now hung on Wade Applegate's rack in the hall.

Applegate moved with silent swiftness. 'Follow me,' he whispered. He led Bryce along a trail to a camp of half a dozen tepees, where a number of squaws were busy around the campfires. Wade Applegate lifted the flap of a tepee and motioned Bryce inside. Glowing coals from a small fire in the center shed a red light inside. Wade Applegate lifted a buffalo robe and his hand came out holding a filled cartridge belt and holstered Colt pistol, which he handed to Bryce, saying, 'You might need it.'

The shooting puzzled Bryce. He was about to ask a question, but when the older man shook his head, the question died a slow death.

The echoes of the shots left a void of silence in the night. A silence charged with danger that tensed Bryce's muscles and screwed his nerves taut as tight-strung, thin wires.

As the two men stepped out of the tepee, the fat squaw came up at a jog trot. Anger blazed in her opaque black eyes as she talked to Applegate in Sioux. When she finished what seemed like an angry tirade, Applegate told Bryce what she'd said. That there were two dead men at the little graveyard, and that two horsebackers rode away

72

after roping the sign over the gate and pulling it down.

Both dead men were strangers to Bryce, but Wade Applegate knew them. They both worked for Kaster and Fogarty.

Both men had been shot in the back as they stood, tracked in the dark shadows of the high willows and buckbrush. Neither man had been given an even chance, both guns were still in their holsters.

'There, but for the grace of God,' Wade Applegate said, 'lie the dead bodies of Bryce Bradford and Wade Applegate.'

'The pair of Avenging Angels?'

'Who else?' The squaw said they saddled a couple of fresh horses and had them tied in the brush while I was showing you where your father was buried. The way I read the sign, the dead men were sent to trail you and while they stood in the brush undecided, Matthew and Stephen slipped up. Mistaking the shadowy forms for you and me, they carried out their orders of destruction, and are now on their way back to Rainbow's End, rejoicing.'

Wade Applegate led the way back to the house. When they had taken a drink together, Bryce told the older man that he'd like him to read his father's letter and another unfinished letter written by a range detective hired by the Wells Fargo Express Company, to investigate the recent hold-ups of the stage. He explained how the letter had dropped out of Quensel's pocket.

Wade Applegate read the first letter aloud in softened tone, while Bryce sat back with half closed eyes as the strange wording of the letter took on a meaning he could now comprehend.

Dear Son. By the time you read this I will be gone. After twenty-five years the Avenging Angels of the outcast

Mormons of Rainbow's End have located me. They are taking me back to stand trial. I will be sentenced and shot down.

These two long riders have given me their sworn promise not to hunt down and destroy my son, on two conditions. First, that I pay them twenty-five years' tithe. Second, that I will take them to Wade Applegate's hideout.

I have the tithe money in a black satchel and am taking it along to Rainbow's End, but regarding Wade Applegate, it is a difficult decision to make.

If I take them to Wade's horse ranch where he has lived in safety all these years, it means the destruction of the best friend a man ever had. On the other hand, if I refuse to betray Wade Applegate, you will be shot down by the two Avenging Angels who are waiting outside while I write this farewell letter to you, my son. Forgive me if I refuse to betray my friend. Wait here at the ranch six months, Bryce. Then put your affairs in order and go to Wade Applegate, whose ranch you can find from the directions I gave you. He will know what to do. May God protect you, my son. Your father, Bob Bradford.

When the letter ended, there was a hushed silence. Both men felt the strange invisible shadow of Bob Bradford's presence in the big room.

'If he had only told me beforehand, given me some warning, told me what to do,' Bryce voiced his thoughts.

'Bob Bradford didn't know himself. A condemned man has no advance warning,' said Wade Applegate.

'I was across the border in Mexico bringing up a drive of cattle I had bought. When I got back to the ranch my father was gone. His letter was on the dresser in his bedroom, weighted down by his gun and cartridge belt.

'I waited six months for his return, then I sold the ranch and the stock. He'd told me to come first to the cowtown of Buffalo Run and make cautious inquiry regarding a squawman who raised Morgan horses. I hit the trail for Montana, travelling light and at night. When I reached Buffalo Run the Avenging Angels had two horses wearing the Square and Compass in the barn. They'd paid two weeks' board bill in advance and pulled out. But I'd already played the damn fool and shot down a tinhorn named Charlie Decker. After I was cleared of the killing, which was in self-defense, I was elected Sheriff of Buffalo Run. That night the stage was held up and I took the trail of the road-agents. When I went to the barn to get a horse, the two Square and Compass horses were gone.'

'Are you calculating on working at that sheriff's job?' Wade Applegate asked.

'Yes sir,' Bryce answered quickly. 'But there's a hangman's rope waiting for me if I have the damnfool guts to return to Buffalo Run.'

Bryce picked up the unfinished letter the detective had written. He handed it to Applegate to read.

When he finished reading it, there was a grim smile under the drooping moustache. 'This letter, properly presented in court,' he said, 'will hang Quensel and Fogarty and Kaster. I hope to be there when Judge Morgan passes his death sentence. Those three hangings should clear the air. Your sheriff's job is to cut out the pattern, a pattern cut on the bias if you capture the three alive.'

'It will take some tricky skull work,' Bryce said doubtfully. 'My brain don't work that way.'

'I'll be around to help you mark the cards and stack the deck. Quensel isn't the only gambler who can handle a double-shuffle.'

'I'd like to bring in the road-agents they sent me after, together with the loot,' Bryce grinned wolfishly.

'I thought you said your brain didn't function when it came to tricks. Fetch Matthew and Stephen in on the hoof, and you'll have pulled a couple of white rabbits from the plug hat.' Wade Applegate got up and filled two glasses from the whiskey bottle. 'This calls for a drink, Sheriff.'

It was when Bryce set down his empty glass that he remembered what Nile had said in her note, that Judge Morgan and Virginia were leaving by stage for Fort Benton. His brows pulled together in a thoughtful scowl.

'Can I get a letter off right now by fast messenger?' he asked.

'An Injun boy can out-travel the Pony Express. Get the letter written.' Wade Applegate brought out pen and ink and writing paper.

Dear Nile. I hope this reaches you in time to keep Judge Plato Morgan in town. If my luck holds out, I'll bring in the road-agents to be tried in his court. Don't tell anyone but the Judge that I'm coming back. I'm trusting you, Nile, with all I got to lose. Bryce.

Wade Applegate's squaw was waiting when Bryce put the letter in an envelope and sealed it. She carried it outside to the Indian boy who sat bareback on one of the rancher's Morgan horses.

CHAPTER EIGHT

A man could buy anything at Chepete's Halfway House, providing he had the money.

That wily, weasel-eyed little French-Canadian half-breed had no fixed price on anything he had to sell in his trading store. Guns and ammunition had a varying value. The rot-gut whisky he made and peddled by the jug or bottle was priced according to the purchaser's urgent needs and the amount of money in his pocket. Everything Chepete had to sell was based on a varying scale.

Sometimes the price ran high, into real money, for such items as the dead body of a man you wanted killed and didn't want to get your own hands bloody. The little 'breed charged according to the danger involved in the actual killing and the risk afterwards.

A man couldn't be too careful and cautious about slip-ups and mistakes that might get him hung by the Vigilantes or shot down by a relative or friend of the murdered man, Chepete would explain it with gestures to a prospective customer.

'Cash on de barrel-head, by Gar.' Chepete's beady black eyes would bore tiny gimlet holes through a man to read the thoughts in his brain. 'Of course,' he would shrug his buckskin shoulders by way of emphasis, 'there would be a bullet left hin de gon for dat man who say he hire dis

Chepete. Mebbe dat man talk lak de magpie with de split tongue when dat man she'll get dronk. Hor mebbe talk in de sleep, han de woman hin de blanket listen. Bimeby dat gossip she spread lak damn prairie fire hin de dry grass. Me, Chepete, Hi'm tak no damn chances, by Gar.'

It was rumoured that Chepete was in the habit of using that second bullet more often than not. His trade in that commodity, involving danger and risk, had fallen off.

The selling of information was another item that was apt to be costly in Chepete's fluctuating scale of prices. It all depended on what a customer wanted to find out and the danger involved.

Chepete's knowledge of what had happened in the past, what was going on now and what was likely to happen in the future was a vast storehouse, kept behind the cunning half-breed's sealed lips. Money was the only key that could unlock his lipless mouth that opened and closed like the jaws of a trap. The grin on his lean, hatchet face was wolfish. His laugh had the sound of a trap chain rattling. His movements were as swift and furtive as the weasel eyes. Chepete was a fast man with a knife or gun or with the three foot length of greased buckskin string looped around his lean middle under the multi-colored woven Hudson's Bay sash he wore, the long fringes of which hung down on one side where he wore his knife scabbard.

Chepete stood five feet in his Cree moccasins. He could stand flat-footed and kick the ash off a cigarette in the mouth of a six-foot man. Or his moccasined foot could break the Adam's apple in a man's throat or break a man's jaw. Sometimes he used both feet to kick a man in the belly or guts or lower down. The little half-breed could handle himself in the toughest company.

It was only on very rare occasions he ever had need to call upon the backing of the score or more 'breeds who camped down the creek with their wives and families. French-Canadian 'breeds like himself who had followed their leader when they had been run across the line under the armed escort of the Northwest Mounted Police. The Canadian government had weeded Chepete and his followers out as undesirables as the aftermath of the Riel Rebellion.

Whenever the notion came, Chepete would 'mak de dance'. All that it took to make a dance was a fiddle and a jug and cornmeal sprinkled on the smooth worn pineboard floor of the log cabin store.

Usually the notion came when Chepete was pleased about something that had put money in his iron safe or benefited his greed for power. He'd uncork his jug and drink till the desire to dance the Red River jig set fire to his blood.

There was such a dance now in full swing at Chepete's Halfway House when the pair of Avenging Angels, Matthew and Stephen, rode up out of the night. They reined up and leaning across their saddle-horns, they peered into the lantern lit room through the open door.

A dozen couples were dancing to the fast beat of the Red River jig. The fiddler stood on a long platform, fiddle tucked under his chin, the resined bow moving swiftly.

Chepete leaped high above the floor, kicking his moccasined heels together. He bounced like a rubber ball, his body twisting backwards in a somersault that landed him on his feet. The shrill laughter of the young 'breed girls could be heard through the shouted acclamation of the men.

Quickly Chepete motioned the fiddler to continue playing. He threaded his way with darting movements through the open door, flattening himself outside in the dark shadow of the log wall, all in a matter of seconds.

79

'Sacre'! The half-breed's voice knifed through the noise from inside. 'She's de 'breed dance, by Gar. What you want at Chepete's, eh?'

It was not the first time that white men with rotgut whisky burning their guts had showed up to break up the 'breed dances at Chepete's Halfway House. Pete Kaster's tough crew of cowpunchers would swarm into dance with the pretty 'breed girls, shoving the men aside. Sometimes it would be Tim Fogarty's bullwhackers and mule skinners. Again it would be a rowdy hoodlum gang of young toughs from Buffalo Run, come to break up the dance.

The results were always the same. A general ruckus, a free for all fight. Knives would cut and slash and stab. Pistols would be drawn and fired. Women would scream and run to hide in the brush.

The drunken white men would prowl the brush, pulling young 'breed girls from their hiding places, their dresses ripped off.

Chepete's trading store would be a blood-spattered shambles. His stock of rotgut white mule corn whisky would be stolen, jugs and bottles smashed. Breaking up the 'breed dances came under the head of indoor sports. Gangs of horsebackers thought nothing of a thirty-forty mile ride to join the festivities.

There was a Colt .45 in Chepete's hand as he stood crouched in the shadows.

'We been here before, Chepete,' Matthew said. 'All we want is a place to lay low for a few days, maybe a week. The same as we did before.'

'Oui, by Gar,' Chepete grinned to himself. 'Ride to the barn, put hup de horse. Hi'm show hup soon.'

'Don't tell anybody we're here, Chepete,' Matthew warned him in a saw-edged whisper. 'Fetch me a jug, the best you got. I got money to pay.'

80

Stephen was bent low along the neck of his horse. His bloodshot crossed eyes had a lustful glassy look as he watched a slim half-breed girl in a red dress and beaded moccasins dancing with a tall, wide-shouldered 'breed in his early twenties.

The tall 'breed was laughing as he swung the girl off the floor. Her skirt swirled up to show brown-skinned, shapely bare legs. Her hair hung down her back in a blue-black mane and her white teeth flashed in a smile, her large brown eyes soft, melting.

'Fetch me that 'breed girl in the red dress, Chepete,' Stephen's voice was thick-tongued, slobbery.

'I bring you one other girl, eh?' Chepete told him.

'I picked the one I want,' Stephen said in a surly voice.

'I bring two, t'ree girls,' Chepete said uneasily. 'You take your pick. Keep all t'ree, eh?'

Stephen's gun was in his hand. 'I told you the one in red dress.'

Matthew spurred his horse into Stephen's and took the gun away. 'We can't afford a ruckus here. Git that into your rutty-brained skull. Pull up the slack in your jaw and wipe your chin off.' Matthew's voice was that of a father speaking to a half-witted son.

'Everything you own has a price, Chepete,' Matthew said. 'Fetch the girl in the red dress to the barn and I'll pay you what she's worth.'

'Qui, by Gar,' Chepete said, shrugging his shoulders.

'Send a man you can trust,' Matthew lowered his voice to a whisper, 'to Wade Applegate's ranch, to pick up what news there is to be gathered. If you don't have a man you can trust, go yourself. I'll make it worth your while, Chepete.'

'Dat Big Gregory,' a sly grin crossed Chepete's face, 'he dance with my girl Marie in de red dress. Sacre, Hi'm mark

81

half de Gregory's debt off de ledger. When he ride hoff, I bring Marie to de barn. One hondred dollars.' He drove his bargain.

'Fifty when you fetch the girl,' Matthew dickered shrewdly, 'fifty when Gregory brings back the news from Applegate's.'

'She's de bargeen! Sacre, damn!' Chepete's chuckle had a dry rattling sound. He motioned the two men away.

Stephen was once more bent over his saddle watching every movement of the girl's lithe, slim body, the bright colored beads on her moccasins sparkling like jewels on her dancing feet.

Matthew crowded his horse close. There was a snarl in his rasping whisper. 'Last time you got outa hand, I tied you up. Git your mind off it!' The quirt in his hand made a hissing sound as it fell across the back of Stephen's horse. For a few seconds, Stephen had all he could do to stay in the saddle.

They rode at a lope towards the big barn and its hayloft hiding place.

CHAPTER NINE

Bryce Bradford and Wade Applegate were up before sunrise, leading the horses in the barn to water at the creek, cleaning the stalls, haying and graining the horses, when Big Gregory showed up.

The two men watched the tall half-breed ride through the gate and come down the hill.

'One of Chepete's 'breed outfit,' the squawman said, 'and up to no good.'

'Long time no see, Gregory,' Wade Applegate said. 'I hear you're going to marry Marie, Chepete's youngest.'

Gregory grinned uneasily, shifting his weight to one stirrup. 'Maybe we get married purty quick now.'

'You're a good picker,' Applegate said. 'Step down. What's on your mind, besides your guilty conscience?'

The big 'breed scuffed his new boots in the dust. Tiny beads of sweat began to show on his high cheekbones as he scowled at the ground in a long, uneasy silence.

'Chepete,' Gregory met the older man's eyes, 'he sent me over here to find out things. Said for me to hang around and listen to any talk and keep my eyes open and my mouth shut. Two white men Chepete had hid in the hayloft will pay me when I get back with the news.'

Wade Applegate cut a meaning look at Bryce, then he spoke to Gregory. 'Did you see the two men? Did one have grey whiskers, the other about your age?'

'Yes, sir. They rode up about midnight. Chepete called me from the dance and said he was hiding the two men out for a few days. They were in the hayloft when I saddled my horse to come here. I got a look at their horses, branded with a brand I never seen.' He squatted on his boot-heels and picked up a stick. He drew the Square and Compass in the dirt.

Wade Applegate told Gregory to put up his horse and come to the house. When the 'breed came from the barn, they started towards the house by way of the graveyard.

'I come here,' the half-breed said, 'to sneak around and find out things. By rights, you should run me off. What are you going to do to me?'

'Nothing. On the way to the house I'll show you two dead men under a tarp. The bodies of Wade Applegate and Bryce Bradford. They were both shot in the back by the two men hiding in the hayloft. The men who rode those Square and Compass horses. You will take the information back to Chepete.'

They went into the house by way of the kitchen door where the squaw was getting breakfast. She eyed the half-breed Cree with cold suspicion. She was a full-blood Sioux and the Sioux and Crees had been old enemies before the coming of the white man. Now the Sioux and Crees were conquered people under the thumb of the white man and the United States Government.

'Keep your scalping knife in its scabbard, woman,' Wade Applegate told his squaw. 'Big Gregory is fixing to get married and he needs his hair left on.'

He led the way to the lean-to shed at the kitchen door where all three of them washed up at the scoured tin basin, drying on the same clean roller towel.

Wade Applegate was relying on his squaw's curiosity and it amused him to watch the way she maneuvered it, detaining Gregory in the kitchen while Bryce and he sat down to breakfast in the dining-room. Before long they heard them talking in a conglomeration of Sioux, Cree and white man's swear words, with a little sign language to bridge the gaps.

The squawman interpreted the talk as he unscrambled it for Bryce's benefit. 'She hates Chepete's guts, but feels sorry for his Cree woman. Chepete's twin daughters work in the trading store. Antoinette, the smart one, keeps the books and handles the men. Marie is quiet and gentle. Both are good-looking girls. Antoinette takes after her father, cunning and treacherous. Chepete has taught her a lot of tricks. She's too handy with a knife. She's never been married to any of the men she's strung along and she's had a lot of 'em. She's a young wildcat, the one called Toni for short. Purrs like a kitten under a man's caresses, while she goes through his pockets. If she's caught, she claws and bites her way out. You see some gent looks like he's tried to tame a wildcat, after he's spent an evenin' with Toni.

'My woman is giving some advice to Gregory. She just told him she'll cut his gizzard out if he ever hurts Marie.'

Big Gregory's face was red when he came to the table. He sat opposite Bryce but was too self-conscious to help himself to the food.

'Tie into that grub before it gets cold,' Wade Applegate told him. 'Clean your plate, or my squaw is apt to scalp you.'

He said conversation ruined a good meal. The table talk should be limited to 'Pass the salt.'

When the meal was finished, they went into the living-room and when comfortably seated, the squawman spoke through his pipe smoke. 'How soon does Chepete expect you back, Gregory?'

'He said the two white men were anxious to get the

news I was to fetch back. He was charging them plenty, but they wouldn't pay till I got back. The sooner I get back the quicker he'll get his money and mark my debt off the ledger.'

'Did he know who the men were?'

'He said they were road-agents who held up the stage two nights ago.'

'Did Chepete offer to cut you in on any deal?'

'You know how Chepete is,' Gregory said uneasily. 'He talks a lot without saying anything.' The young 'breed was beginning to sweat a little.

Bryce knew that it had to be fear of some kind that was holding him back from talking. Bryce felt a little sorry for him. In spite of his better judgment, he had taken a liking to the 'breed.

'How many times, Gregory,' Wade Applegate asked quietly, 'have you helped Chepete with his chores?'

'Chepete has me across the barrel,' the words were forced out. 'He lets me go in debt at the store. I owe him for a Miles City saddle that costs forty dollars. A pair of chaps. A silver mounted bit and spurs, a Stetson hat. I wanted to make a showing so Marie would like me.' Gregory was sitting on the edge of his chair, hands clenched. Wade Applegate let him sweat.

'Chepete let you get over your head in debt,' he finally said. 'Then what happened?' The softness in his lazy drawl was no longer there.

'You know what happened then,' Gregory exclaimed. 'I was one of the 'breeds Chepete sent to steal twenty-five head of your yearling colts from the weanling herd at Haystack Butte.' His voice cracked and broke on a high note.

'Why didn't you call me in last fall with the other 'breeds you brought here for punishment?' he asked.

'I had my own reasons, Gregory. The others were old

offenders. I let them off easy and told them what would happen if I ever caught any of them again stealing my stock.'

The 'breed wiped the sweat from his face with the back of his hand. Wade Applegate's eyes were cold as blue ice.

'Before Chepete sent you here, Gregory,' he said. 'He made you a proposition. What was it?'

'He said the two men he was hiding out had a lot of money in a canvas bean sack. He saw them take it up the ladder to the hayloft. Chepete said he was going to get that money they stole when they held up the stage. He said he'd have them dead drunk by dark tonight and he wanted me there to back his play if he got into a tight. He said they were killers. He said he'd cut me in on the money. He had me over the barrel,' Gregory whined.

'So you took him up on the proposition.' Wade Applegate's voice was gentle.

'He had a knife in his hand,' the 'breed said. 'I had to agree. I was sick with fear. He told me to saddle up and ride here. He said the two men had killed you and the new sheriff of Buffalo Run. He wanted to make sure you were both dead.'

'What else?'

'He said those two road-agents had propositioned him to hire a few 'breeds and run your horses south. Chepete said if I helped him kill the two men in the hayloft, there was nothing to stop us from stealing your horses and he'd cut me in on the profits.'

'It must have been a surprise to find us alive,' Wade Applegate said, his hard lips twisting in a sardonic grin.

'Yes, sir, it was, but I was glad to see you both alive.' Gregory rose to his feet and stood there wiping the sweat from his face with his shirt sleeve.

Applegate let him stand while he filled his pipe from a buckskin pouch. When he got the tobacco lit, he smoked for a while in thoughtful silence. In the early morning sunlight that came into the room through an open window a meadow-lark warbled its song from a tree top.

Bryce looked at the tall young half-breed, dressed in a bright red shirt and new pants and new squeaky boots. Humiliation was clearly stamped on his face as he waited with quivering belly to receive whatever punishment was meted out.

When the song of the meadow-lark ended, Wade Applegate spoke.

'All you've really done, Gregory,' he said, 'is to confess the crimes Chepete had in mind, so supposing you return to Chepete's place and tell him you saw Wade Applegate and Sheriff Bryce Bradford lying dead under a blood-stained old wagon tarp at the end of the graveyard. Tell Chepete that and nothing more. Whatever you do after that is strictly up to you, Gregory.'

Bryce had got to his feet and stood facing the 'breed to whom he said, 'Wade Applegate is giving you a chance to prove yourself, Gregory. He's giving you a chance to marry your girl.'

Gregory's sagging shoulders straightened and he looked into the squawman's steady blue eyes.

'I'll do whatever you tell me to, Mister Wade,' he said humbly.

'All you have to do is to take a few lies back to Gregory,' Applegate told him, then asked, 'How much do you owe Chepete?'

'Almost a hundred dollars. Toni showed me the ledger. But I got to pay him two hundred that isn't on the books.'

'What for?'

'If I don't pay him the two hundred dollars, he won't let me marry Marie. That's the price he has on Marie.'

Wade Applegate crossed the room to the roll top desk in the far corner of the room. A moment later he returned with a roll of bills. 'Here's three hundred, Gregory. That'll get you off the hook.'

'I can't take money from you, Mister Wade, unless you let me work it out.'

'If that's the way you feel about it, I'll give you the contract for putting up the hay. I'll furnish the teams and mowing machines and hay wagons. You hire what men you'll need and I'll pay them their wages.' Wade Applegate smiled. 'Get Marie away from Chepete's and bring her here. That woman of mine will take good care of her. When the haying's done I'll need a man in that winter line camp. You can move in there with your bride. You've got a job with me as long as you want it, Gregory.'

'You mean,' Big Gregory forced a wry grin, 'that you're trusting me?'

'Why not? That woman of mine claims you're a good man even if you got some Cree blood in you. I've never yet known her judgment to be wrong.'

Gregory was caught off-balance by Wade Applegate's understanding and generosity, and Bryce Bradford was sharing his emotions as they both looked at the white-haired man.

Wade Applegate seemed a little embarrassed by the frank admiration in the eyes of the two younger men. He looked at the clock on the mantelpiece. 'It's time for you to get going, Gregory.'

Big Gregory grinned widely and shook hands awkwardly with them both. They watched him ride away.

'I reckon,' Bryce said quietly, 'it's about time for me to saddle up and hit the trail.'

'You realize the danger that lies in wait, Bryce. Take care of yourself. This is your home. Come back to it.' The blue eyes were misted with unshed tears, and Bryce knew that there would be a prayer in the older man's heart as he rode away.

CHAPTER TEN

Bryce Bradford was timing his arrival at Chepete's Halfway House for sometime after dark. He had given Big Gregory more than a half hour's head start. The young half-breed must have kept up a long trot because Bryce had not caught even a distant glimpse of the rider.

Bryce tried to figure out some plan as he rode along. He told himself all he had to do was hold back and wait for Chepete to make his killer-play for the loot. Let wolf eat wolf, then when the gunsmoke cleared and the dust settled, he could pick up the kindling. That was, Bryce told himself, what the average sheriff on a man hunt would do, play both ends against the middle. It would save a lot of wear and tear on the system.

But Bryce wasn't going into this in the capacity of a law officer. Matthew and his cross-eyed son were the Avenging Angels who had hounded his tracks. They'd shot down two men in the dark, believing they were killing Bryce Bradford and Wade Applegate, who never in his life had packed a gun. So Bryce wasn't going to let Chepete or any other man on earth do his gun chores for him.

He decided there was no use in mapping out any plan of attack until he got there. By the time he reached Chepete's Big Gregory would have delivered the news and no one would be expecting him to show up.

The rolling prairie had flattened out at late dusk. The shadows of night were blanketing the sage-brush and greasewood wasteland of Alkali Flat. Chepete's place was at the far end where the stage road crossed Alkali Creek.

Bryce took his bearings from the evening star. A big yellow lop-sided moon pushed up over the skyline as he was crossing the five mile stretch of Alkali Flat, and a prairie wolf somewhere in the night sat on gaunt haunches, long nose pointed skyward, and gave voice in a salute before starting its night prowl.

The wolf howl had no echo in the flat country, except in the heart of Bryce Bradford who knew the danger he was riding into, his hand on his gun, his hat slanted to throw his face in shadow.

Ahead showed the yellow blobs of light of Chepete's Halfway House. As he rode up, everything was quiet and peaceful and there was no sign of life anywhere. The double doors of the barn were closed, the door of the hayloft open. Bryce rode up from the blind end and swung down, dropping his bridle reins to ground-tie his horse.

He kept close to the shadows of the barn as he edged along, his gun ready. Every nerve in his body was taut as he shoved one of the big doors inward, wide enough to slip through. He stood flattened against the door he had closed, listening, eyes squinted into the darkness. The wooden butt of his Colt .45 felt moist in the sweaty palm of his hand.

He could hear the movements of the horses in their stalls but that was all. He was about to move when a dry scuffling came from the hayloft and particles of dust and hay came down into his eyes as he looked up.

'Quit that clawin' and bitin',' Stephen's voice had a nasal whine. 'Open them purty lips so's a man can pour some of your old man's rotgut into you. I'm fillin' that little belly of yours full of booze to set your guts afire and maybe you'll listen to reason and quit clawing me. I'll get you so drunk you can't move, you little bitch.'

'Hand me the jug. I'll do my own drinking,' the girl said. 'It won't be the first time I've drunk Papa's rotgut. Quit pawing me. I'll give in when I'm ready. . . .'

Bryce's eyes had focused to the dark. He could make out the ladder rungs nailed to the log wall and was edging his way cautiously across the hard-packed dirt floor when he heard a dull crashing noise above, like a man had fallen heavily.

Stephen's harsh outcry saw-edged inside the barn. Then bare or moccasined feet padded swiftly across the hayloft, then ceased abruptly. Then cowhide boots thumped overhead and Stephen spat out a string of obscenities.

Stephen was coming down the ladder now. Bryce, crouched to one side in the dark, waited until his feet touched the floor, then he was on his back, pitching him forward on his face.

Bryce grabbed at the shock of sweat matted hair and jerked Stephen's head around, twisting his face up to look into the cross-eyes. 'Know me, you slimy bastard? I'm Bryce Bradford!'

The gun slashed down in short chopping blows on the unprotected face and Stephen's high-bridged nose flattened out, spurting blood. His scream was choked off as Bryce's gun smashed the discolored yellow teeth into a gaping maw.

Bryce let go the sweaty hair. He shoved Stephen's battered, bloody face into the dirt, then got to his feet. He rolled Stephen over on his back and kicked him roughly in the crotch. Stephen let out one agonized scream, then was silent.

Darkness concealed the hate that masked Bryce's face as he stood straddle of the Avenging Angel from Rainbow's End. He was breathing heavily as he waited for the tight, twisted knot inside his belly to loosen.

Low, moaning sounds came from inside the barn and it took Bryce a little while to locate Big Gregory in the last empty stall. His hands were tied behind his back and his legs tied with a halter rope. When Bryce cut him free and struck a match, he saw the battered face of the big half-breed, who looked up at him from swollen slits of eyes.

'Marie,' Gregory's voice was a croaking whisper. 'Chepete sold her to the old man with the chin whiskers. He bought her for his son.'

'I'll get her for you, Gregory', Bryce told him. 'Just take it easy. Who worked you over?'

'Chepete and the old man were in the saloon drinking whisky. I told them you and Wade Applegate were both dead and I gave Chepete the money. I said I was taking Marie away tonight. The old man laughed and said his son had Marie in the hayloft.

'I ran for the barn. Chepete jumped my back as I was opening the barn door. He kicked me in the face and belly, then everything went black. I got to find Marie,' he croaked in a racking sob, and struggled to his feet.

Bryce led him to the front end of the barn and eased him down to a sitting position with his back against a manger. Stephen lay near the ladder, out like a light. 'Take it easy till I get back. Ride herd on that bastard. If he comes alive, yell for me.'

Bryce went up into the loft. It was empty. When he looked out the loft door he could see the girl on the ground in a motionless, twisted shape.

It was a fifteen foot drop from the loft to the ground. Bryce hung by his hands for a moment, then let go. He kept his body relaxed so that his knees hinged when he struck ground. He let himself go and rolled over and on to his feet almost on top of the girl.

Her head jerked up. For a brief instant Bryce got a look

at the white face and the black fire in her wide eyes. Then her fingers were clawing at his face. He made an instinctive grab at her shoulders, pulling her close against him, lowering his head to protect his face.

'Take it easy,' Bryce told her as her clawlike fingers grabbed his hair and yanked. 'I'm not Stephen. I'm not going to hurt you. I'm taking you to Gregory.'

The girl was fighting like a young she-wildcat .Her teeth bit into the side of his neck and as he lifted his head, she spat a mouthful of his own blood in his face.

'Quit it,' Bryce panted, getting a grip of her long black hair to hold her face away. 'I came to take you to Gregory. Can't you get that through your head? I'm here to help you both, Marie.'

The black fire died out slowly in her eyes. She was no longer fighting, but the tenseness was still present.

'Who are you?' she asked.

'Bryce Bradford. You don't know me.'

'The new Sheriff at Buffalo Run?' she whispered tensely.

'I reckon so.' He forced a grin as he let go her hair.

'You're a liar, mister. Bryce Bradford is dead. Those two men shot him and Wade Applegate at the squawman's horse ranch.'

'This is no time to argue with a woman,' Bryce said. He picked her up in his arms, expecting the clawing and biting to start again, but she made no effort to resume her wildcat tactics. Her body felt limp as she let her head fall back, her long hair almost touching the ground. Her large eyes were black depthless pools. The color was back in her face and in the red lips that parted in a smile. Then her arms went around his neck and she pulled his head down, fastening her lips on his.

Her teeth bit into his lip. Bryce felt his knees tremble. He had to tighten his arms to keep her twisting body from slipping. The blood was pounding into his throat, hammering against his eardrums. Her clinging mouth slid away and he heard her soft mocking laugh as he pushed the barn door open and carried her inside, kicking the door shut.

'Here's your girl,' Bryce told Gregory as he slid the girl down beside him. 'Take her. I got a job to do.'

'Marie.' The name was ripped from inside Gregory as he stumbled to his feet.

'I'm Toni,' the girl said. 'Marie's hid out. I put on her red dress. Cross-eyes didn't know the difference. Who's the man who carried me in?'

'Bryce Bradford,' Gregory said dazedly.

'Oh,' the girl's voice had a hint of defiance in it. 'I'm sorry I called you a liar, Sheriff.'

Bryce opened the door. 'Don't let Stephen get away,' he warned as he went out and closed the door.

Bryce was still trembling as he headed for the saloon, keeping close to the shadows of the buildings as he ran. He lifted the door latch slowly, then shoved the door open and stood back from it, his gun in his hand. When he peered into the lamplit room, the saloon was empty. He headed for the store and flattening himself against the log wall, he looked in through an unwashed window.

The small statured, wiry built man in the buckskin shirt squatted in front of the big black safe, working the combination, had to be Chepete.

Bryce made out the lanky, rawboned figure who stood back in the shadow beyond reach of the glow of the lamp on the counter above Chepete's head. Matthew's thin lips were skinned back and his pale eyes slivered. The gun in his hand moved a little in a short gesture as Chepete swung open the safe door.

'Dig into 'er, you runty bastard. I want all you got.' Matthew's short laugh sounded like seeds rattling in a dry gourd. 'Put the money in that sack I gave you and hurry it up. Me'n Stephen is pullin' out directly he gets his ashes hauled.'

Matthew moved out from the shadow and came slowly across the floor to approach the squatting Chepete from behind.

Chepete was working in feverish haste to fill the sack. His head kept twisting around as Matthew came towards him, his grey chin whiskers jutted out and murder in his eye.

'The safe, she's hempty, by Gar.' Chepete's head twisted upward. 'Hall de money I got in de worl' ees een dat sack.'

'You won't need money where you're goin', you runty 'breed.' Matthew grinned as he thumbed back the gun hammer.

Bryce's six-shooter barrel smashed the window-pane, whirling Matthew around. In that same split-second Chepete came up from the floor as if his legs were levered springs. His wiry little body twisted in mid-air and his moccasined feet struck Matthew full in the face just as the gun spat flame.

The kick slapped Matthew's head back on its skinny neck. His long legs gave way and as he went over backwards a flailing arm knocked the lamp off the counter. The next instant there was a sheet of flame, ceiling high.

Chepete grabbed up the canvas sack of money from the floor and bent over, he moved swiftly, crabwise towards the back door. His face was a ghastly, slimy mask, the beady black eyes burning in deep sockets.

Bryce smashed the window in and threw one leg across the sill. If he moved fast he could drag Matthew out the back door Chepete had left open, before the place became an inferno.

He was less than twenty feet from Matthew, whose head was twisted sideways on its broken neck, his gun still gripped in his hand. Matthew's eyes opened and into their hate-glazed depths came recognition of Bryce Bradford. No muscle moved in the inert body and the hand holding the gun was rigid. Bryce wasn't aware that the six-shooter was cocked until flame spurted from its black muzzle.

Bryce shot at that instant, tearing a black hole above Matthew's high-bridged nose. Death fixed the hate in Matthew's eyes.

The bullet that had creased Bryce's ribs was like a hot branding-iron. He staggered forward a step, then caught his balance. He was wading in a puddle of flames and smoke choked his throat. He grabbed Matthew by the feet and dragged him as he backed out the door and fell down the three steps to the ground, pulling the dead man clear.

Bryce coughed as he crawled away from the burning building. The flames licked the dry log walls and the exploding stock of cartridges stored inside the store sounded as if a gun battle was being waged.

Bryce saw Chepete bent over double as he carried the money sack to the log cabin where he lived with his squaw and two daughters.

The cabin door was open and the squaw stood motionless in the doorway, watching Chepete, but making no effort to lend her husband a helping hand, even when he stumbled and fell to the ground.

Chepete was spewing out a strange mixture of Canuck French and Cree blasphemy as he sat up, blood spilling from clenched teeth and down the corners of his ghastly grin. The sack was slowly spreading with crimson stain from the gunshot Matthew's bullet had torn.

Big Gregory ran out of the barn into the red glow of the fire. He called for Marie over and over with each unsteady, lurching step, like a mechanical man-sized talking toy.

Bryce stood facing the barn. He was squinting sweat from his eyes when he saw Stephen spur his horse out of the barn, a short-barrelled Winchester carbine gripped in both hands. The Square and Compass gelding was gun broke, trained by expert hand, and savvied the pressure of its rider's knees like the touch of a bridle rein.

Stephen charged his horse at Bryce, to ride him down. 'Stay dead!' he shouted. 'This time stay dead, Bryce Bradford!' Bryce felt the whining snarl of the 30-30 bullet past his head as the big gelding swerved sideways to avoid trampling Bryce, which is a horse's natural instinct unless it happens to be an outlaw horse turned man killer.

The sudden sideways jump of the horse threw Stephen off balance, making him grab the saddle-horn with one hand. Bryce shot at the quick moving target but missed.

Stephen suddenly let go the saddle gun and his hand slipped its frantic grip on the horn. As he fell, his boot caught in the ox-bow stirrup and a terror-filled scream came from his gaping mouth as he hung by one foot.

Then the scream was blotted out by a shod hoof as the running horse kicked loose. The momentum rolled his body over so that it lay face down, and it was then that Bryce saw the buckhorn haft and a few inches of steel of the bowie knife between the dead man's shoulder blades.

Bryce gulped down mouthfuls of clean fresh air as he fought back the nausea. He was moving like a sleep walker through the fire glow of his nightmare. The taste of death was in his mouth and the blast of gunfire was an aching drum in his brain. He forced himself to keep moving.

Somewhere beyond the barn lay the creek. He'd keep

going until he found it. Never had water seemed more precious. The smoke-coated thickness of his tongue had swollen like a mouthful of dirty flannel, and as the waves of nausea came his eyes no longer focused. Only the will to get to water kept him on his feet.

He neither saw nor heard the girl in the torn red dress take hold of his arm and guide him. She held on to him while he sat belt deep in the water and lowered his head and face into the creek. Consciousness returned slowly and he became aware of somebody holding him, to keep him from toppling.

Bryce twisted his head around to see who it was. The half-breed girl was almost waist deep in the water, her red dress clinging wetly to her slim body. With the red glow of the blaze reflected on the water, she looked like a pagan goddess of fire standing in a river of molten flame that was by some conjuring trick, cooling. The deep black fire in her eyes held him trapped in a strange, gripping nightmare of unreality.

Bryce became dimly aware of men shouting and the resined scrape of a bow across fiddle strings while the fiddle was being tuned, then the quickened sound of the Red River Jig.

The spell was broken. 'Nero fiddled while Rome burned,' Bryce spoke without thinking.

Toni let go her hold on his shoulders. 'Stay where you are, mister, while I get your horse. I kept your gun dry. It's on the bank with your cartridge belt and hat. You're getting the hell away from here before those half-breed cronies Chepete left behind get drunk and start prowling. They don't like the color of a white man's skin around here.'

Bryce watched her wade through the shallow water and vanish from sight in the tall willows. He crawled up on the bank and sat down to drain the water from his boots, shivering a little as the night breeze penetrated his wet clothes.

He put on his hat and buckled on his cartridge belt, feeling the reassuring weight of his gun. Remembering he had fired it, he ejected the empty shells and shoved in fresh cartridges. Then he worked his way cautiously through the willow thicket and tangled underbrush, to get a look at what was going on.

Beyond reach of the heat from the still burning log building, Bryce could see the younger 'breeds with girls in their arms, dancing around a barrel of whisky that had been rolled out from the saloon. A pile of tin cups were in a bushel basket nearby. The fiddler stood on the whisky barrel, his fiddle tucked under his chin, the dancers moving in quick step.

Men, women and children were standing in family groups watching the dancers, while a group of several young 'breeds were drinking from a passed jug in the barn doorway. They were all armed and their saddled horses stood ground tied. The bodies of Matthew and Stephen still lay on the ground.

Bryce sought in vain for a glimpse of Big Gregory. Chepete's body was gone and his squaw was nowhere in sight.

Despite the fiddle music and the shrill squealing of the 'breed girls as their partners swung them off their feet, there was an undercurrent of tenseness beneath the surface of gaiety. A potential danger that formed a black whirlpool in the armed group of younger 'breeds. It was only a matter of time until the rotgut started working and then all hell would tear loose.

The sound of breaking brush on the far side of the creek turned Bryce around, his thumb on his gun hammer.

'Move fast, mister,' Toni's voice was sharp edged. 'Get over here.' She had on a shirt and overalls and her hair

101

was piled up under the high crown of a wide-brimmed black hat. A filled cartridge belt sagged around her slim waist and she was mounted on Stephen's Square and Compass horse. She led Bryce's saddled horse by the bridle reins.

Bryce waded to the other side of the creek and stood close to her horse's withers. 'Chepete's cronies are holding a wake. Get a-horseback, mister.' Her red lips peeled back to show her teeth.

Bryce noticed the bloodstained canvas sack she had tied to the back of Stephen's saddle. When Bryce made a tentative gesture to re-tie a loosened string, and she slid a wet moccasined foot from the stirrup and without any indication of warning, kicked him, flat footed, in the face. It was more like a quick shove than a kick, but hard enough to send Bryce back a step, off-balance.

'Hands off, mister,' the 'breed girl's voice had a cat-like snarl.

Bryce was looking into the black muzzle of a Colt pistol in her hand. The black flame was in her eyes.

'It's mine,' she spat the words in his face. 'I earned every rotten dollar of it.'

'I don't want your damn money,' Bryce said. 'I was just going to tie a saddle string that came loose.' He turned his back on her and reached for the latigo strap to tighten his saddle cinch.

'I didn't see any sign of Gregory,' Bryce said over his shoulder. 'Did he get Marie and pull out?'

'To hell with that big ox and that cry-baby Marie. When I told him where I'd hid her, he left the barn like a turpentined dog.'

She shoved the gun back into its holster and twisted sideways in the saddle to tie the sack on securely.

'I'm getting to hell and gone away from here,' she

whispered from behind clenched teeth. 'Get a-horseback, like I said.'

'I'm staying behind,' Bryce told her. 'I got a couple of chores to finish at Chepete's place.'

'What about the money?' the girl asked.

'As Sheriff of Buffalo Run I set out to fetch back a couple of road-agents who held up the stage and got away with a lot of money. I'm taking their dead bodies back.'

"What about the money?' the girl asked.

'It's hidden somewhere,' Bryce eyed the girl narrowly. 'I'll prowl around till I locate it.'

Her short laugh had an ugly sound. 'There's half a dozen 'breeds with the same idea, mister. They're working on rotgut booze. You ride over there now and you'll last as long as a snowball in hell. I told you Chepete's cronies don't like a white man.'

'All right, Toni. You're trying your damndest to scare me away from Chepete's place. Why?'

'I don't want to see you shot down, that's why,' she answered sullenly.

'If I had one guess coming,' Bryce's grin twisted, 'I'd say you know where the money is hid. You got the information from Stephen before you stabbed him in the back with Gregory's Bowie knife.' Bryce watched her warily, ready to slap the gun from her hand if she pulled it.

'If I had another guess, I'd say you were coming back for it when the 'breeds finished their drunk and went home to sleep it off. That's how I got it figured, Toni.'

'I told you those 'breed cronies of Chepete's would be hunting for the booty from the stage hold-up.' Her eyes were half-lidded, crafty.

'Nobody but Chepete knew that Matthew and Stephen held up the stage, until you got Stephen to brag about it.' Bryce reached out suddenly and grabbed her wrist as her hand moved towards her gun. 'Chepete kept his mouth shut. So did you, Toni. There isn't a damn 'breed drunk or sober, man or woman, who knows about the hold-up money cache.'

Toni was breathing fast. She made no effort to free her wrist. 'Pick up the marbles, mister. I found the money in the hay and I've cached it where nobody but me can find it', she admitted. She leaned from her saddle and her lips brushed his. Bryce released her wrist.

'You're wrong about one guess, mister,' she said. 'When I leave here tonight, I'm travelling fast and I'm never coming back.' Her hand caressed the sack behind the high cantle of the saddle. 'I got my getaway stake here. If you'll come with me to Canada, a few months from now I'll tell you where I hid the stage money.'

'I told you I had a job to do here, Toni.'

'Quensel's Stranglers are waiting for you with a hangman's noose,' her voice was gritty, 'and it's not Quensel who gives the orders but Nile Carter. Nile has given orders to hang Sheriff Bryce Bradford if and when he brings in his prisoners and the loot. Does that change your mind about those chores you got in mind?'

Bryce shook his head. 'I got a letter signed by Nile Carter, warning me not to come back to Buffalo Run. What you just told me is old news, Toni.'

'What I'm telling you now,' the breed girl said, 'is older yet. It dates back to one Christmas Eve when Nile Carter was on the stage-coach that was held up by two masked road-agents. Three men were shot down in cold blood, but Nile Carter's life was spared. The next day she tried to buy a half-interest in the El Dorado.'

'What's wrong about that?' Bryce asked with provocative calm.

'Nile Carter was broke,' Toni's voice was vibrant.

'How do you know how much money Nile had?'

'Because I saw all she had in her purse. It was noon and snowing when Jerry O'Toole drove to Chepete's for dinner and a change of horses. I talked a lot to Nile Carter that day. I wanted to be what she was, wearing beautiful clothes. When I told her that, she told me she was just an adventuress who made her money from cheating men. She opened her purse and showed me all the money she had to her name, but said that she had no intention of starving as long as there was a sucker left.

'But on Christmas Day she wanted to buy a half-interest in the El Dorado. What do you make of that?' Toni asked, but Bryce had no answer.

It all fitted into what Wade Applegate had told him last night as they sat and smoked and talked. Toni was repeating in her own words what the old man had told him. Nile Carter held a lot of hidden secrets locked somewhere inside.

Wade Applegate had told Bryce that Chepete knew a lot about the Christmas Eve stage hold-up. That he'd sell the information for a price. That if the play came up, Bryce could get the information from his daughter Toni, but to take care she didn't knife him in the back.

Bryce remembered the knife between Stephen's shoulder blades. When he looked at the half-breed girl, the black smoldering fire was back in her brooding eyes.

Bryce felt the cold knot that twisted his belly. 'The three men,' he kept his voice even toned, 'who were passengers on the stage. Did you talk to them?'

'No, I didn't. When I asked Nile about them she said one was a prisoner and the other two were guards, and that was all she knew. Why?'

'One of the men,' Bryce told her, 'the one who was a prisoner, was my father.'

'Oh.' The girl stared at him. 'He was killed, so you're tracking down the killers.'

105

'My father was murdered, shot down in cold blood. Nile Carter was there and saw it all,' Bryce forced a mirthless grin. 'That's another reason I'm taking the two dead men back to Buffalo Run. I want to have a talk with Nile Carter.'

'Are you in love with Nile?' Toni asked bluntly.

'What difference would that make?' Bryce said curtly.

'It would make a lot of difference,' Toni spoke with brutal frankness. 'If I were a man like you in love with a woman like Nile, I'd kill that tinhorn Quensel where I found him. You shot the wrong man when you killed Decker. He hated Nile Carter's guts.' She spoke vehemently.

'You shot Decker on account of Virginia Morgan,' Toni continued with a sneer. 'Don't tell me you're stuck on that high-toned little trick, mister.' Toni laughed, a short bitter laugh. 'Once again you shot the wrong man. It's Quensel who wants that little delicate magnolia bud from the south. He tossed Nile into the discard. That's how come Nile made a play for you.' Toni smiled thinly. 'It takes another female to figure out the treacherous tricks of the trade when another woman makes her move.'

Bryce's grin was twisted, bitter as the taste that came into his mouth. He had nothing to say.

They both heard the loud drunken shouts of the 'breeds on the other side of the creek.

Toni crowded her horse close. 'I've got to get gone,' she said. 'That drunken coyote pack are hunting for me right now. Help me get away, mister, and I'll tell you where I cached that money.' She reined her horse around.

'Head for Wade Applegate's ranch,' Bryce said as they rode away.

'I'm heading for the Canadian line,' Toni told him. 'For the Cypress Hills country.' She spurred her horse to a run and there was nothing for Bryce to do but follow.

After an hour's hard ride, they came to a deserted log cabin, well hidden in the brush. The girl reined up and swung to the ground, loosening the saddle cinch. Bryce dismounted and waited while Toni went into the cabin. He could hear her prowling around in the dark.

After a short while she came out into the moonlight, wiping dirt from a quart bottle of whisky on the front of her shirt. 'One of Chepete's crocks', she said. She pried the cork out and handed the bottle to Bryce.

'Ladies first,' Bryce grinned faintly.

'I'm no lady, mister,' Toni said bitterly. 'I'm a half-breed slut.' She lifted the bottle and drank a large swallow.

The front of her shirt was gaping open. Her faded overalls fitted skin-tight to the slim legs and around her lean flanks and small buttocks.

Back at the creek, in the red glow of the fire on the water, Toni had looked strangely beautiful in her red dress, in a wild pagan way that was clean and untouchable.

Now there was an unclean obscenity to her half revealed breasts, the tight fitting overalls. Her breath stank of whisky and her elfin face, with the large black eyes, the white teeth outlined by parted lips, and faintly swarthy skin, taut across high cheek bones, had changed to the cruel hard lines of her father's hatchet face. Her eyes were glinting slivers of black agate, cruel and cunning.

The soured stench of rotgut booze now mingled with the musky odor of her body. The look in Bryce's eyes must have revealed his thoughts because the girl turned away and walked over to sit on a fallen log.

'I lied about the money,' she said. 'That goat-whiskered old man was too foxy to bring more than a couple of hundred dollars to the Halfway House. I never saw the money and neither did Chepete. I lied to get you to come with me. But here is where our trails fork. You go your way. I'll go mine.'

'To hell with the money,' Bryce blundered. 'You think you can make it to the Canadian line from here alone?' he asked.

'Hell, yes. Quit crying about it.'

'Then you'd better get going,' Bryce tightened his saddle cinch. 'I'll hang around here for a while in case some 'breeds show up. It'll give you a head start.'

'You'll find the hold-up money buried in the dirt floor of this cabin, unless that cross-eyed Mormon lied with a knife twisted in his back.' Her laugh was short and nasty sounding. 'Take the money and the dead men to Buffalo Run. Maybe Nile Carter will pin a leather medal on you before she ties your rope necktie.'

Toni walked over to her horse and slowly tightened the saddle cinch. 'I figured if I got you this far,' she said without looking around. 'I could get you to go the rest of the way. We'd dig up the money and travel to hell and gone. Together.'

There was something in the tone of her voice and the way the 'breed girl said it, that kept Bryce tracked and without a word to say, until she had ridden out of sight.

He was unaware of the bottle in his hand until he started for the cabin. Then he threw it, smashing it against the log wall as he went in.

The dirt floor was hard packed. He went outside and prowled around till he found a broken shovel in under some brush.

He lit the stub of candle in the neck of a whisky bottle and started digging. Half an hour later he had the money dug up. He opened the canvas sack to make certain it was there before he tied it on behind his saddle cantle.

He headed back for Chepete's place with his Win-

108

chester carbine across his saddle in front of him. The first streaks of dawn were spreading the skyline when a lone rider came into sight. He came from the direction of the Halfway House.

The rider was Wade Applegate. Never had Bryce been so glad to see any man.

CHAPTER ELEVEN

The slow grin on the leathery face of Wade Applegate touched his eyes as he looked Bryce over from head to foot.

'It's good to see you, boy.' His quiet voice was vibrant. 'Good to see you alive.'

Bryce Bradford was strangely moved, touched deep by the older man's emotions. He nodded, too choked to trust his voice. Both men were trying to cover up any outward display of feelings as they dismounted.

'There was quite a gun ruckus at Chepete's place,' Bryce told the older man.

'I heard about it. When Big Gregory showed up with his girl, I saddled up and brought him back with me. Between us we managed to get the whole story from the older 'breeds and the women. I left Big Gregory there to swamp up. I picked up your trail. What happened to the 'breed girl?' Applegate asked.

Bryce untied the money sack. 'This is the money from the stage hold-up,' Bryce said. 'Toni took me to where Matthew and Stephen buried it at an old deserted log cabin. She told me where to dig, then she pulled out. Said she was heading for the Canadian line.'

'The girl got away with Chepete's money, so the 'breeds say.'

'I know. Toni said she was claiming it, that she'd earned every dollar of it,' Bryce said defensively.

'She has every right to the money,' Wade Applegate said. 'She hid her sister in the dug-out cellar, put on her red dress and substituted her body for Marie's.'

'I don't know how Toni got hold of the money. Last time I saw the sack of money, Chepete was hugging it against his gunshot belly,' Bryce said.

'Chepete's squaw took it into their cabin when she dragged her dead husband in,' Applegate told Bryce. 'Toni slipped in by the back door, changed from the red dress to overalls and shirt. She had a cartridge belt buckled on and a gun in her hand, ready to shoot down anybody who got in her way. She took the money sack with her. Marie found her squaw mother lying on the bed. She was dead.' Wade Applegate said grimly.

'You think Toni killed her own mother?' Bryce asked.

'It was the squaw's skinning knife that killed her. She wanted to give the money to Marie because she was like her in every respect, even-tempered, dull-witted. She hated Toni because she took after Chepete. I figure that when Toni took the money, the squaw tried to stab her.'

'She's a wildcat', Bryce said. 'She wanted me to go along with her. I still don't feel right about letting her ride off alone.'

'Forget the 'breed girl Chepete trained to steal and cheat and kill.' Wade Applegate looked at Bryce. 'Toni is plenty capable of taking care of herself and she'd have knifed you like she put a knife between Stephen's shoulder blades and did the same to her own mother after they'd fought over the money.'

They left it like that. But the half-breed girl and the memory of her would never be forgotten by Bryce Bradford.

112

Bryce handed the money sack to Wade Applegate, who tied it on his saddle. Then both men squatted on their boot heels facing one another.

'I'm taking the dead bodies of Matthew and Stephen to Buffalo Run', Bryce told Applegate.

'The 'breeds threw the two bodies into the burning building,' Applegate told him. 'The fire cremated those two Avenging Angels.'

'Saves me that trouble, then', said Bryce. 'But I'm headed for Buffalo Run anyway. I found out a few things at the Halfway House that ties in with that other Christmas Eve stage hold-up.' Bryce told Wade Applegate everything that Toni had told him.

The older man filled his pipe and put it in a corner of his mouth. 'Have you figured out your method of approach when you get there?' he asked.

'Only that I'm going to get the truth out of Nile Carter and Quensel.'

'Don't forget the stagedriver, Jerry O'Toole, also Big Tim Fogarty and Pete Kaster. They know plenty.'

'I want to find out who killed my father,' Bryce said. 'And what happened to the tithe money he had in the black satchel. Also if Nile Carter was in cahoots with the two road-agents.'

'That's a big sized order for one man to handle.'

'It's strictly a one man job,' Bryce replied.

'How about your sheriff's job? Are you going to use your legal authority to back any play you make?' asked Wade Applegate.

Bryce Bradford's laugh had an ugly sound. 'When I locate the two men who murdered my father, I'll kill them where I find them. Regardless.'

They were silent for a while, then Bryce said, 'I was sent out to catch the road-agents and bring them back,

113

dead or alive, together with the loot.' Bryce smiled thinly. 'I'm going back empty-handed.'

'They'll be waiting with a hangman's rope for you, Bryce, so watch yourself,' the old rancher warned. His pipe had gone out. He knocked the cold ashes into the palm of his hand and blew them down wind.

'I figure Jerry O'Toole, the stagedriver,' he said, 'knows who held up the stage that Christmas Eve. I was in town when he drove in. Nile Carter was on the driver's seat beside him. That old rascal has a roving eye for the ladies and he was drunker than usual. A girl of Nile's calibre could twist Jerry around her little finger. If he knew who the road-agents were it's a cinch bet that she shared his secret by the time they reached Buffalo Run.'

'I sure played into her hands when I killed Charlie Decker,' Bryce grinned ruefully. 'She claimed Decker's share in the El Dorado. Made me a proposition to kill Quensel and become her partner.'

'You turned her down?'

'I told her I was drifting on.' Bryce took Nile's note from his pocket and handed it to the older man.

Wade Applegate read the note that warned Bryce never to return to Buffalo Run, and that Morgan and his daughter had left for Fort Benton.

'How does it add up in your tally book, Bryce?' asked Wade Applegate, returning the note to Bryce.

'A Strangler's necktie party when I get there,' Bryce answered with a twisted grin. He remembered the half-breed girl's words; 'Nile might pin a leather medal on you before she ties your rope necktie.'

'Did it ever occur to you that Nile Carter's life might be in grave danger?' Wade Applegate's question drove the remembered thoughts from Bryce's mind.

'Nile Carter probably had a reason for sending you that note of warning,' Applegate said. He walked to his horse and swung into the saddle, then said, 'I'm riding to Buffalo Run with you.'

Bryce mounted and together the two men rode side by side into the dawn, its leaden grey sky streaked with crimson that looked like fresh blood on a dirty grey blanket.

CHAPTER TWELVE

It was somewhere around midnight when Bryce Bradford and Wade Applegate reached the little cowtown of Buffalo Run.

They had decided to stop at Nile Carter's house at the edge of town first. Lamplight showed behind closely pulled blinds in the living-room and bedroom and in the kitchen.

They rode around back. Wade Applegate told Bryce to stay in the saddle as he dismounted and handed him his bridle reins.

Bryce had an uneasy feeling as he watched the squawman stop at the kitchen door and rap. He was unarmed.

The kitchen door opened a crack and the moon-faced squaw peered out. The squawman spoke softly in the Sioux language and the door opened wide enough to let him in.

Bryce waited impatiently, his nerves taut. It seemed a long time before the squawman came out, carrying a bag. 'Do you recognize this?' he asked holding it up to Bryce.

Bryce took the satchel from him and after examining it, he said, 'It belonged to my father. He kept his tithe money in it.'

'Nile Carter told the squaw to give it to you when you showed up. The money has never been touched. She left a message for you to take it and hit the trail back to wherever you came from.'

Bryce Bradford's lips skinned back in a sneering grin as he wedged the satchel between his belly and the saddle-horn. 'Anything else?' he asked, his bloodshot eyes splinters of steel.

'There's to be a wedding here at midnight,' Applegate said. 'I got a glimpse of the bride waiting alone in a big armchair. It's Virginia Morgan and she's going to be married to Jack Quensel.'

Bryce started to get off his horse, but Wade Applegate put an arm out to hold him in the saddle. 'No use you blundering in there. The squaw told me Quensel had sold out to Nile Carter and that he and his bride were quitting Montana, never to return. He's taking Virginia to New Orleans to live.'

Bryce Bradford sat wedged in his saddle. His heavy brows knit in a scowl as he forced clarity of thought through his confused, bewildered brain.

He and Wade Applegate had made a long, hard ride to Buffalo Run, to save Nile Carter from threatened danger. Now Nile was in power here. She and Quensel had made some kind of a deal. It was Virginia Morgan who was in danger and in need of help. It looked as if her drunken father had sold his daughter down the river.

If Nile Carter had a notion she could buy him off, scare him out of the country, she had the wrong man.

'I'm going on to the El Dorado,' Bryce's voice was deadly quiet.

'You could be walking into a gun trap, Bryce. Set by Quensel and baited with two women.'

A few minutes later they rode into the wide doorway of the barn to stable the horses that had packed them a long way. They swung to the ground.

'Good Gawdamighty!' Old Dad Jones's whisky voice came from the dark shadows of the barn. 'It's Bryce Bradford come back, and Wade Applegate with him. Time you got the snakes out of your boots, Jerry.'

The grizzled barnman and the tipsy stagedriver came out of the barn. Bryce took the black satchel from his saddle and waited until the two cronies came close before he spoke.

'Who were the two road-agents who held up your stage on Christmas Eve a year ago?' Bryce looked straight at Jerry O'Toole and waited for his answer.

The half-drunk stagedriver recoiled a step. 'Fer the love of Judas, how could I tell who was behind a black handkerchief mask?' he whined.

The squawman took a quick step forward. His strong, gnarled hands fastened on the collar of his flannel shirt, twisting it tight as a rope around O'Toole's neck.

'Love of Judas!' Jerry's eyes rolled towards Dad Jones. 'Are you goin' to stand there, begobs, like a dumb bastid and let this squawman choke me black in the face? Lend a hand.'

'Tell the man, Jerry.' Old Dad spat tobacco juice on the floor. 'Get it off your mind. Hell, you ain't gone to confession since you was an altar boy in County Cork. Do you good. Like a dose of caster oil.' The barnman winked at Wade Applegate.

'They'll hang me,' wailed the terrified stagedriver.

'I'm choking you down right now,' said Wade Applegate, putting pressure on the twist of the shirt collar.

'It was Charlie Decker,' grasped Jerry O'Toole. 'Decker and Quensel.'

'Wade Applegate cut a look at Bryce as he slowly loosened his twisting grip.

'Where did Nile Carter fit into the deal?' demanded

119

Bryce. 'Was she in cahoots with Decker and Quensel?'

'Hell, no,' Jerry snorted. 'And that I'll swear to. Decker shot the two younger men and Quensel shot the older man when he reached for a gun. Nile Carter witnessed the killings and Decker wanted to kill her, but Quensel drawed the line at killing a woman. Especially a colleen as purty as that one.'

'Go easy!' Dad Jones's whisky breath blew hot in Bryce's face as he stood close. 'Quensel's expecting you back tonight. I was to keep you here till Jerry had time to get to the El Dorado to say that you had arrived.'

'I'm much obliged to you, Dad,' Bryce told him.

Jerry O'Toole's bleared eyes bugged out when he saw the black satchel. 'That satchel belonged to the older man Quensel shot', he volunteered.

'Go on. Who got the satchel?' Bryce snapped.

'Nile Carter had it when she rode with me on the driver's seat. I handed it down to her when we reached Buffalo Run,' he said.

The two men unsaddled. Wade Applegate took the money sack from his saddle. The barnman and the stage-driver led the two horses into a double stall and piled hay in the manger, giving each horse a gallon of grain.

Bryce and Applegate stood there wordless, each thinking their own thoughts, the black satchel and the canvas sack at their feet on the floor of the barn.

Bryce's eyes narrowed when he saw the big brown gelding in the Square and Compass brand in the first stall. 'That's the horse the 'breed girl made her getaway on,' he told the squawman, puzzlement in his eyes.

Old Dad Jones said quickly, 'One of Chepete's girls stabled the horse. The wild one, Toni. She told me it was money she had in the bloody-looking sack she carried across the shoulder of her red shirt. Said she was going to buck the tiger at the El Dorado, show Nile Carter the difference between foolin' around and playin' for keeps. Last I seen, she was headed that way. She had a six-shooter buckled on.'

Wade Applegate picked up the money sack and reached for the black satchel. 'I'll take the satchel,' he told Bryce, 'to balance the load. You might need both hands.'

'There'll be a Hot Time in the Old Town Tonight,' Old Dad piped up, a little off-key.

Bryce Bradford and Wade Applegate peered through the windows of the El Dorado. Tobacco smoke hung in thick layers and blobs of yellow light showed foggily from the half dozen big nickled Rochester lamps that hung by chains high above the heads of the milling crowd lined up at the long bar and clustered around the gambling layouts.

The orchestra pit below the level of the stage was empty. The keys of the upright piano were covered. No kerosene lights burned in the row of floodlights. The red drapes of the half dozen boxes on either side of the barn-like vast room were pulled back, except the front box above the stage. The curtains on it were pulled together. It was the private box where Nile Carter had taken Bryce Bradford on the first night in the cow town.

At the far end of the room the packed crowd was standing motionless, backed up a dozen deep behind a roped-in enclosure. Inside the heavy rawhide rope corral was a big roulette wheel, and spinning the wheel was Nile Carter. The high stool behind her, where the lookout usually sat, was empty.

Nile wore a sleeveless, low-cut evening gown of charcoal black satin. Her tawny hair was plaited in heavy braids and coiled around her head like a crown of burnished gold. Even through the smoke haze, her amber eyes

123

glinted. A bitter, contemptuous smile twisted her red lips as her long, shapely, ringless fingers spun the wheel.

Toni, the half-breed girl, was the only player inside the roped-in enclosure. Her high crowned dusty black hat was on the floor behind her, half covering the canvas money sack. Her black hair hung down her back in two squaw braids. Her scarlet silk shirt was open at the throat. The blood had drained from her face and her black eyes glowed like smoldering red coals in the smoky lamplight. Red lips were peeled back to show her white teeth as she reached both hands into the almost empty sack to scoop out a double handful of crumpled bank notes and gold coins.

Toni dumped the pile on the table, bunching it together in a tight wad over the color red. She played only the red numbers, disregarding the others.

The spinning wheel slowed down. The little ivory ball bounced a few times and fell into a slot and stayed there, the white ball showing against the black.

Nile hooked in the pile of money with an ebony handled rake.

The half-breed girl upended the canvas sack on the table.

Jack Quensel was nowhere in sight. Judge Plato Morgan stood alone at the far end of the bar, a half-filled bottle of whisky and a pitcher of cracked ice in front of him. He held a filled glass in his hand as he stared into space with unseeing eyes. There was something tragic about the black clad erect figure in the black Confederate hat.

Big Tim Fogarty and Pete Kaster stood together at the bar. Both looked freshly barbered and were dressed in their best clothes. They held drinks in their hands and each had a whisky bottle in front of him. They watched the crowd with shifting, restless, wary eyes.

The hands of the big clock over the back bar showed the hour to be thirty minutes past eleven o'clock.

Nile spun the wheel, sending the ivory ball in the opposite direction. A hush fell like a smoke pall while the white ball dropped into a black slot.

Two pairs of eyes, one greenish-yellow, the other red-black fire met and held across the wheel.

'Red for blood,' the almost whispered words hissed from behind Toni's bared teeth. 'Black for death.' The Colt pistol in her hand was pointed at Nile's breast.

Nile used both hands to shove the big pile of money slowly towards the half-breed girl. 'The wheel's fixed for suckers', she said in a voice as cold as the glint in her eyes. 'Put the money in your bloody sack. Then get out. Don't come back Injun.'

Nile turned her back on the gun in the 'breed girl's tense hand. The crowd parted as she crossed the floor towards the stage and disappeared inside the curtained box above.

Toni reached for the empty sack. Holding it open below the level of the table she used the long barrel of the six-shooter to scrape the money into it. She pulled the string to close the bag and picked up her hat, slanting it on her head. Her jaws were clamped till the muscles bunched and quivered, her lips pulled taut. A thin, greyish film hooded the black eyes as she slung the sack over her shoulder. Every man in the place was watching her as she crossed the floor, the gun in her hand. Toni opened the door to the back alley and went out without a backward glance.

The tense-packed crowd slowly relaxed. The shuffling of booted feet mingled with men's voices that were low toned, hushed.

'Stay here, Wade,' Bryce said. 'I'm going to find Quensel.' His hand was on his gun as he shouldered through the swinging half-doors, leaving the older man alone outside.

Fogarty and Kaster sighted Bryce the second he came

125

in. They stiffened, exchanging quick meaning glances. Neither man made a move towards a gun as Bryce stopped just beyond the long reach of Big Tim.

'Where is Jack Quensel hiding out?' Bryce put the question to both men, the tone of his voice deadly.

The two men moved apart as if to make room for Bryce at the bar.

'By Gawdamighty,' Fogarty mumbled and belched into Bryce's face, 'that's what me'n Pete are beginning to wonder. Belly up to the mahogany, Sheriff. Have a drink.'

'Where's Quensel?' Bryce repeated, ignoring the invitation to drink.

Bryce had seen the quick exchange of glances, the slight shift of Pete Kaster's shoulder and arm. He ducked his head with a quick jerk as Kaster threw the contents of his whisky glass into his face. Bryce's hat caught the splash of whisky.

Bryce moved in swiftly, covering the scant three feet distance in one quick jump that slammed him into Kaster. The short, burly man was thrown off-balance by the hard impact as he slid a .45 from its holster.

Bryce grabbed the thick wrist as Kaster thumbed back the gun hammer. He jerked the wrist downward in a twist that put the muzzle deep in Kaster's paunch just as Kaster squeezed the trigger. The soft-nosed bullet ripped through the hard layers of fat into the man's belly, tearing a ragged hole at the base of his spine.

The bared grin was frozen on Tim Fogarty's red jowled face. His heavy, ham-like fist clenched around the thick shot glass as he swung a wild haymaker at Bryce's head. Bryce threw the gutshot Pete Kaster at Fogarty and the big man's fist crashed into the twisted face of the dying man before he could pull the punch.

Bryce moved in and the barrel of his gun chopped down behind Tim Fogarty's ear. It was short and savage

126

enough to make Fogarty's knees buckle, and he pitched headlong across the body of his side-partner who lay sprawled against the brass foot rail.

Bryce backed away, his gun ready. He was half-crouched, feet balanced to twist or jump in any direction, his eyes slivered, dangerous. He was set and ready to shoot. The packed crowd of men stood frozen, held by the levelled gun, the killer's look in Bryce's eyes.

Without turning his head, Bryce was aware of Wade Applegate standing near him.

Bryce looked up over the heads of the silent crowd. Nile Carter had parted the drapes, to stand there in her black satin sheath, her pale amber eyes fixed on him, a cold smile on her lips.

The creak of a pulley squealed like a rat. The stage curtain raised slowly, pulled by unseen hands back stage. Men twisted their heads, shuffling their booted feet around. An almost inaudible mutter swept the crowd, like a dry, invisible fox-fire.

There on the stage was a wooden gallows, its thirteen steps leading to a high platform, a hangman's rope hung down from the ridge-log. You could tell by the surprised hush that gripped the men, that they were seeing the gruesome stage setting for the first time.

Bryce cut a quick look upward. His eyes met Nile's fixed stare. Then her hand beckoned him. The drapes fell back into place.

Big Tim Fogarty raised himself from the floor. His big hands reached up to grip the edge of the bar and pull himself up. Blood from a torn ear trickled down to stain his starched shirt bosom. His eyes found Bryce Bradford and a wide grin spread across his face.

'I warned Quensel,' the big man's chuckle came from deep inside him, 'that he had a grizzly by the tail.' He reached behind him and grabbed a whisky bottle by the neck. He smashed the end on the edge of the bar.

'Any you sonabitches want the sheriff, start movin'! You gotta pass me to get to him.' He waved the jagged bottle in a sweeping gesture. 'Them as don't want Bryce Bradford hung, belly up to the bar.'

The crowd moved as one man towards the bar.

Bryce shoved his gun into its holster. There was a grim set to his jaw as he took the satchel from the older man's hand.

'You saw her,' Bryce said in a tight voice. 'I'm going up there.'

'You could be walking into a death trap,' Wade Applegate told him.

'It won't be the first time,' Bryce said.

'I'll be having a drink at the bar,' the older man said. 'I'll keep my eye peeled for any trouble up there.'

CHAPTER FOURTEEN

Bryce Bradford carried the black satchel in his left hand, to keep his gun hand free, as he went up the enclosed stairway and along a narrow passageway to the last box.

He parted the drapes with the pistol barrel and peered inside. Nile Carter was the sole occupant. She was sitting at a small table, an iced bucket of champagne on the floor beside her chair, and two champagne glasses on the table.

Bryce stepped into the box and put the satchel on the table. Nile looked at him across the table, then said softly 'The man who owned that bag was shot down in cold blooded murder. I saw it happen.'

'That man was my father,' Bryce tried to keep emotion from his voice.

'I found that out after you were gone,' Nile said. 'That is why I did everything I knew to keep you from coming back here.'

'Even to marrying off Virginia Morgan to the killer who shot my father,' Bryce retorted bitterly.

'Not that.' Her cold smile tightened her lips. 'Quensel arranged that. I don't know what threats he used by way of persuasion.'

'Who arranged the stage setting below?' Bryce sneered.

'Quensel's men moved it in, while he and I were drawing up the sale papers for the El Dorado at my cottage. Quensel's price was the black satchel of money. The pay-off was to be at midnight tonight. He gave his gambler's word he'd leave Buffalo Run tonight and quit Montana for good.

'Then when I returned to the El Dorado, that half-breed girl came in. She said she had enough money in the sack over her shoulder to buy the El Dorado, lock, stock and barrel. She insisted on gambling me for the place. Either I'd gamble or she'd kill me. She had a gun in her hand and meant business. She wanted to buck the wheel, play the red. She kept looking at the dress I have on, saying, "Red for blood. Black for death." I don't scare easily but the look in her black eyes had cold shivers running down my spine.'

'I know what you mean,' Bryce said grimly. 'I want to know everything you can tell me about my father's murder, Nile.'

'Decker and Quensel held up the stage-coach. It was Quensel who shot your father. I could have told you that the first night we met, but you never asked me.'

'I didn't know about it until the half-breed girl told me about the Christmas Eve hold-up.' His eyes narrowed. 'Were you in on it?' he asked.

'No. I never saw Quensel or Decker until that Christmas Eve.' Nile reached for the satchel. 'I've never tampered with the lock on this bag. You can see that the lead your father poured into the locking mechanism has never been broken. I live on the money I make dealing cards.'

Bryce bent over to examine the lock and verify her statement.

'I used that satchel to blackmail Quensel,' she admitted. 'I used it tonight to drive Quensel out of Montana.'

'Why?' Bryce asked.

'I got word that Bryce Bradford was coming back to Buffalo Run. I didn't want Quensel to kill you.'

'Where is Quensel?'

'He dropped from sight a few hours ago. The last I saw of him was when he left my cottage with the agreement we'd made up, which was to be signed when I laid the satchel of money on the line at midnight.' Nile looked at her watch. 'It's fifteen minutes till midnight. Quensel's wedding and the pay-off is set for that hour, his favorite time to do business.'

'There'll be one uninvited guest at Quensel's wedding,' Bryce said.

'How do you know that Quensel is not expecting you?' Nile stood up, reaching for the champagne bottle. There was a card wired to its neck. She held it out for Bryce to read.

'For Nile Carter and Bryce Bradford; to drink a toast to Jack Quensel and Virginia Morgan on their wedding night.'

'It was here when I finished spinning the wheel for the half-breed girl and came up to the box.' Nile smiled faintly.

Bryce put his hand on the satchel. 'You were going to double-cross Quensel on the pay-off.' It was a flat statement but there was a puzzled question in it.

'There was an element of chance,' Nile smiled enigmatically. 'Both of us were aware of it. Both of us high stake gamblers playing a cut-throat game. Neither of us knows how much money is in the satchel. It could be filled with rocks.

'That black satchel has become a symbol, an evil, deadly symbol. Tainted with the crime of murder and the more insidious evil of a blackmail threat. Quensel was buying my silence.'

'Honor among thieves,' Bryce said brutally.

'Ouch!' Nile smiled. 'I asked for that one.'

131

'You two gamblers don't trust one another', Bryce said. 'While Quensel made secret plans to marry Virginia Morgan, using some kind of threat to put the squeeze on the Morgans, you made secret plans to turn the satchel over to me when I showed up. Thank God I'm no gambler,' Bryce said contemptuously.

'Your return was a gamble,' Nile told him. 'When you came in here with the satchel, you took chips in the game.'

Bryce laughed shortly. 'You used the satchel as a threat against Quensel. You used it to buy me off, leaving word with your squaw housekeeper for me to run away from Quensel and the Stranglers of Buffalo Run.' His voice was tense with anger. 'You were out to save Nile Carter!'

Her amber eyes looked at him for a long moment, studying him, probing deep into his mixed emotions. Whatever she found there brought a faint smile to her lips.

'I've been taking Nile Carter's part for a long time. When a woman has the guts to battle for existence, she uses her sex as the deadliest weapon of all. Whatever I've done, I was out to save the body of Nile Carter, regardless, and to hell with her soul.' Her voice was vibrant.

Leaving Quensel's card wired to the bottle neck, she lifted the champagne from the bucket of ice and began twisting the cork. It popped like a pistol shot.

The drapes stirred gently. Wade Applegate stepped into the box, alarm in his eyes. He still had the sack of money in his hand.

'Forgive the intrusion', he said. 'I was waiting for Bryce in the passageway when I heard what sounded like a shot.'

There was a mocking smile on Nile's lips and a challenge in her eyes as she handed each man a filled glass of champagne. Then she took a third glass from a shelf in the corner of the booth and poured herself a drink.

'To whatever the future may hold,' she said as they

raised glasses and drank. Her voice was level toned as she looked at both men.

Bryce felt the sharp, cold, needle-like sparkIng wine as it went down his throat, quenching the parched thirst within him, cooling his temper and heated blood.

'The chips are down,' Wade Applegate said as he set the empty glass on the table. 'Within the hour the game will be over.'

Nile twisted the hollow stem of her emptied glass. Her eyes flicked the sack of money in Applegate's hand. 'What's that?' she asked.

'Tithe money,' he told her. 'It was collected from Quensel by two Avenging Angels sent out by the outcast Mormons of Rainbow's End. It's the money Quensel was expecting on the stage that was held up.'

A dark shadow crossed Wade Applegate's eyes as they looked inward. He said slowly, 'The two Avenging Angels are dead. There will be no more sent out from Rainbow's End. Bryce does not belong to the Mormon Church, therefore, he owes no tithe. His father's tithe in the black satchel has been cancelled out by the hand of God. The money now belongs to the boy.'

'What becomes of the money you have there, Mr. Applegate?' Nile asked.

'This money belongs to me,' he said, holding the sack up. 'I'll try to explain it. Decker and Quensel robbed the stage on Christmas Eve a year ago and got away with seventy-five thousand dollars I had consigned to the Bank at Fort Benton. The sixty thousand in this sack belonging to Quensel was lifted by those two Avenging Angels and recovered by Bryce. I'm claiming it from Quensel to repay part of the money he stole from me.' The eyes of the white-haired man were cold as winter ice as he looked at Nile Carter.

Nile Carter's amber eyes paled. She reached into the low-cut neckline of her dress and now held a snub-barrelled .38 belly gun in her hand. 'Get the hell out of town, both of you.' The gun was levelled at Applegate's waistline.

'When I've killed Quensel,' Bryce spoke tensely, 'I'll be glad to leave Buffalo Run. But not until then.'

'You both saw the gallows set up on the stage below. If I were to give the word, those Stranglers down there would hang you both.' Nile's mouth flattened into a thin, lipless slit. 'Tell the damned fool to get away, Applegate, or I'll kill you where you stand.'

The squawman's blue eyes were cold, calculating. 'Which one of the two men, Bryce or Quensel, are you trying to save?' he asked quietly.

'What difference does it make?' Nile's voice had a scratchy sound.

'Decker wanted to kill you when the stage was held up', Wade Applegate said, ignoring her question. 'You owe your life to Quensel.' He paid no attention to the gun in her hand. 'It's a shame to let that vintage wine go wasted', he said, a slow grin on his mouth.

'Damn you, Wade Applegate,' Nile's voice broke like a shattered wine glass. She slid the gun into the front of her dress and looked at her watch.

'Ten minutes till midnight,' she told them. She splashed champagne into the glasses. 'The hour set for Quensel's wedding, and Nile Carter's wedding gift.' She nudged the satchel with the bottle, then dropped it into the bucket.

Nile Carter stood facing the two men, the blood drained from her face, a film of unshed tears in her eyes, her lower lip caught and held between her teeth, bitten down until a drop of blood showed.

None of them saw the half-breed girl standing just inside the drapes. Her moccasined feet had made no sound.

Her heavy hair had come unbraided and fresh wet blood streaked her pale face. Her red shirt was sodden with sticky blood that oozed sluggishly from a bullet rip across her collar-bone. She clung with one hand to the drapes, holding the .45 in the other blood-smeared hand. The croaking sound she made whirled Bryce around.

He made a dive for the gun as Toni let go the curtain to lift the gun with both hands. The gun was pointed at Nile. Bryce grabbed the barrel and twisted it upward just as it exploded.

Bryce caught the girl as she swayed and pitched headlong into his arms. Her eyes were pain-seared in the dim lamplight. He eased her to the floor and knelt on one knee. 'Who shot you, Toni?' he asked gently.

'Quensel. Nile Carter's tinhorn. He's drunk.' Toni whispered.

Nile knelt beside the girl. She soaked the towel around the champagne bottle in the ice water and laid it across the bullet wound.

'Tell us what happened, Toni,' Bryce said.

'Judge Morgan bumped into me as I went out into the alley. He asked me to help him get Virginia away from Nile's house. The squaw and I sneaked her out the back door. She acted like she didn't know where she was or that we were taking her away. We hid her out in the squaw camp across the creek. The squaw stayed with her. I went back to the house where Judge Morgan was.'

Bryce held the champagne bottle to Toni's mouth and let her swallow. She forced a smile. 'Bottle-raised on Chepete's rotgut. Never got weaned.' She pulled the bottle away to talk again.

'Quensel was in the house, drunk as a 'breed fiddler. The old judge went after him with a sword cane. Quensel shot the judge, then grabbed me before I could get away. I clawed loose and ran. He took a couple of pot shots at

135

me, but I kept on going. I was after Nile. She'd put me on the Injun list.' Toni took another swallow.

'Quensel's out to kill you, Bryce. I had to find you to tell you before I died. You're a hell of a good man, Bryce.'

'You're not going to die, Toni,' Bryce tried to make it sound convincing.

'The hell I ain't. I'm a no-good half-breed slut.'

Nile took the wet towel and rinsed it in the ice water and wiped the blood from the girl's face. 'You're a half-breed, Toni, but you're no slut. You got more guts than any female I ever met.' Nile smiled at her, and asked. 'You still got that sack of money, Toni?'

Toni nodded, but her eyes narrowed with suspicion.

'You'll need it for a bank-roll to run the El Dorado. I'm giving you the place. I'll put it in writing.' Nile told her.

'I tried to kill you', Toni said.

'I humiliated you. So you took a shot at me. That crosses it off the books. You now own the El Dorado, but don't try to thank me. I hate the place. I was going to set fire to it at midnight tonight.'

The half-breed girl lay back. The champagne had brought the natural colour back into her face and red-lipped smile. The black fire smouldered in her eyes as she realized the fulfilment of her dream of owning a place like the El Dorado.

'I'll change the name,' she whispered. 'Toni's Place, in big red letters. I'll wear a black dress like yours.'

Toni reached up and pulled Bryce's face down to hers and fastened her red lips on his mouth in a bruising kiss. Then her lips slid away and her head fell back.

'Quensel,' she told him, 'is at the squaw camp in the te-pee where we took Virginia Morgan. He's drunk and wrapped up in an Injun blanket with his bride.' Toni's laugh pierced his eardrum as she raised her head to his. 'You did me a favor, remember? I pay my debts, good and bad. I set Quensel up for you, easy as shooting a duck on a pond, Bryce.'

The 'breed girl's laugh was like the scratch of a broken needle across a dark window-pane. Her fingers, sticky with fresh blood, fastened into Bryce's hair as she held his head down against hers.

'I hid the sack of money under a buffalo robe in the bride's tepee. Fetch it back to me when you kill Quensel.' Her mouth fastened on his again, then she lay back, a bitter, twisted smile on her mouth, the black fire dying out of her eyes. 'Good huntin', Bryce,' were her last words.

Chepete's half-breed daughter had died dreaming, all debts paid off according to her lights.

Nile covered Toni's face with a thin black scarf that had covered her bare shoulders. She turned to face Bryce Bradford. 'Before you go, Bryce,' her voice was barely audible, 'I want you to know this. Nile Carter has never given herself to any man on earth.' She put both hands on his shoulders, holding him away, and said, 'I'll be waiting for you Bryce.'

Bryce pulled Nile into his arms. The sob she had been holding back found release as her parted lips met his. Bryce felt the long shudder of her body as it pressed close against him in a woman's complete surrender. There was no need for spoken words during those long, lingering moments of parting. Perhaps it was to be a final parting. Both were aware of that dread thought as Nile's arms tightened, holding him there in a final, desperate effort.

Never had life seemed more precious to Bryce Bradford. He had found everything he had ever dreamed of as he held Nile Carter in close embrace. He was too young to die, too filled with the zest for living now to be shot down.

It took a lot of will power for Bryce to pull himself away. He looked around dazedly. Wade Applegate was no longer there.

Nile looked at her watch. It was five minutes till midnight.

'Toni's gun is gone,' Bryce spoke in a harsh whisper. 'Wade Applegate took it along.'

'What's wrong with that, Bryce?'

'He never owned a gun, never shot a gun in his life. It was a part of his religion. He's doing this on my account. I'm not going to let him. It's my job to kill the man who murdered my father.'

Bryce's eyes were slivered, bleak, as he pulled the drapes aside and strode out of the box, running blindly. 'Stay here, Nile,' he called as he ran. 'Wait there till I come back for you.'

CHAPTER FIFTEEN

Pale moonlight flooded the hundred yards of clearing. Beyond it showed the white picket fence and the white-washed log cottage that belonged to Nile Carter. Lamplight showed from every window.

Bryce was well aware of the desperate chance he would have to take to cross the clearing. There was no sign of movement around the house but there could be hidden guns in the lilac hedge that laned the walk.

There was only one way to play it, to Bryce's way of thinking. That was to walk out into the open as if he feared nothing and no man this side of hell. Take his time. Don't run like he was scared of being shot down. On the other hand, don't drag his feet like he was forcing himself to face something that chilled his guts.

The trick was to step out like he was asking for a show-down. Like he didn't give a damn, win or draw. If Quensel were bushed up, watching, let the tinhorn get a good look at a man who had the guts to come out in the open. If he lacked the courage to fight out in the open, let him do his bushwhacking, and to hell with it.

Bryce was checking it to Quensel. If he was the high stake gambler he claimed to be, let him prove it. Bryce kept telling himself that with every step he took. But he didn't believe any part of it.

139

Quensel was a cold-blooded killer. He did his gambling with a cold deck, the cards marked and the odds always in his favor. Quensel never gave a sucker a break, and Bryce Bradford was a sucker, every step he took.

Quensel had shot Bryce's father down in cold blood. Tonight he had shot the white-maned Judge Morgan. He had shot the half-breed girl. Quensel would never give a man like Bryce an even chance. Amen to that.

Bryce told himself that he was whistling in the dark. A stiff-lipped grin forced its way across his face. He reached for the gate, clicked it open and walked down the gravel path. The tall lilac hedge on either side cast dark shadows in front of him. Bryce slid his gun out and gripped it in a moist palm, but nothing moved and no sound broke the hushed quiet.

Bryce stepped up on the vine-covered porch. When he was sure no one was hiding there, he peered into the living-room window. Through the lace curtains he saw the body of Judge Plato Morgan lying sprawled, face down, on the carpeted floor, his cane gripped in his dead hand. The fringe of his thick white hair was tipped in the puddle of blood that stained the carpet.

There was no sign of Wade Applegate or Big Tim Fogarty, or the man Bryce had come to kill. But Nile's squaw housekeeper was in the kitchen, a sawed-off scatter gun across her wide lap. Bryce felt the full impact of her stare as he entered by the back door.

'Quensel is in the tepee with his woman,' she said when she recognized Bryce, speaking in a guttural voice that was startling. 'That white man crazy. You kill him. You go to tepee, cross the bridge. Quick as hell!'

Bryce lost no time. He was across the bridge and following a dim twisting trail through the brush that hid his cautious movements. He saw the high lodge poles of a tepee ahead along a creek bank. The tepee flap was propped half open, held in place by a long stick.

Bryce shifted his gun to his left hand and wiped the sweat from the palm of his gun hand along the seat of his britches. He could see shadowy movements inside the dark tepee, then he heard the flat sound of Quensel's voice.

'. . . you appeared like a frail, beautiful ghost that came out of a dead past to haunt me. You rose from the grave of a girl I once loved. A girl of delicate beauty, with hair like pale moonbeams spun on a golden spinning-wheel by the hands of angels.' A short laugh that had a bitter metallic sound came from inside the tepee, then the voice went on.

'. . . the same pale translucent skin as yours that comes from generations of line breeding, to keep the same blue blood of the first families of Virginia untainted. . . .' The voice broke off. A cork twisted from a bottle.

'I was a beardless young Captain of the Confederate Cavalry then but not good enough for a Virginia blueblood. When she refused my offer of marriage, insane with jealousy and hurt pride, I organized Quensel's Guerrilla Raiders and we did some plundering, raping and burning before I lost interest and came west.' The laugh sounded again, the laugh of a man gone insane. 'I turned her over to my raiders to rape and murder. I killed her father, her brother who'd been my class mate. I set fire to the colonial mansion.' An empty bottle was flung out of the tepee, crashing against a rock. A string of foul blasphemy spilled out and again that crazy laugh.

'I left my true identity in the south. I chose the name of Quensel from a tombstone in a New Orleans graveyard. I disbanded my guerrillas after I'd sobered up from a long debauchery with John Barleycorn. I had regained some of my sanity when I reached Buffalo Run. Then you came out of the past. . . .' Quensel laughed again. Then lurched out of the tepee.

He stood in the moonlight on wide-spread legs, his eyes burning in a greyish twisted mask of insane hatred. His hand gripped a gun.

Bryce Bradford stepped out into the moonlight, his gun-barrel tilted, ready to level down and fire. They faced one another across a fifty foot distance, their eyes held gripped for a long moment.

'When I count three,' a calm voice spoke from the foot-bridge, 'shoot at will.'

Wade Applegate stood on the bridge, bareheaded, the moonlight on his shock of white hair. Tall, erect, grim-faced. Toni's gun ready in his hand. He had come to see that Bryce got an even chance when he and Quensel met.

'One . . . two. . . .'

Quensel fired at the count of two. Bryce felt the thudding hot pain in his shoulder. He squeezed the trigger of his gun just as Quensel shot a second time. Bryce's bullet tore a hole in the gambler's heart. Wade Applegate had fired at Quensel's gun hand, causing his second shot to go wild.

Pain shot from Bryce's shoulder down his arm to his fingertips. It hung numbed at his side as he walked towards the fallen gambler. When he made sure Quensel was dead, he followed Wade Applegate who had gone into the tepee and had lit a tallow dip candle.

Virginia Morgan lay stretched out on a tanned buffalo robe. Her eyelids were closed and her thin hands folded. A beautiful bride asleep. But it was the sleep of death. The buckhorn handle of a bowie knife, deep through her heart was almost hidden under her folded hands. Virginia Morgan lay cold, beautiful in death.

Quensel had been talking to the dead girl, whom he imagined had come as a ghost out of his past to haunt him.

Then Nile Carter was standing beside Bryce. She took the gun from his loose grip and shoved it into the empty holster of his thigh. Linking her arm through his, she led him back to her cottage.

Bryce sat straddle of the kitchen chair while Nile cut away his blood sodden shirt and undershirt with long bladed scissors. He flexed his fingers slowly, moving his arm from the shoulder socket. The bullet had ripped through the muscle, grazing the bone. There was no serious injury beyond the loss of blood and Nile worked in swift, sure silence to stop the crimson flow with gauze sponges and bandages.

Strangely, Bryce felt little pain. Only a dull, throbbing numbness. His eyes were dark with inward thoughts, remembering what Quensel had told about his back trail as he spewed out the slow poison that had been hidden deep within him during the long bitter years. Someday he'd tell Nile about it.

Wade Applegate came in and closed the door softly behind him. He told them that Virginia Morgan had taken her own life. She was dead when Quensel found her. He handed a paper to Nile. It was the agreement for the sale of the El Dorado which the gambler had signed before the midnight pay-off hour.

Nile told them that she'd met Big Tim Fogarty after Bryce had left her and had told him he was welcome to the El Dorado. 'Tim never packed a gun', she said. 'His fists were his only weapon. He's never killed a man and never liked being tied up with Quensel and Kaster.'

Wade Applegate had brought Toni's money sack with him. He said he'd bank the money to the credit of Big

143

Gregory and Marie, to give them a new start in life. He told Bryce that Virginia Morgan had left his money belt with Nile's squaw to give to him.

'I'm leaving for home now,' Wade Applegate said, looking kindly at them both. 'I'll have a buckboard waiting outside and I want you two to come to the ranch for a few days.'

When he had gone, Nile said they'd leave as soon as she signed over the El Dorado to Tim Fogarty.

'We're leaving Buffalo Run, Bryce, and we're never coming back.'

VIOLENT
MAVERICK

Chapter I

Cattle rustlers were stealing old Wig Murphy blind, and
there wasn't one dog-goned thing that Wig could do about
it. The big cowman had made his start with a fast horse, a
good rope, and a running iron that was heated several
times a day; he liked to brag about how he got his start
from a bunch of 'wet' cattle that he stole out of Sonora,
Mexico. And even now, after some forty years in the cow
business, Wig Murphy was not too proud nor too honest
to pick up a little bunch of good cattle that some fast-
riding rustler fetched across the border and delivered on
his range.

It wasn't that Wig Murphy needed to steal or buy stolen
stuff. The old rascal was one of the biggest cowmen in
Arizona. He had more money than any man needs in this
world. He had a fine ranch, a big brick house in Phoenix,
outside interests that brought him in big dividends, city
property that was jumping in value. Wig must have been
worth close to a million. Yet he would ride forty miles on
a rainy, chilly night to dicker with some renegade cowboy
for a dozen head of stolen cattle that came up out of Mexico.

He was as bold, and swashbuckling, and lawless, as any
pirate that ever sailed the Spanish Main. Huge of build,
with a bellowing voice, a pair of hard fists, and an eye that
could change in the fraction of a second from merry
twinkle to steely hardness. He was generous toward his
friends, relentlessly uncompromising in his dealings with
enemies. His cowpunchers would fight for him at the
least bidding. They would follow old Wig anywhere and
on any sort of mission.

Along the Mexican border, from Nogales to El Paso,

Wig Murphy's Flying W iron was known. Wherever cowboys gathered around a camp fire, some tale concerning the old cattle baron would spice the evening's yarning. Some of those stories concerning Wig were true. Other tales hung on his name and his Flying W brand, were undoubtedly false. But all aided in the colouring of his reputation along the Mexican border. And because the old swashbuckler enjoyed his unsavoury reputation, he denied none of the wild stories that were listed to his credit or discredit.

And now some rustler gang was robbing the Flying W range! Old Wig Murphy bellowed and pawed dirt aplenty. He stormed and raved, there at the home ranch, when Billy Carter told him. Billy was Wig's foreman. A short, wiry-built, freckled man, with bowed legs and stubby features was Billy Carter. Rated as one of the best cowhands in the business, he ran the Flying W for Wig, who was getting too old to take active part in the round-ups. Wig had raised Billy Carter, had taught him all the thousand-and-one tricks and kinks of handling a cow outfit. And because Billy was more like a son than a foreman, Wig felt privileged to storm at the young cowpuncher whenever he chose. And Billy listened undisturbed.

Now, when old Wig had bellowed himself hoarse and had sought the solace of a drink, Billy sat smoking, apparently deaf.

'Well,' growled the old cowman when he had taken his nip of "corn-likker," 'why don't you say somethin' instead of settin' there like a wart on a hawg's back?'

'From what I could get of it, Wig,' grinned the unruffled Billy Carter, 'you didn't leave much of anything to be said on this here subject. You done said her all, and I couldn't add one part of a word to it that would be of much value. Some gents are a-whittlin' on the Flyin' W cattle, that's all. And what I mean to tell the cockeyed cow country, they're as slick as ever I seen work. All we got to show for five hundred head of white-faced cattle is a mess of stale sign that crosses over into Mexico. Last week them cattle was there on the Concho River, fat, and in prime shape. Now there's only a few culls scattered along the river. And I thought I'd better have a medicine talk with you before I done anything.'

8

'If you was half as handy with a Winchester as you are with that Flyin' W check book,' roared old Wig, 'you'd be a jim dandy. But the minute somethin' turns up, you come a-yelpin' to the old man for to help you. If I was twenty-five years younger, I'd ride down there into Mexico. I'd follow that sign till I found my cattle. And when I found them cattle, I'd fetch 'em back, and I'd make it mighty sorrowful for the Mexicans that thought they were men enough to outfox me.'

'I took five of the boys and went down there,' said Billy calmly. 'Night ketched us there at Black Springs. We made camp there and was a-cookin' supper when down rides two-three hundred Mexicans and Yaquis with none other than Pablo Guerrero with 'em. Polite as a preacher, Pablo tells us that he and some more of the Mexican folks is thinkin' of startin' another revolution, mebbe, and that we're in his road down there. And that it might be a good idea if we saddled up, come mornin', and went back home. Because him and his men is needin' that part of the country to hide out in, and we make it kinda crowded. He sends you his best regards and says that on account of his bein' busy trainin' these Yaquis, he won't have much time to deliver you any wet cattle for a few months. And that if he wasn't so busy just now gettin' ready to take over the Mexican gover'ment, he'd be glad to help us get back them stolen cattle and kill off a few rustlers. And without sayin' so, he makes it awful clear that me and the Flyin' W boys is due for some bad luck if we let the sun set on us down there.'

'I thought the federals killed Pablo Guerrero down at Mazatlan.' Wig Murphy's tone was milder now. From time to time, across the span of the past ten years, Pablo Guerrero had come north of the border and on to the Flying W range. Usually, Pablo brought with him a few of his most able followers and a bunch of stolen cattle that would already be in the Flying W iron. Pablo was thorough in his methods, and quite a stickler for detail. He would suavely explain that these freshly branded cattle were some of Wig's that had strayed across the border. He had brought them back to their owner. He and his men would be glad to accept any reward Wig Murphy might see fit to offer for the return of his strayed stock.

Whenever a revolutionary movement was afoot, Pablo was in the thick of it. He had a following among the ferocious Yaquis. Their services went to the highest bidder. Whichever faction laid out the highest cash bid, they joined. Two months or so ago, down at Mazatlan, official report had it that Pablo Guerrero had faced a firing squad. Wig Murphy had taken much pains to have this report verified, because he owned interests in the Eldorado Mining Co. in Mexico and, to protect these interests, he had been paying, each month or two, a fat sum of money to Pablo Guerrero. It amounted to blackmail, to be sure. Pablo had, in his suave, apologetic manner, made it quite plain to Wig and Wig's partners in the mining venture that whenever these blackmailing taxes were not paid in gold, then Wig and his business associates could expect trouble at the mines. Therefore, Wig had reason to wish that harm might overtake Pablo Guerrero. It was rumoured that a certain man who represented the Eldorado Mining Co. had paid over a tidy amount of money for the delivery of Pablo's head in a sack, the day following the report that Pablo had faced a firing squad at Mazatlan.

Now, Billy Carter brought back the disconcerting news that Pablo Guerrero was not dead. That, on the contrary, Pablo was very much alive. And this bit of vital news had the effect of silencing Wig's bellowing complaint about those stolen cattle that had vanished from the lower range on the Concho River.

In black silence, Wig Murphy eyed his foreman. The old border buccaneer had made a habit of never confiding in Billy Carter except in matters that concerned the Flying W Ranch. He never mentioned his outside interests to Billy. He absolutely and firmly discouraged any talk on Billy's part concerning the Eldorado Mining Co. He liked to make himself believe that Billy Carter was ignorant of what went on down there. But now, as he regarded the bronzed face of his foreman, he was wondering just how much Billy Carter knew of his dealings with Pablo Guerrero. He wondered if Billy guessed that when Pablo came across with those bunches of wet cattle, the freshly branded 'critters' represented the amount of tribute that the polite-mannered Mexican bandit was asking.

If the cattle numbered twenty head, then Pablo expected ten thousand dollars. Five hundred dollars per head was the amount that Wig Murphy had been paying Pablo Guerrero for those wet cattle!

That was Pablo's idea of humour. It tickled his Mexican vanity to ride across the border and make Wig Murphy pay. In gold or unmarked United States currency, the swashbuckling old cowman would pay five hundred dollars per head for whatever cattle Pablo brought across. None but the two ever saw the money that was paid. They alone knew. And because Pablo always came with a bodyguard of several heavily armed Yaquis, Wig had never dared open hostilities. Not only would Pablo be well guarded, but he would make it quite plain that he was otherwise protected from harm.

Sometimes he would kidnap one or two of the mine officials and have them held hostage back in the hills until he returned safely. Or he would inform Wig that all his peons at the mine had gone on a holiday from which they would return when Pablo Guerrero again showed up at some place in the Mexican hills. And until those peons returned, the mines were in absolute possession of the Yaquis, who could destroy machinery, and cause many thousands of dollars damage if anything should happen to their leader. Or Pablo would calmly inform Wig Murphy that the wind was so blowing that if the range were to be set on fire at certain spots where Pablo's men were stationed, both range and cattle would be doomed.

Pablo Guerrero was a clever general. Any harm that might befall him would be avenged by the wild Yaquis who lived in the remote part of the rough mountains. He was a power in that section of Mexico because he commanded the finest body of fighting men in the northern part of the republic. His was a power that could break the backbone of any revolt. He was the most feared, most respected man in that state. News of his rumoured death had been both glad and evil tidings. His friends had mourned, his enemies had made it the occasion for a fiesta.

'Pablo Guerrero is dead,' repeated Wig Murphy. 'He was shot at Mazatlan.'

'Then it musta bin his ghost that sent word back to you that he knowed how happy you'd be to know he was alive

11

and that he himself had collected the ten thousand dollars for a head that was supposed to be his. He got a big laugh out of it when he told me how he'd growed a swell bunch of whiskers and swapped his fancy clothes for peon pants and shirt and a pair of sandals. So that the gringo that paid him the money for that head never recognized him. He said the head belonged to a cousin of his. A Mexican named Morales. This Morales was a dead ringer for Pablo in looks, but not in brains. Morales takes over the job of turnin' Pablo over to the federals at Mazatlan. Pablo gets wise to the racket. He makes Morales swap clothes with him. Then he gives Morales his choice of two things. Morales kin get captured and shot, like a gentleman. Or, if he don't like that easy way of dyin', Pablo will have his Yaquis torture him for a few days until he's dead. So Morales picks the easy way out. He gets shot in Pablo's place, and Pablo delivers the head in a gunny sack and gets the ransom money offered by the Eldorado Mining Co. Wig, I ain't much of a Mexican-lover, but there is somethin' about that son of a gun that I can't help but like.'

Chapter II

Some twenty or thirty miles below the border, a lone cowpuncher sat eating his supper of jerky and brown beans. His horse, a splendid bay gelding, grazed at the end of a picket rope. The light of the camp fire showed the man to be a tall, rawboned fellow of perhaps thirty. Light of hair, blue-eyed, with strong, rugged features. His overalls and denim jumper were badly faded. The chaps that lay on the ground near his saddle were brush scratched. A Colt .45 was shoved in the waistband of his overalls, and a carbine lay against the saddle that was covered with a stained Navajo blanket. Now and then, as he squatted by the fire, he seemed to pause in his meal, apparently listening for something.

He had just finished eating, when, through the moonlight night, there came the thud of hoofbeats. The man stepped back out of the glow of the fire and picked up his carbine. Then he vanished into a patch of mesquite that fringed the water hole. The big bay horse stood alert, ears forward, as if he shared his master's suspicion of the newcomer's intentions.

Now, accompanying the thud of the approaching hoofs, sounded the tinkle of spurs and a man whistling a Mexican waltz tune. The rider boldly entered the rim of firelight.

He was slender, of medium height, dressed in Mexican fashion; silver decorated his huge sombrero and his trappings. He looked boyish as his teeth flashed in a white smile and he lifted his hands above his head.

The lone camper stepped from the brush, his carbine covering the Mexican.

For a long moment the two eyed one another. The Mex-

13

ican was smiling, the sandy-haired cowpuncher masking his feelings behind a faint scowl. Then the cowpuncher lowered the muzzle of his carbine.

'That ees much better, señor.' The Mexican's voice was soft of texture, a little mocking in its pleasantry. Without invitation, he dismounted. The white man eyed him carefully, with eyes that glinted with suspicion.

'You are Pablo Guerrero, I reckon?'

'Si, señor.'

'Why did you follow me?'

'To have a little bit of talk, Señor Pat Roper.'

'You know who I am, then?'

'Part of the business of Pablo Guerrero, señor, ees to know all about any man who comes to my hills. Especially, señor, when that man brings down five hondred head of Flying W cattle. Cattle that belong to my friend, the Señor Wig Murphy.'

'Yo're plumb welcome to them cattle,' said the cow thief. 'Eat 'em or sell 'em. Sell 'em back to the old rascal, if you've a mind to.'

Pablo shrugged his slim shoulders and smiled. 'Per'aps, señor, I weel do that very theeng. Quién sabe? He ees, like you say, the old rascal.'

'You and yore men had me shut up in a trap, back there in the hills. I figgered I was a goner. Them Flying W men come in right behind me. You sent them all back. Then you let me ride out without even tryin' to stop me. Why didn't you stop me back there, instead of follerin' me?'

'Because I am not the beeg fool, señor. You would fight, and my men would shoot you, sure. So I say to them that you are the good old friend of mine from El Paso and Juarez and over in Chihuahua. You are the Señor Pat Roper. One time, five years ago, in Chihuahua, you save my life. Pablo Guerrero never forgets the small favour like that.'

'I don't recollect ever savin' yore life. You mebbe got me mixed up with some other gent.'

'No. One does not forget a theeng like that. You are the foreman for the OX outfit then. You find a Mexican tied to a post to die een the sun, while his two bad enemies sit een the shade and dreenk water that the prisoner cannot have. You, Pat Roper, chase away those two hombres.

14

You make free the tied man and you give to heem water and grub and a horse and a rifle weeth cartridges. Maybe, when that horse ees not return', that thees ongrateful son steal that horse, no? Not so, señor. The horse, he got keel' when I follow those two evil hombres. They shoot the horse, but I shoot them. The man you are so generous to that day, my friend, ees me, Pablo Guerrero.'

'And now you return the favour,' grinned Pat Roper. 'Fair enough. And I'm obliged.'

Pablo waved away the other's thanks with a graceful gesture. Then he smiled quickly.

'You do not like thees man, Wig Murphy?'

'No,' came the stout reply, 'I don't. But they say he's a friend of yours.'

'The Señor Wig Murphy has been very generous to Pablo Guerrero. But sometimes I get ver moch annoy' weeth heem. The Señor Wig, he get some very stupid ideas.'

'He'll bear watchin',' replied Pat Roper grimly. 'He's as crooked as a new rope. Full of kinks. The worst cow thief along the border, and that's takin' in some mighty snaky folks.'

'He steal from you, señor?'

'Cleaned me out, you might say. I had a little bunch of cattle on the Mexican side. He includes them on one of his raids. Mebbe he didn't do the actual stealin', but he bought every head that these men he hired could steal and deliver to him. I'd gone up to Denver on business for the OX spread. When I get back, two-three weeks later, I find that my range has bin cleaned, and after some fair to middlin' detective work, I learn that them cattle in my iron is now at the north end of the Flyin' W range.'

'Soch things make one very angry, no?' smiled Pablo.

'Angry is right. I hired me a few good men and made a raid on that stuff old Murphy was pasturin' on the Concho. We worked the river plumb clean. I sent back the boys that he'ped me, come on alone, and shoved those cattle into the hills. I don't want the cattle. All I want is the satisfaction of makin' that old cow thief suffer where it hurts the most.'

Pablo Guerrero nodded thoughtfully. There followed

15

several minutes of silence. A silence which the handsome Mexican broke with a soft laugh.

'Listen to a plan which I have made up out of my brains, señor,' he said, in reply to Pat Roper's mute question. 'Reject thees plan if you weesh, or take the advantage of eet. First, a question. Do the Señor Wig, or Billy Carter, or any of the Flying W vaqueros know you?'

'I don't reckon so. I belong over in Chihuahua and Texas.'

" 'Sta bueno. Very good. The next question ees this. You are not scare' of Wig Murphy?'

'No.' Pat Roper grinned crookedly. 'No, I don't reckon I'm too much scared of him.'

'Once more, 'sta bueno. Like you say it, okay. Now watch while I make with a stick on the sand, a map picture. Here ees the Flying W rancho.' Pablo drew lines in the dirt with a mesquite stick.

'The lower Concho marks Wig Murphy's boundary. Joining the Flying W range ees the Two Block rancho. Twenty-five thousand acres of good feed and plenty water. Not so many cattle, but enough for a start. You would like to own that rancho, my friend?'

'Ask me somethin' harder,' Pat Roper smiled wryly. 'You don't seem to understand that when Wig Murphy gutted my range, he broke me. I got my horse and saddle and the clothes on my back. I paid my last money to those boys that helped me run them Flyin' W cattle off Wig Murphy's range. I gotta go back workin' for wages.'

'No, my friend. If you care to own the Two Block outfit, then it belongs to you. Ees like this, señor. For three years I 'ave own' that Two Block outfit. Nobody know that I am own it. Not even Wig Murphy know. He think that Jim Boudry, who runs the outfit, ees run it for the bank een Phoenix. Boudry likewise ees think the same theeng. So I make out a bill of sale to you. You take that paper to the bank and they will give to you the proper documents that make you the one and only owner of the Two Block outfit. But watch thees man Boudry. I do not trust heem.'

'Excuse me,' said Pat Roper solemnly, 'but are you plumb sure the sun ain't touched yore brain some?'

Pablo Guerrero laughed softly and from his saddle pocket he took a leather case. From this case he took a

paper which he handed the cowboy. It was a bill of ownership to the Two Block outfit, including all cattle and
horses in that iron, and twenty-five thousand acres of
land. While Pat Roper scanned the document, Pablo took
fountain pen and paper and wrote swiftly in a neat hand-
writing. He wrote in Spanish. It was a document that made
transfer of ownership of the Two Block outfit to Pat
Roper.

'This has all the earmarks of a swell dream,' said the
cowpuncher dazedly. 'Why are you doin' this?'

'Because, señor, I am a very selfish man. And likewise
for some other reasons. First, I have not forgot that you
save my life. Second, I have a very personal wish that you
should have this ranch which will make you the very close
neighbour of Wig Murphy. Third, I do not feel too pleased
with that Jim Boudry because he has stolen many cattle
from the Two Block iron and sold. Fourth, because I am
very busy now helping to make a revolution. If my luck
does not turn out so good, I may be stood against the
adobe wall and shot down. Or the federals may chase me
hard, and I wish to have, across the border, one good
friend who weel give me welcome and shelter. That ees
why I have that rancho. That ees why I give it to you, my
good friend, who save my life. There are not so many
men, señor, that one can trust when one is get into trouble. I find that out many times. You weel do me the kind
favour to accept this little gift from Pablo Guerrero?'

Pat Roper's protests were dismissed with a grand
gesture. Pablo took a thick sheaf of bank-notes and
handed them to Roper without troubling to count the
money.

'Expense money, my friend. There is much more where
that comes from. And here ees a note to my attorney at
Phoenix who will take care of you on the papers. Now I
must go. Thees business of making a revolution takes up
one's time.' He held out a slim, well-kept hand. 'If the
Señor Dios ees kind, you and I shall meet again, my
friend. Quién sabe? Who knows how the luck weel run?
Adios señor, my friend.'

Pat Roper gripped the Mexican's hand. There was so
much he would like to say to this impulsive caballero. He
could find no words that seemed sufficient.

'Whenever I can be of help, Pablo, call on me. You know, the Two Block Ranch is mine only till you want it again.'

'I may need help,' smiled the Mexican. 'Who of us does not find that he needs a friend sometimes? Watch that Jim Boudry. Keep an eye open for trouble. Do not place too much trust in Wig Murphy. But if you need the counsel of a friend, call upon Billy Carter. *Adios, amigo!*'

As he had come, so left Pablo Guerrero. The music of his song came drifting back to the cowpuncher who stood there alone. And while the little song was one of gay notes, still, there crept through its melody a plaintive, wistful sadness.

Pat Roper stowed away his bill of sale and the roll of yellowback currency. He noted that the letter to Arturo Gonzales, attorney-at-law, was sealed. He put it away carefully. Then he threw some sticks on the fire and sat there smoking and thinking, trying to realize his good fortune, striving to reason out why a stranger had made him a gift that amounted to a neat fortune. Could he have read the contents of that bulky note to the Mexican attorney at Phoenix, he might have had further food for thought. And he would have glimpsed another side of Pablo's nature that would further prove the crafty generalship of this leader of the Yaquis. Because in that note to the attorney was given a shrewd reason for making Pat Roper the owner of the Two Block Ranch that adjoined the Flying W range.

Chapter III

Two weeks later, Pat Roper rode across the lower Concho and crossed over on to the Two Block range. He still wore the same faded overalls and jumper. He was riding the same big bay horse. There was a week's stubble of sand-coloured whiskers on his square jaw.

Below the ridge where he sat his horse, some men were working a bunch of cattle. Pat watched them for half an hour before he rode down the ridge and into the dry wash below.

Five men were holding the worked cattle—cows with big calves, ready for branding. A heavy-set man of reddish complexion rode around the little bunch of cattle to meet the newcomer. There was a heavy scowl on his hot face, and his pale eyes were slitted with ugly suspicion.

'Which way did you come here?' he asked, without the formality of any greeting.

'Across the Concho and along the main trail. Why?'

'You musta seen a notice posted there that would tell you this is Two Block range and that any rider on this side of the boundary is trespassing. Are you one of Murphy's new men?'

'No.'

'I asked to see if you'd lie about it. You was wise not to lie.'

'Mebbyso, mister, lyin' ain't one of my habits.'

'Yore habits don't hold no interest for me. That horse of yourn looks stout enough to carry you back the way you come. Hit the trail.'

'Supposin' I don't?' asked Pat Roper gently.

'In that case, you range bum, I'll put the skids under you.' The red-headed man jumped his horse against Pat's.

His doubled rope lashed out viciously. Pat ducked and swung the big bay against the other man's horse. He reached out and grabbed the big man, quitting his own horse after the fashion of a man bulldogging a steer. His quick movement jerked the red-haired man from the saddle, and their twisting bodies struck the earth with a crashing thud.

Pat's fists swung in short, powerful jabs. The big man fought with clumsy ferocity. He reached for his gun and grunted with pain as Pat twisted his arm down and back in a hammerlock. The pain blanched the red face of the big man. Pat released his grip, grabbed the man's six-shooter and flung it away, then leaped to his feet.

'Now wade in, big un, and get it.'

The big fellow rushed with lowered head. Pat straightened him up with a left and right, then beat him to his knees with a volley of blows that made the red spurt from a smashed nose. Blind with pain, the big man rose again from his sagging position. Pat timed his swing with the nice precision of a skilled boxer. There was a hundred and eighty pounds of rawboned weight behind the left fist that crashed against the big man's jaw. With a moaning sigh, the man dropped like a shot beef.

The cattle had scattered in swift flight. The cowboys sat their saddles uncertainly. Pat faced them, his hand on his gun. His blue eyes were glittering.

'Which of you boys is Jim Boudry?' he asked gratingly.

'That's him you knocked out, stranger,' volunteered a grinning cowboy.

'When he comes alive, hand him this check. He's paid off. You boys kin come in to the ranch for your time. My name is Pat Roper, and I've bought the Two Block outfit, lock, stock and barrel. Jim Boudry is fired. So are any of you that claim to be his friends. I'll be waitin' at the home ranch when you get there. And don't bother gatherin' any of them cows and calves. The gent that was dickerin' fer the calves has bin took with a bad case of chilly feet. I crossed his trail back yonder a ways and had a talk with him. Last I seen of him, he was travellin' yonderly at a high lope.' He started to ride off, then halted. His mouth grinned twistedly.

'I plumb forgot to ask any of you if you wanted to take

20

up that fight that Boudry wasn't man enough to finish.'

'Not me, boss,' grinned the young cowpuncher who had identified Boudry for the new owner. 'And I don't know as the other boys is hankerin' to take on any of them jabs an' swings. Me, I wouldn't git down off my horse to pick Jim Boudry outa the dirt. And if you kin stand my company, I'll ride on in to the ranch with you now. As long as I'm canned, I'll git my bed rolled and hit for town this evenin'. And unless you know the trail, mister, you might get kinda lost.'

'Then come along,' Pat invited the boy. They rode away together.

'Don't never turn yore back on them gents,' whispered the young cowboy. 'Ride off sideways. I'll keep between them and you.'

'That,' said Pat Roper, and he slid his carbine out so that it rested across his saddle, its muzzle towards the group of sullen-looking cowboys, 'ain't necessary, kid. But it was white of you to tip me off.'

'Keep the odd change, boss. I just hate to see any dirty stuff pulled. And two of them boys is thick with Boudry, and Boudry shore fights dirty. Too bad you made an enemy outa him, mister.'

'Why?' asked Pat, when they had put some distance between them and the others.

'He stands in with a bad gang and they'll whittle on yore cattle somethin' scan'lous. Alongside Jim Boudry, old Wig Murphy is a honest man.'

Pat Roper chuckled. He liked this honest-eyed boy who seemed to always grin.

'What's yore name, kid?'

'Sid Collins. I'm just a button, but I kin ride some and was raised in this country. Born here at the Two Block Ranch. My daddy run the outfit up till he died of lead poison. He was shot in the back about four years ago. I got no mammy. I could work for Billy Carter, but I wanted to ride for the Two Block. Two of them men back yonder, and Jim Boudry, worked here when my daddy was murdered. I've always wondered how much they knowed about how dad was killed, and why. So I went to the bank folks at Phoenix and they fixed it for me to work here. Though Boudry has made things mighty tough for me.

21

Sometimes I shore wanted to quit. But I hung an' rattled and took Jim Boudry's abuse, rode sorry horses and broncs, cooked, wrangled horses, and built fence. And all the time I kept my eyes skinned and my ears a-standin' out. And I'm hopin' to learn, somehow, who murdered my dad.'

'And when you do find out, what then?'

'I reckon, mister,' said the boy quietly, 'that it'll be up to me to kill him. Though I ain't much force with a gun.'

'How'd you like to stay on here, Sid?'

'Ain't I bin talkin' in hopes you wouldn't fire me along with the others?' grinned the boy. 'I'd be proud to stay, and I'll work cheap. And I'll do any kind of odd jobs there is to do. I'd shore like to stay.'

'All right, Sid. Now that's settled, and yo're hired at regular wages, I'll let you pilot me around. And mebbyso some day, we're gonna find out who killed your dad. And it'll be a heap better to turn the murderer over to the law. This killin' business is goin' outa style.'

'That's what "Tommy" Murphy says.'

'And who is Tommy Murphy?'

'Old Wig Murphy's daughter. Gee, you shore are a plumb stranger! She's away a lot of the time. Her name is Colleen, but Wig and the cowpunchers always called her "Tomboy," or Tommy, for short. She goes to college back East, but she'll be home in a few days. You had ought to see her rope and ride, though. Man, she's a peach! Purty, too, you bet. And havin' money and schoolin' ain't spoiled her, neither. She's got as much sense as a cow pony. And Wig shore gets the rough knocked outa him when Tommy's around. He can't bluff her, you bet. Don't know as he would try, nohow. He thinks that Tommy is just about the swellest thing in the world. Wait till you see her, mister. Only you'll have to go over there. She never comes here to the Two Block because she hates Jim Boudry. Only a few times, when I thought I was on to some clues, she come over at night and we spied around some. And what we run on to is a secret that we can't tell nobody. But I'm tellin' you, mister, this is shore a spooky old place sometimes. But say, I'm talkin' too much. I got a bad habit of runnin' off at the head a lot. Slap me shut when I get to blabbin'.'

22

Pat chuckled. "Mebbyso you talk a lot because you ain't had a chance to unload much conversation around Boudry and his men.'

'Gee, mebbe that's it! It gets awful lonesome sometimes. You bet Boudry usta slap me shut.'

'I didn't know Wig Murphy had a daughter,' Pat mused aloud.

'Just wait till you see her,' repeated Sid with enthusiasm.

'I'll do my best to wait, Sid.' But the tone lacked warmth. Pat Roper was thinking of old Wig and how he would even his score with the old buccaneer. He hoped the girl would stay away. A range feud is no place for a woman.

Chapter IV

Now, Wig Murphy was in a bad humour. He had just received a very polite, very carefully worded communication from a Mr. Arturo Gonzales, attorney-at-law, Phoenix, Arizona. Mr. Gonzales, so read the communication, represented Señor Pablo Guerrero, of Sonora, Mexico, and other points south of the international border. The letter suggested that it might be to the advantage of Mr. Murphy's interests, if he would call upon Mr. Gonzales at his office in Phoenix at his earliest convenience.

Enclosed with the letter was a clipping from a Mexican newspaper. This clipping stated that, some time during the past two weeks, the elusive and agile Pablo Guerrero had paid a personal visit to the editor of the paper to correct the erroneous account in that paper, some time ago, of the execution of a man who died under the name of Pablo Guerrero. The daring Pablo, after his own peculiar way, hereby branded that man who had so bravely faced the firing squad as a rank imposter seeking notoriety. Pablo stated that the authorities should be careful about such mistakes. That he would not be held responsible for the burial expenses of such impostors. Such an error of identification might very easily start an epidemic of similar deceptions. There would be so many graves holding the earthly remains of a Pablo Guerrero that, when it came time for the real Pablo to die and be buried, posterity could never be absolutely sure which of the several graves held the authentic remains of Sonora's greatest bandit. In closing, Pablo naïvely stated that there might be many beautiful señoritas wishing to visit his grave, bringing flowers, and praying for the repose of his soul. That it would be doing these many lovely señoritas a grave injustice if they had to choose, at random, one of several graves that supposedly held the bones of Pablo Guerrero.

The newspaper article further stated that the wily and tactful Pablo, when questioned concerning his political leanings in the present situation of growing discord among the men high in Mexican politics, had been non-committal. He had, so he claimed, been somewhat out of touch with things the past couple of months. He had been on a visit to New York and San Francisco. Now he was quite busy doing this thing and the other, and had little time to spare. Pablo felt rather certain that, in the event of a revolution, he and his Yaquis would favour the side that was in the right. But that, in order to ascertain which faction was really right, he would have to confer with certain political heads of the state.

Finally, Pablo Guerrero stated with grave emphasis that the great government of the United States could be positively assured that he and his followers, the finest fighting force in all Mexico, perhaps in all the world, would, as they always had, protect American interests.

Whoever had written the article, and in all probability the writer had been none other than Pablo himself, had accomplished a masterpiece of that sort of delicious ridicule so dear to the heart of the Mexican patriot. It was, in fact, an open declaration that informed Pablo's many friends that he was alive and active. That his services and the services of his Yaquis were at the command of the highest bidder. Also, that he was once more about to levy a tax on the American interests in Mexico.

Wig Murphy read the newspaper clipping twice. Across his square, weather-beaten face there spread a slow grin of admiration for this gritty little Mexican who snapped his fingers at death. Then he touched a match to the clipping and the communication from Mr. Arturo Gonzales, attorney-at-law.

Hoofbeats from outside brought old Wig Murphy to the long veranda. Three men on horseback reined up. The one who dismounted was none other than Jim Boudry.

His legs widespread, thumbs hooked in the armholes of his frayed vest, Wig scowled at the big red-haired man from the Two Block. Old Wig's scowl halted Boudry at the bottom step that led up to the shaded veranda.

'Whatever you come here to say, Boudry,' he growled, 'say it from there and spit it out in a hurry. Then take them two men and get off my range.'

'Treatin' me bad won't buy you nothin', Wig. I just stopped to tell you that I've quit the Two Block. Me and these two boys is startin' in business for ourselves.'

'That don't interest me, not one bit, Boudry. I know the kind of business yo're startin' in. And I'll tell you this right now, that I ain't in the market for wet cattle. And if my boys ketch you or your men on my range, they'll make bunch quitters outa you. Drag it!'

'I'll drag it in a minute. Don't get your shirt in a knot, Wig. I'm gonna give you a tip. Not because I want to help you, but just so you'll not lay any too easy on the bed ground tonight. You got some cattle on the upper Concho that has a big PR on their left ribs. The brand is vented and they're in the Flyin' W iron. But you know and I know, Wig, that you never bought them cattle from the owner. I seen 'em delivered there on the lower Concho. Pablo Guerrero delivered them cattle.'

'You can't prove a thing, Boudry, if your game is black-mail.'

'That ain't my game, Mister Murphy. How you got them cattle is no hide off my nose. But the new owner of the Two Block is a gent named Pat Roper. He owned them PR cattle down in Chihuahua. And now I'll drag it. So long, Mister Wig Murphy.'

Old Wig stood there, his narrowed eyes following Jim Boudry and the other two men out of sight. He crammed some plug tobacco into a short-stemmed clay pipe and lit it. Then he paced the veranda for fully half an hour. Now and then he swore in a rumbling undertone.

Two bits of bad news in one day. That letter from Gonzales meant that the foxy Pablo was up to some shrewd game. And Wig would have bet his top horse that Pablo's game had to do with this new owner of the Two Block spread, there beyond the lower Concho.

Between Tim Collins, former ramrod for the Two Block, and Wig Murphy, there had been an amicable rela-tionship. Tim had been an honest cowman who would meet a neighbor half-way. Tim and Wig Murphy had been

26

honest in their dealings with one another. Then Tim had been murdered. A lot of fools said that Wig had been behind the killing of Tim Collins. And evidence had borne out that theory rather strongly. But beyond those several bits of strong circumstantial evidence that lacked the power to stand in court for conviction of Wig Murphy, nothing had come of it. Tim's death was just another black mark against the old border buccaneer. And while Wig had never denied the charges, still he had felt the sting of that rumour that said he had murdered a man who was his friend. Wig Murphy had his faults, but such a crime was not among them.

After Tim Collins had passed, the Two Block had mysteriously changed hands. A Phoenix bank had taken it over. Jim Boudry had been put in charge. Wig Murphy offered a big price for the outfit, but was flatly informed that the Two Block outfit was not for sale at any price.

Because of its locality in relation to the border which it joined on the south, the ranch made an ideal pass into Mexico. Smugglers, gun-runners, rustlers, could slip across the line without much trouble. Wig had always suspected that this change of ownership had been brought about by the big guns who engineered the smuggling and gun-running along that section of the border. He had often wondered if Pablo Guerrero had a hand in that deal, because Tim Collins, affiliated with the border patrol, had his men posted along the border to check the smuggling and gun-running. Tim was a member of the rangers and worked hand in hand with the border patrols. Except for a few leaks, the border along the Two Block range had been closed during the period of Tim's foremanship.

But Jim Boudry was a different breed of man from honest Tim Collins. Boudry had been bought by the smuggling fraternity. The south line of the Two Block range was as full of holes as a colander. Patrol men rode that part of the line with their guns in their hands and in bunches of three and four. And when Boudry rode over the Flying W Ranch one day, old Wig Murphy was forced not only to talk to him, but to compromise with him. Because the Flying W cattle were at the mercy of the Two Block men. The lower Concho, though rough country, was the choice part of Wig's range. And in spite of the long drift

27

fence that separated the two ranges, the cattle on the lower Concho were easy pickings for Jim Boudry.

'You mind your own business, Murphy, and you'll brand more big calves at round-up time. If you go on poking into my game, your fool drift fence will be cut faster than twenty fence crews kin built it up. You ain't foolin' with an old fogy like Tim Collins when you tackle me. What I do is my business. You and Billy Carter keep your men off my range. Else you won't have good luck with your stuff on the lower Concho.'

So old Wig Murphy had been made to eat crow meat. After all, Boudry's connection with the gun-runners and smugglers was nobody's business but Jim Boudry's. Old Wig was getting too old to fight. Billy Carter was a good cowman, but not a fighter. So they had compromised along those lines. There had been no alternative for Wig Murphy.

Now came this news that Pat Roper had bought the Two Block. And on the same day came that letter from Mr. Arturo Gonzales who was as smooth a lawyer as ever drew up a tricky document.

Wig Murphy quit pacing the veranda. He went into his bedroom and packed his bag. Without bothering to shave or change his clothes, the grizzled cowman carried the packed bag out to the battered old buckboard he used by preference. His loud bellow brought Taller, the old ranch cook, from the kitchen.

'Taller, tell Billy when he gits in that I've gone to Phoenix. I'll be back when I git here. Tell him I said to gather them PR cattle and throw 'em up on to the upper range, and to run off any Two Block men that come acrost the line. Tell him if he sights Jim Boudry, to set him afoot, then whip him plumb outa the country. Tell him I said he wouldn't be gettin' these orders if he'd bin doin' some ridin' instead of bein' bushed up somewhere with his head under him.'

'You won't be back for supper, Wig?'

'Not unless I kin sprout wings and fly back an' forth from here to Phoenix and back again. Your fool brains is made of the same sour dough as your bread.'

'You ain't forgot that Tommy's due home tonight, have you, Wig? I'm bakin' the big cake now.'

Wig Murphy had forgotten that telegram that said his

28

daughter was due at the ranch that night. For a moment the old cowman sat behind the wheel of the light truck, a harassed, worried look on his face.

'Tell Tommy,' he said in a mild tone that brought a grin to the seamed face of the old round-up cook, 'that her old man will be back as fast as he kin get here. This is somethin' I can't put off, Taller— And listen, Taller, mind that the little rascal don't get a look at her new hoss till I get back. Tell Billy I'll shoot him if he lets her sight that black hoss I bought her. And break it to her gentle that I'm gone, understand or I'll smother you in your dough pans.'

'I'm to say you've gone to Phoenix, Wig?'

'Yeah. To Phoenix. To make a dicker for the Two Block outfit.'

Chapter V

Every Two Block man, the cook included, had been fired by Pat Roper. He and the boy Sid Collins finished their supper and washed the dishes. It was almost dark and the two sole occupants of the Two Block Ranch sat in rawhide-upholstered chairs watching the moon rise above the jagged skyline. Tomorrow the cowboys that Pat had sent for, boys he had known in and around El Paso, would arrive.

The new owner of the Two Blocks was deep in thought when the distant sound of hoofbeats broke the still evening. He looked at Sid inquiringly. The boy was on his feet, head tilted sidewise, a tense look on his tanned face as he listened intently. Then he turned to Pat, a light of excitement dancing in his hazel eyes.

'We better duck,' he hissed. 'They'll be here purty quick. They're coming a-gallopin',' and I don't mean perhaps. We better hide, Pat.'

'Hide from what, kid?'

'Them friends of Jim Boudry's. I guess they don't know he got fired and they're bringin' a load.'

'A load of what, Sid?'

'Guns,' hissed the boy dramatically. 'Boudry always sent me off somewheres when they was due. But a couple of times I snuk back and spied on 'em. They're fetchin' guns.'

'To go quail huntin' outa season?' asked Pat Roper solemnly. The boy looked at him quickly.

'I reckon yo're funnin' me, ain't you, Pat?'

'I reckon I am, son. And I likewise reckon that you had better pick a good hidin'-place. So if anything happens to me, you can take the bad news to town.'

'There'll be three of 'em.'

'There'll be more than three shells in my gun, young

'un. Now hide out. Yonder I see 'em, there against the hill.'

Sid Colllins was shivering with excitement as he slipped into the shadow of the buildings. He could see Pat Roper sitting there on the porch, his chair tilted back against the wall, a Winchester across his lap, the tip of his cigarette glowing in the dusk.

The buckboard swung around the corner of the barn and the horses slid to a halt. There were two men in the front seat, one in the rear. The vehicle was so close that Pat could almost reach it with the gun that now covered the three startled occupants.

'Reach for the moon, gents!' grated Pat's voice. 'I'll kill the man that makes the first move. Climb down and I'll look you over.'

The three men obeyed sullenly. Pat sat in his chair. His cigarette still glowed as he breathed. His gun covered them with a sinister steadiness.

'Which of you is called "Slats" Mussik?' he asked.

For a long moment there was a most deadly silence. Pat Roper smiled crookedly.

'Sid,' called Pat in a slightly louder tone, 'don't answer me or show yourself, but line your sights on the tall, slim jasper. Aim at his heart. If he don't talk by the time I count to three, let him have it. One—two—'

'I'm Slats Mussik,' blurted the slim man.

'So I figgered. You usta run a crap game at Juarez. Just shed your hardware, Slats. You other two hombres foller suit. Because if you don't do just like I say, you'll all go back to town in pine boxes. Drop your guns on the ground. If you feel awful lucky, try to get me. Sid and me just hates to take prisoners. I'm thinkin' of a couple of friends of mine that was found shot from the brush. They belonged to the rangers. And I never yet heard of a case where a man done time for killin' such stinks as you three. Shed the artillery. Pronto!'

The three men obeyed quickly. This man spoke like a law officer. Perhaps he was a ranger.

'Now,' drawled Pat, 'just dump out that cargo of guns you have there. This is one batch that won't get across the line. And work fast, because I'm gettin' awful impatient. So is Sid.'

31

Five minutes later the buckboard was emptied. The three gun-runners were dripping with perspiration as the last case of guns was placed on the ground.

'Now, Slats,' said Pat, and his voice was harsh, 'I'm askin' you one question. You kin answer it here, and I'll let the three of you go. Or you kin refuse to answer and the three of you will be fitted into them pine boxes I spoke about—Who killed Tim Collins?'

'So help me, brother, I—'

Pat Roper was on his feet like a flash. His carbine clicked to full cock.

'When I kill Mussick, Sid, you get one of the others. I'll finish the third.' His voice was a snarl. The snarl of a man about to kill.

'Don't!' shrilled Slats Mussik. 'Don't for heaven's sake! I'll tell! Wig Murphy killed Tim Collins!'

From somewhere back in the shadow came the quick, sobbing intake of the hidden boy's breath.

'Get in that buckboard,' snapped Pat, 'and don't quit driving till yo're out of Arizona.'

The three obeyed with alacrity. A few moments and they were gone. As the beat of hoofs dimmed in the distance, Pat Roper walked slowly back to the deep shadows between the buildings. He found Sid Collins stretched out on the ground, terrible sobs shaking his slim body.

'Don't take it like that, son. Don't do that, Sid, old man. We'll fix that Wig Murphy before we're done.'

'You—you don't savvy, Pat. Wig Murphy is—is Tommy's dad. She thinks he's the finest man on two laigs—and Tommy is the best friend I got—Don't you see how I can't go on through? Don't you savvy?'

'I savvy, son. Why, shucks, boy, mebbe that polecat lied. Mebbe he put over a fast un on us.'

'Nope. He was too scairt. He was as bad scairt as I was. I'd never shot me a man, and I was shakin' awful, Pat.'

'You mean that you had a gun, kid?'

'Shore. My—my dad's gun.'

Pat Roper took the big old .45 from the boy's hands. There was a queer look on his face when he lifted Sid to his feet.

'Most kids would'a' run. I didn't know you was so

32

close, boy. And I shore certain didn't know you was a-totin' this cannon. My gosh, I was just a-bluffin' them three snakes!'

'You looked awful scary for a man that was only foolin'.' Sid grinned as Pat poked a thumb in his ribs.

'This gun-throwin' business is a lot like poker, boy. You get in a good bluff, act like yo're holdin' all the aces in the deck, and chances is that you won't ever need to pull a trigger. Speakin' of guns, you better let me keep this hardware of yourn. Guns, Sid, are a mighty serious kind of ornament. They kin get a man into a sight of trouble in one second. Trouble that may hang on to a man all his life. I have knowed a case where the man that won a gun fight was the man that got killed.'

'The man that lived couldn't ever forget that he had killed a man. It worried him of a night, somethin' awful. He'd always be kinda dreamin' about it, you might say. And while he lived in that section of the country, he was always seein' somethin' that reminded him of that man he'd shot. He was too high-strung and sensitive, you see. He couldn't ever wipe it off his conscience. He moved away from there, but he wasn't much better off. A man can't just get up an' run off from his conscience. It follows him along. It followed that man from Mexico to the Klondike and all over half the world. And when he died, he died a-hopin' he'd meet that pore fellow he'd killed and somehow square things up. That's what one little jerk of a gun trigger did for that man. It wrecked his life, Sid. It robbed him of a nice fortune, and it made him an old man before he'd reached forty. It broke his mind and his body. In the end, it killed him, slow and hard.'

Pat Roper's voice drifted into silence. He seemed to have forgotten the boy who listened so raptly. Until Sid broke the long silence that followed that sermon on guns.

'You kin have that gun, Pat, for always.'

'Uh? Your gun, boy? Thanks, old-timer.'

'That man you told me about must 'a' bin a real man, wa'n't he? Because if he wa'n't, he wouldn't of cared a darn. I bet he was a mighty fine kind of a man.'

'I always thought so, Sid. You see, he was my daddy.'

Chapter VI

'The mountain,' smiled a black-haired girl with laughing brown eyes, 'would not come to Mahomet, so Mahomet went to the mountain. Sid Collins, you stubborn little rascal, come here and tell me why you stayed away when you knew I'd got home.'

Tommy Murphy stepped down from the back of a handsome black horse and approached a very red-faced boy who sat with Pat Roper in the shade of the Two Block bunkhouse. Sid seemed all hands and feet as the girl, with a laugh that held a teasing lilt and also an undertone of wistfulness, put her arms around him and kissed him heartily.

Pat Roper had got to his feet. The sheer beauty of this girl, who wore the chaps and jumper and boots and Stetson of the cowboy, had made him gasp a little. Tommy's beauty was not the rose-petal loveliness of the city-bred débutante. Her skin was sun-tanned, glowing with radiant health. Her nose was a trifle too short, her mouth the least bit too boyish, her white teeth a mite too strong-looking, to be really beautiful. Her thick mop of cropped black curls added to her boyish appearance. But to Pat Roper, Tommy Murphy, in weather-worn, cowpuncher garb, was the most wonderful girl he had ever seen.

'Sid, you little tramp, is this the only shirt you own? I bet you've had it on a month. And you need a bath and haircut and a general overhauling. I'll take you back with me and turn you over to Taller. But I want to know right now why you've stayed away. I've been back two weeks. Tell sister, or sister will duck her little Sidney in the crick. Come clean, cowboy.'

34

'I reckon, ma'am,' Pat sought to come to Sid's rescue, 'that it is more my fault than it is Sid's.'

'I don't doubt that,' Tommy Murphy's brown eyes hardened. 'I take it for granted that you are Pat Roper, and from the various things I have heard about the new owner of the Two Block, the sooner this boy gets away from your influence, the better for him.'

'That ain't so, Tommy!' flared Sid. 'Pat is a real feller. You gotta take that back, Tommy. Please! Gosh, if you knowed—knew—him like I do, you'd like him. Just because he wouldn't sell this ranch to Wig Murphy is no sign he's ornery. And because he wouldn't let Billy Carter bluff him the other day when Pat and me rode over on the Flyin' W range, is no sign he was over there to steal somethin' like Billy claimed he was.'

'I don't care to go into all the details of Pat Roper's character, Sid,' said the girl, her cheeks showing two red spots that Pat read for danger signals. 'I came to take you home with me. You aren't quitting me cold, are you, pardner?'

'You bet I ain't, Tommy. But please don't go hoppin' on Pat. He has bin awful good to me. Look at these swell shop boots he got me. And a full-stamped saddle and a pair of chaps. And I got a string of top horses to ride. And he took my gun to keep for always, because he don't want me to get into trouble. And next fall, after the round-up, I'm goin' to a real military school so's I won't grow up ignorant like most cowpunchers. I guess if he was mean an' ornery, he wouldn't be doin' that for a kid. Would he, now? Would he, Tommy?'

'You're too much of a kid,' replied Tommy, 'to understand some things. I didn't say that Pat Roper was mean or ornery. A man can be despicable without being a bully. If he is so honourable, ask him why he came here to the Two Block Ranch. Ask him who stole five hundred head of Flying W cattle that were turned over to Pablo Guerrero down in Mexico.'

'Sid,' drawled Pat Roper, 'since the lady needs an interpreter, will you tell her that I plumb decline to answer them questions. And tell her that, before she pulls out for home, she'd better fix that saddle blanket of hers because it's worked back too far.'

35

Tommy Murphy stamped her foot impatiently. It was a small foot, encased in a high heeled tan boot that must have satisfied the pride of some expert bootmaker. Her silver-mounted spurs chimed as she stepped to her horse.

'Are you riding back with me, Sid?' she queried.

'Tell her you shore are, Sid. Us Two Block men don't let girls go ridin' around alone on this range. It'll be dark before you kin make the Flyin' W Ranch, and I'm beginnin' to think that it ain't exactly safe for folks to be ridin' alone after night.' Pat shoved a forefinger through a round hole in the high crown of his white Stetson. 'That's how close some fun-lovin' cuss come to my bone head the other night as I was comin' home,' he grinned. He turned to Sid.

'Don't keep Miss Murphy waitin', old-timer.'

With an eagerness that was a little pathetic, Sid made for the barn. Left alone, Pat Roper and Tommy Murphy ignored one another with an aloofness that would have been humorous to a third person. Only once was the awkward silence broken.

'I'd shore set that blanket ahead, if I was you, ma'am.'

'I'll tend to my own rig, Mr. Roper. When I think my blanket needs fixing, I'll fix it without your suggestion or your assistance.'

Sid led out his horse, a wiry little dun horse with notch ears. Tommy knew that pony to be one of the fastest, wisest cow ponies in the Two Block remuda. Sid's new chaps and saddle were the best that saddle-maker could produce. The headstall was spotted with silver conchos, and the curved shank bit was crusted with etched silver. An outfit and horse that might be the dream of any youth whose love lay in the cow business. Sid swung up into the saddle, flushing proudly, his eyes bright with excitement. He looked from the girl to the man with helpless appeal. Pat grinned good-naturedly.

'Have a good time, old trapper. Stay as long as you like. And git that scrubbin' and fresh duds. So long.' He turned to the girl.

'I'm mighty sorry, miss, that me and you has struck such a bad snag, right at the start. I was hopin' we could be friends.'

'You hoped for a great deal.' Tommy mounted the rest-

36

less black gelding. Without a backward glance, she rode away, Sid by her side.

Pat Roper watched them out of sight, a hurt look in his eyes. Then he went to the barn and saddled his own horse. Before he left the ranch, he shoved a carbine into his saddle scabbard. And at a slow trot, he followed the girl and her boy escort, taking care to stay well behind them.

Chapter VII

As Pat Roper rode alone in the twilight, he turned over in his mind the several things that had happened during the two weeks that he had been owner of the Two Block outfit.

Old Wig Murphy had ridden over alone to the ranch. Without any preamble, he told Pat that he had been to see Arturo Gonzales at Phoenix and that the suave Mexican attorney had told him, among other things that Murphy did not explain to Pat, that if he wanted to buy the Two Block outfit, he must see Pat Roper.

'What's your price, Roper?' he had growled.

'I'm not sellin', Murphy. Not at any price.'

'That means you figger to work on my cattle that range on the lower Concho. And as a sideline, you'll cross over guns to your pardner, Pablo Guerrero. It's a purty trick you and that Mex pulled on me, young feller. But I'm gonna take pains to see that you don't win a thing. I'll fight you and Pablo until either the Two Block or the Flyin' W goes bust. If it's war you want, Roper, war is what you'll get. And somebody is gonna get a mouthful before the chips is all cashed in. Don't let me ketch you or Pablo or any Two Block men on my side of the drift fence. My men has their orders to run you off. That goes as she lays.'

Pat had nodded grimly. 'I could take a stock inspector over on your range, Murphy, and gather every head of stuff in the PR iron. You know that. It's bin three years now since their hair dried when your rustlers shoved 'em north of the Concho, but they're still mine. And what's more, I'll gather every hoof of 'em.' He pointed in the direction of the Flying W ranch. 'Your ranch lies acrost yonder. Pull out.'

And Wig Murphy had turned his horse and ridden away without a word.

A few days later, Pat Roper rode boldly up the Concho River and on to the upper range. Sid was with him. They were looking through a bunch of Wig Murphy's cattle when Billy Carter and half a dozen Flying W men rode up.

Hot words passed like pistol shots between the indignant Billy Carter and Pat Roper.

Pat had been hotly accused of coming there to rustle cattle.

'The old man don't know it, Roper, but I know that it was you that stole five hundred head of prime beef steers and delivered 'em to Pablo Guerrero. One of Jim Boudry's men watched you. Deny that if you kin.'

'I won't try to, Carter. I took them cattle and turned 'em loose down there. I didn't git a dollar for 'em. I didn't deliver 'em to Pablo Guerrero or any other man. Do you want to know why I run those cattle off? Then ride through these cattle with me. I'll show you upward of fifty head of big white-faced cows in this little gatherment that wears a PR brand on their left ribs. Those are part of better than three hundred head that was stole from me down in Chihuahua and trailed here. Two hundred head was three-year-old cows. They'd each have a calf every year. With an eighty per cent calf crop, them cows has made Wig Murphy money. The steers, a hundred head, he sold at a fair price somewhere. Figger out for yourself, Carter, if I was stealin' when I taken five hundred head of two- and three-year-old steers from the lower Concho.'

'That sounds fine, the way you tell it, Roper. Only you don't tell the whole story. Wig has tried to keep me from knowin' a few things that has gone on the past several years. But I'm not as dumb as I look. I happen to know that Pablo Guerrero has bin blackmailin' the old man for a long time. I likewise know that it was Pablo that stole them PR cattle an' delivered 'em this side of the Concho. I know that Pablo got them five hundred head of cattle you run off a few weeks ago, because I was down there an' he as much as admitted he had 'em. And I bet that you can't deny, without lyin', that it was Pablo's money that bought you the Two Block Ranch. There's snake tracks there, Roper. Yo're in cahoots with that slick Mexican to help

39

him rob Wig Murphy. And while I don't pretend to deny that the old man has done his share of dealin' in wet cattle, still, he's bin like a daddy to me and I won't stand idle and watch him git robbed. He's gittin' old. Too old to get out and fight for what's his. But I ain't old, mister, and I'll fight for that old son of a gun until I'm stopped by a bullet. From now on, you and your men keep off the Flyin' W range. And what I mean to state, Roper, plumb off. Or somebody is gonna get hurt bad.'

'You've give me somethin' to think over, Carter,' Pat had told him. He knew that Billy Carter had not lied when he said Pablo had delivered those PR cattle north of the Concho. What, then, was Pablo's present game? Was he trying to use Pat as his tool in attacking old Wig Murphy? It looked that way. He'd better go on back to the Two Block Ranch and figger this thing out some way.

'I'll think 'er over, Carter,' he had promised the Flying W foreman, 'and when I've come to a decision, I'll ride over and let you know what my stand is. Until then, we'll all of us keep to our own sides of the drift fence.'

So Pat Roper and Sid had ridden away, Sid hotly refusing Billy's request that the boy stay with the Flying W spread.

And it was while Pat and Sid were homeward bound that late evening, and while they were still on the Flying W range, that a rifle had cracked from a patch of brush and boulders above the trail, tearing a hole in Pat's hat. When Pat, sending the boy to cover with a quick command, jumped his horse up the steep slope toward the brush patch, the would-be murderer had ridden away at a run, keeping to the brush-choked trail that screened his flight. Pat found the man's sign up there among the rocks. Sign that told him the bushwhacker had waited there several hours, figuring Pat would be returning along that trail. Pat examined the tracks carefully. Imprints showed that the man's high-heeled boots turned under at the heel. Both run-down heels slanted outward. The boots were large size and old. He smoked a pipe and had knocked the ashes from it a dozen times during his several hours of waiting. The empty shell from the rifle was a .30-40 calibre. Contenting himself with those meagre clues, Pat had rejoined the excited Sid and they had ridden on home without further incident.

Now, as Pat Roper followed behind Tommy Murphy and Sid, he reviewed those things. And got no further in his piecing together of the sinister puzzle. Then a woman's sharp cry and a confusion of other sound broke abruptly into Pat's musing. He jerked his gun as he jabbed home the spurs. It was almost dark. He heard a man's gruff voice shouting; the thud of hoofs. Then Sid's voice, filled with pain and helpless rage.

'Hold 'em, old-timer!' called Pat, fear gripping his heart with a clammy hand.

A horse tore by, kicking viciously at something under its belly. Tommy's black horse, the saddle turned, the terrified animal stampeding! Sick with anxiety, Pat gritted out a few brief words of prayer. Then he found himself returning the shots that ripped at him from the darkness. A man on horseback was shooting at him, racing away. His shots droned past Pat's head. Pat, his lips pulled apart in a snarl, shot blindly at the man whose horse carried him swiftly beyond range. He would have given chase but for that terrible dread that he would find that beautiful girl ripped and maimed by the black gelding's shod hoofs.

'Sid!' he called, in a voice that was hoarse with fear.

'Here!' sobbed the boy's voice out of the dark. 'Over this way!'

A moment later Pat Roper was bending over the blanched face of the girl who lay in a twisted heap on the ground. A crimson trickle marred the whiteness of the forehead fringed by black curls. Vaguely he saw that Sid's face was smeared with red and that the boy was trembling as if with a chill.

'It was Jim Boudry!' panted the boy. 'Is Tommy dead, Pat? Is she dead?'

'No. No, she ain't dead. Hurt, though. I can't tell how bad. You fetch my horse and yourn. We gotta get her home as quick as we kin. It ain't over five miles there.'

Sid brought the horses and they started for the Flying W Ranch. Pat carried the limp girl in his arms while the big bay horse travelled at an easy, pacing gait. They had gone some distance when Tommy moved with a spasmodic jerk and her eyes opened. For a brief moment, she fought with sudden fury. Then she realized that it was not Jim Boudry, but Pat Roper, who held her. He had swung off to the ground and stood there grinning queerly, supporting the standing girl. Down his face trickled thin threads of red where the girl had scratched him.

'Gee whiz!' gasped Sid, who was on the ground now and holding on to Tommy. 'Don't go fightin' Pat. Gosh, he's the one that chased that darn Boudry off! Are you hurt, Tommy? Are you hurt bad?'

'Dizzy, Sid,' she said weakly, 'and I feel all pulled apart, but not hurt. Could I sit down a minute?'

'You bet you can.' Pat eased her to a sitting posture on the ground. 'I'm sorry there's no water handy.'

'If I'd been less stubborn about that saddle blanket,' Tommy admitted with a wan smile, 'it wouldn't have happened.'

'Boudry tried to kiss her, Pat,' explained Sid. 'When I went at him with my quirt, he smashed me one on the beezer. I sure did see stars. Feels like she's busted, but I don't reckon so. Then Tommy's saddle turned, and then you hollered and Boudry run for it. Then the shootin' commenced.'

'The big beast was drunk,' added Tommy, 'or he wouldn't have dared touch me. Did Arab get away?'

'If Arab is your horse,' grinned Pat, 'he was doin' about sixty miles a minute and kickin' that purty saddle of yourn into small pieces. I wouldn't worry about—Shhh! Somebody comin'.'

Pat stepped to his horse and slid his Winchester from the saddle boot. Two men were coming at a long trot along the trail. Pat halted them with a rasping, 'Who are you? Speak up?'

A rumbling roar of colourful profanity gave reply.

'Dad!' called Tommy. "It's my dad, Mr. Roper!'

'Roper?' roared the old cowman. 'What in—'

'Dad, quit swearing so. Everything is all right.'

'All right, huh? With shots that sounds like a war busted open? We ketched that black hoss back yonder with what's left of a saddle under his belly. And here's this Roper trespassin' on my range. It'll take some tall explainin' to save him from the best thrashin' he ever got. Billy, shed your coat an' get ready to wade into that cow thief.'

'Billy,' said Tommy Murphy sternly, 'before you begin to shed your coat, think it over some. Because from what I gather from Sid, Neighbour Roper is some handy with his fists. Any man that can whip Jim Boudry with his two hands is a big job. And, anyhow, you have no cause to fight him. Just because he rides up in time to save me from being pawed over by that big, drunken, red-headed Boudry, is that any reason why you and Dad must begin throwing big fists and little ones? And swearing like that, Dad, is a bad example for Sid and me.'

'You keep outa this, Tommy', growled Wig Murphy. 'Billy, this Roper snake has hornswoggled the girl into thinkin' he's a white man. Step down and trim his wick. Can't you see his game? Tryin' to soft-soap his way on to my range by playin' up to Tommy.'

'That's a lie!' cried Sid.

'Spoken like a regular stage actor, Sidney,' said the girl. 'And like a regular guy. Dad, you're all wrong. Pat Roper may be a cow thief, or a burglar, or a pickpocket, or what have you, but he's not a coward, and he's trespassing on your land only because he was being decent to a girl that had treated him like a sheep-herder. And if your other charges against him are as silly and unfounded as this one, then you'd better have your thinking machinery overhauled.'

'Thanks, Miss Murphy,' grinned Pat Roper, 'for takin' my side. But I reckon it's time I took my own part in this argument. I didn't come here on the Flyin' W range to hunt a fight, Murphy. I kinda trailed along behind your daughter and Sid because I knowed that Jim Boudry and some of his friends has habit of ridin' at night and I didn't want any harm to come to Sid and her. I'm not tryin' to crawl backward on this. If you and Billy Carter is bound to have trouble, I'll do what I kin to'rd accomodatin' you. But unless you're both dead set on whippin' me, I'll turn back from here and go on home. I sure haven't one single reason that I kin think of, Murphy, for likin' you and Carter any more than you like me. But somehow, here

43

and now don't seem exactly the right place to settle our dislikes. However, that is strictly up to you two. Lay your coin on the line, gents.'

'Roper's right, if you ask me, Wig,' said Billy Carter, a look of relief in his eyes. The Flyin' W boss, his first anger cooled, had no relish for a fist fight with the man who had so thoroughly whipped the hard-boiled Jim Boudry.

Wig Murphy snorted. 'Just let the play go as she lays, Roper. But don't come again.'

'I won't come for pleasure when I do, Murphy,' said Pat, stepping up into his saddle, 'and I'll come in broad daylight when I make the visit. So long, Sid, take care of yoreself, old-timer.' He turned and rode away at a leisurely gait.

'Good night, Pat Roper,' called the girl, 'and thanks an awful lot for doing what you did.'

'Keep the change, ma'am. And don't forget to scrub Sid's ears.'

Chapter VIII

There was a light burning in the house when Pat Roper reached the Two Block Ranch. A strange horse and pack mule were in the corral. The visitor had unsaddled and jerked his bed off his pack-horse and had made himself at home after the free-handed manner of the cow country where the unwritten law says that the tired and hungry traveller need not stand on formality. If his host be absent, he helps himself to food, after his horse is fed. When he leaves, he leaves the dishes clean and the wood box filled. If he is so inclined, he may sweep the kitchen floor or do what chores there are to be done.

Pat stabled his horse and, not without some little uneasiness, went to the house. His carbine was in the crook of his arm as he stepped inside the house. His eyes were a trifle cold as he eyed the cowpuncher who was eating a cold supper.

The visitor was a wiry little man somewhere in his fifties. Bow-legged. a trifle shabby, with puckered grey eyes, battered features, and a head that was bald save for greyish fringe that needed trimming. He grinned as he got to his feet.

'I shore made myself at home, mister. But my horse and mule was about tuckered out. Are you Pat Roper?'

Pat leaned his carbine against the wall and tossed his hat in the corner. 'I'm Pat Roper, yes.' There was neither welcome nor hostility in his tone.

'I come here to get a job, if you ain't full-handed.'

'I'm not full-handed,' said Pat evenly, 'but I'm not hirin' strangers. Finish your supper, mister.'

The wiry little man resumed his seat and went on eating. Pat took a chair and built a cigarette. Not once did he turn his back to the man. There was never a moment when he was not watching his visitor. The man ate in the fast, businesslike manner of the cowboy. Eating, for the working cowpuncher, is more of a routine task than a pleasure. He is hungry, and he needs to satisfy his hunger as soon as possible, washing his crude fare down with strong black coffee. Neither man spoke until the visitor's plate was emptied and wiped clean with the last piece of cold biscuit. He drained the last of the black coffee, pulled his fingers across the legs of his overalls, and reached for tobacco and papers.

'If you ain't hirin' strangers, Roper, it looks like I'll ride the grub line till I strike some outfit that kin use me. I heard you needed cowhands, so I drifted this way.'

Pat nodded without speaking. There was no offence in his silence. Men of the cow country are, with rare exceptions, silent in the presence of strangers. The visitor lit his cigarette. Pat noticed that two fingers on his left hand were missing, and the back of that hand wore an ugly scar. There was an odd twinkle in the little man's grey eyes as he spoke again.

'Them cowboys of yourn is awful free about their target practice, Roper.'

'Meanin' what, mister?'

'As I come along the crick, about ten miles south of here, along about dusk, they sure fogged me up. Must 'a wasted a dozen ca'tridges on me before I got outa range.'

'Where was that, again?'

'Below here. I'd say about ten miles.'

'My men are all on the upper end of the range. They're holdin' a herd there. Whoever shot at you was not any of my men.'

'Then you must have some enemies around here?'

Pat Roper smiled grimly. 'I wouldn't be su'prised.'

'A man don't like to be bushwhacked that a'way, Roper.'

The manner in which the little man said it brought a grin to Pat's face. The stranger grinned back.

'Even when he's shot at and missed,' the little fellow chuckled, 'it makes a man kinda mad. Them rascals had me a-dodgin' like a coyote. That fool pack-mule of mine ain't used to bein' shot at, and he gits me wound up in his

46

hackamore rope. It gets under my pony's tail and he sinks his head and tries his best to upset me. Between gittin' untangled from that rope, tryin' to set that fool horse, and doin' my best to knock off one of them gents with my six-gun, I was about the one busiest human in Arizona for five or ten minutes. When I got over bein' scairt, I got mad. But my madness buys me nothin'. I swallers my hurt feelin' and come on here. But if some good hand with a pencil could've drawed the picture of that scene, he'd've had somethin' worth lookin' at.'

'Did you sight any of 'em?' asked Pat.

'Not clost enough to do much good. Bein' sorta occupied, as the feller says, with several things at once, my powers of observation gets more or less gummed up.'

'I kin understand that,' grinned Pat. 'They're probably a bunch of gun-runners or smugglers. My south line is full of holes those renegades has bin usin'.'

'They was headed south to'rd the border. Had about eight-ten loaded pack-mules.'

Pat got out of his chair and walked into the adjoining room. He struck a match and went to the far end of the room, returning in a moment, a comical look of chagrin on his face.

'I don't know who you are, stranger, but I don't reckon yo're one of them gun-runners. I had some cased guns in that room that I taken off that gun-runnin' layout. I'd sent word to the sheriff to come and get 'em, but he hasn't got around to it. I left here right before dark. They must 'a' bin watchin' the ranch. When I'd gone, they rode down, loaded their mules, and pulled south. You happened to be comin' up the trail and they smoked you up.'

'Looks like both of us had bin treated kinda dirty,' said the little cowpuncher quietly. Pat felt the sharp scrutiny of the man's grey eyes. He wondered a little if the stranger thought he was lying. It made him a little irritated, but he said nothing. They smoked in silence. Presently the visitor pinched out the short stub of his cigarette and began washing his dishes. Pat got a dish towel and dried them.

'About my bedtime,' announced Pat. 'You kin spread your bed in the bunk-house or in the next room.'

'The bunk-house suits me, Roper, and it'll save you from shootin' me. I snore somethin' scan'lous, so I'm told.'

47

'See you in the mornin', then.'

The little man nodded as he paused in the doorway. 'You won't be expectin' company tonight, will you, Roper?'

'Not as I know of. Why?'

'Bein' bushwhacked has made me kinda jumpy, I reckon. It always kinda startles me when I'm woke up at night by somebody comin' in the house. If you don't mind, I'll just lock the bunk-house door.'

'Shore thing,' grinned Pat.

He noticed that the visitor, though under medium height and not especially husky-looking, had no difficulty in carrying his bed from the corral to the bunk-house. Pat called to ask him if he needed help, but the bow-legged little man replied that he did not. He also declined Pat's offer to put his horse and pack-mule in the barn. He explained that he had put some hay in the corral for the animals and they were all right where they were.

'Queer little duck', mused Pat, as he extinguished the lamp and crawled into his own bunk in the house. 'He don't seem anxious to tell his name or where he's from.'

Chapter IX

It must have been well after midnight when Pat Roper awoke with a start. A light sleeper, he was fully awake even when his bare feet hit the floor. His six-shooter was in his hand as he crouched there in the dark room beside the window that gave him a view of the barn, the corrals, and bunk-house, plainly visible in the moonlight. Tense, his wits sharp, he peered out. He wondered what unusual sound had awakened him, and he could not rid himself of the feeling that something was wrong, out there beyond the house. Now his eyes were focusing better. There, in the black shadow cast by the bunk-house, something moved.

It was a man, crouched low under the bunk-house window, moving stealthily along the wall of the building. Now came the sound that must have awakened Pat. It came from a hundred yards or more down the creek where the trees and brush grew thickly. The nicker of a horse, muffled abruptly. The man who belonged to that horse had smothered that telltale nicker. Now, from the corral, the little bow-legged man's horse gave unrestrained reply. Pat grinned mirthlessly and slipped on his overalls as he watched that creeping man pause. He pushed his feet into a pair of old slippers and waited for the climax of that moonlit drama.

Nor had he long to wait. He saw the crouching man hesitate, then turn and run back the way he had come, toward the spot where the horse had nickered. Then another shadowy form jumped out from behind the wood-pile and blocked the running man's escape.

· 'Not so fast, Bender,' rapped the voice of the second man. 'I got you all right!'

'Not yet!' gritted the runner, and fired point-blank

without checking his speed. But the other man had anticipated that shot and dropped to the ground. As he dropped, his gun cracked. The shot must have hit a vital spot, for the running man stumbled, pitched headlong, and lay still. The other was on his feet like a jumping jack. Without paying any more heed to the man he had shot, he turned and ran swiftly down the creek. There were several shots; the pound of hoofs. And before Pat Roper had begun to reason out the why and wherefore of this gunplay, the victor of the swift duel had again appeared. Pat now recognized him as his odd guest.

'Better come here, Roper,' he called briskly, 'and look this man over. I think he's dead. The other one got away. I hope I haven't shot one of your men.'

Pat came on the run, his six-shooter in his hand. He found the little man bending over the dead one. He thought he saw the stranger slip something into his trousers' pocket.

The little man struck a match, and Pat noticed that his hands were steady. He also took note that his queer guest was fully clothed, except for his hat and jumper. Around his waist was a sagging cartridge-belt and a carbine lay nearby him on the ground.

'Know the man, Roper?'

'Why, he's a man I fired when I took over the place. One of Jim Boudry's men.'

'One of the gun-runners, perhaps?'

'He might be. Boudry's men are all bad uns. Didn't I hear you call him Bender?'

'Did I? Musta bin nervous, Roper. Excited. The name musta slipped out. I used to know a man named Bender, and he must have bin in my mind. Queer what a man will say when he's excited.'

'Yeah,' Pat's voice was coldly sarcastic. 'It shore is queer. Mighty queer. I thought you was asleep there in the bunk-house?'

'I couldn't sleep good,' came the even reply of the diminutive cowpuncher, 'so I went for a little walk.'

'With a Winchester and a six-shooter?'

'I was nervous about that bushwhacking, so I took along my guns. Lucky for me that I did. These men didn't come here for fun.'

50

'No. Did they follow you here?'

'Why should they want to foller me, Roper?'

'That,' said Pat, 'is just exactly what I'd like to find out. Here's a case for the coroner. This man is dead. There's one or two little things that I'd like to clear up. First, who are you, and what fetched you here to my place?'

'Such questions is usually asked by the coroner, ain't they?' The stranger's tight lips smiled. 'And you ain't the coroner.'

'No,' said Pat, a little heatedly. 'I'm not the coroner. I'm just the gent that owns this ranch. You come here with a yarn about bein' shot at by some men that's stole stuff outa my house. You prowl around my place at night with a gun. Then this crook comes slippin' around. His pardner or pardners stays back in the brush. Your horse nickers. Horse down in the brush answers his howdy. Just like they might be friends, from the same remuda. You call out to this man to show up, that you got him. You call him Bender. When I made out his time, he was on the books as Pete Bender. All of which tells me that you and your horse is known to Jim Boudry and his remuda. So, unless you kin give me a mighty plain story, mister, I'll just ask you to hand over your guns until the sheriff and coroner arrive on the scene.'

The little man meekly unbuckled his gun-belt and handed his holstered .45 and his Winchester to Pat. His grey eyes were bright, steady. He was smiling faintly.

'There's the guns, Roper. Take good care of 'em because I may need 'em again soon. Now, we better do something with this dead man. He'll have to lay there till the coroner sees him. Got an old tarp handy?'

'There's one in the bunk-house. Better get it. And watch your step, mister. Don't try to put over any fast tricks.'

'All I care about puttin' over, Roper, is a few hours of shut-eye. I kinda feel like I could sleep now, without bein' so scared.'

He came out of the bunk-house with a tarp. And Pat did not overlook the fact that when he went in for the tarp, he used a window instead of the door. Either to keep out intruders, or to perfect his trap to catch Bender, he had bolted the door from the inside and gone out by way of the window, to hide behind the woodpile until Bender should arrive on his deadly mission.

They covered the dead man with the tarp. Bender had been shot through the heart. The little man yawned.

'Killin' a man don't seem to upset you much, even if you are such a nervous man.'

'It was him or me, Roper. He shot first. I come out lucky. There is nothin' about killin' a man like him that should keep me from sleepin'.'

'Mebbyso Bender ain't your first one?'

'Well, now, mebby he ain't. Good night, Roper.' He swung off toward the bunk-house on his bow-shaped legs, chuckling in a grisly fashion.

Pat, back between his blankets, found that sleep would not come. He felt fidgety and upset. He almost regretted that he had not brought his queer visitor back to the house where he could watch him more closely. The fellow might be up to some bit of trickery, but if the killing of his host was his aim, he could have accomplished that as Pat rode through the gate. There were no guns in the bunk-house. The man's horse was too weary to carry him far, even if he wanted to run away, which Pat, somehow, doubted. The barn door was secured with a heavy padlock so that he could not steal Pat's horse.

Finally, Pat fell into a fitful slumber. And it was Tommy Murphy, not the bow-legged stranger, who haunted his dreaming. It was sunrise when Pat woke.

He dressed hastily, washed at the basin outside the kitchen door, and made for the bunk-house. No reply came when he called. He stepped inside. The place was empty. There was a note on the table, weighed down with a .45 cartridge. The message read:

FRIEND ROPER: Sorry I could not wait for the coroner and sheriff, but have a deal on that I want to close. Am taking Bender's horse, which his yellow pardner left in his hurry to get away. When I can get to it, I will come back for my horse and mule, and my bed. If I never come back, they belong to you.

Take my tip and do not ride alone after dark. Jim Boudry and some others are out to kill you. Like Bender aimed to kill me when he come here. If you need tobac-

52

co money, collect the bounty on Bender's scalp. His right name is Charlie Jackson and he is wanted for train robbery and murder. You are plumb welcome to the money, if you will take good care of my horse and mule. But do not walk in close behind the mule or he will kick the buttons off your vest. If you set afoot and need to ketch the horse or mule, take along a biscuit and whistle 'Turkey in the Straw'. They'll come up to you.

Mind what I tell you about riding around at night. And do not bother about trying to plug the holes in the border where the Boudry gang is going through with guns. They are watching for you down there. Tend to your cattle and stay off Murphy's range. Them PR cattle kin be gathered later without a gun pulled, because Billy Carter is on the square and will do the right thing by you when he learns some facts. Hang and rattle and step careful. This is a lot of free advice to give a man, but I think you are big enough to take it. When Pablo Guerrero handed you the Two Block on a silver platter, he handed you plenty trouble for seasoning. But if the breaks go right, you kin win out. You see, I know aplenty about you. I did not come here for a job. Only to size you up. Because some folks think that you are in cahoots with Pablo on some queer stuff. I am glad to find them folks are all wrong. Your daddy, Bill Roper, was a good friend of mine. I worked for him when you was a baby and was there when he got into the gun fight that busted him. Bill was good to me when I was a kid and I would hate to see his boy get in bad. That is one reason I come here.

I asked you to do me two favours. First, when the coroner and sheriff come here, you take the rap for killing Bender. No law can lay a finger on you for it, because under the name of Charlie Jackson, he's wanted dead or alive. Second, I want you to gather five hundred head of Two Block steers and turn same over to Wig Murphy. You made the wrong move when you run them Flying W cattle into Mexico. You played right into Pablo's hand. Pablo is a fox and he aims to use you plenty. If you hope to win out here on this ranch, pay off Murphy with Two Block cattle. And I'll gamble that you will win ten dollars for one on the deal.

If I could sign this with my name, you would know I was giving you a right tip. But it is better for us both if you do not know me. I have said too much already. Burn this. So long and good luck.

Chapter X

The sheriff had come from town in answer to the summons that Pat Roper had sent him. With the sheriff came the coroner. The law officer, a somewhat pompous sort of man, with an eye that held more suspicion than warmth, returned Pat's greeting with discouraging coldness. The coroner was a moist-eyed individual who continually took off a pair of steel-rimmed spectacles and polished them with a silk handkerchief.

After a brief examination of the dead man, the sheriff took Pat aside.

'Who killed that man, Roper? he began abruptly.

For the fraction of a moment, Pat hesitated. He hated lying. Yet that letter left by his strange guest had rung true.

'Here's the gun that did it.' He pulled the stranger's .45 from his overalls waistband and handed it, butt first, to the sheriff. 'The hammer ain't bin lifted off the shell.'

'What was your idee in killin' him?'

'He came here in the dead of night after he'd had orders to stay off the place. His gun is still in his hand. You'll find an empty shell under the gun hammer. It was self-defence.'

'Do you know who he is?'

'He was on the books as Pete Bender.'

'Pete Bender, eh? Well, that ain't his right name. Not by a jugful.'

Pat Roper nodded. 'Alias Charlie Jackson, then.'

The sheriff snorted indignantly. 'Charlie Jackson, eh? Next thing I know, you'll tell me he was Jesse James. Your little game don't go with me, Roper. You've killed an officer of the law that come to arrest you for being mixed up with these gun-runners and cattle rustlers. I've had an eye on this layout for a long time. Just when I'm ready to nab Jim Boudry, the men higher up get rid of him and put you in here.

'The dead man layin' yonder come to me not three days ago. He showed me his credentials and told me his plan to clean up this Two Block nest of bad eggs. Now he's murdered, and you try to tell me that he is Charlie Jackson. And you think I'm durn fool enough to swaller a bait like that. Just put out both hands, Mr. Pat Roper, and we'll try on these bracelets.'

'What do you mean, sheriff?'

'You're under arrest, that's what I mean.'

Pat's eyes narrowed. Was the sheriff right? Had the bowlegged man killed some law officer who had been trailing him? He now recalled, with a sudden sinking of heart, that the man who had killed Bender had taken something from the dead body as he knelt beside it just before Pat had reached the spot. He had noticed the sheriff point out to the coroner a tear in the dead man's shirt where something pinned to it had been torn away.

'Put out your hands, Roper,' growled the sheriff, his gun shoved in Pat's ribs.

Pat's hands went out slowly. The sheriff's left hand reached out with the nickelled handcuffs. Suddenly, Pat's left hand gripped the sheriff's right wrist. The gun exploded, so close that the powder burned the cowpuncher's shirt. The next second a terrific left swing sent the officer staggering. Pat followed it with a second jolt to the pit of the sheriff's stomach.

Without paying heed to the wild shots that the agitated and near-sighted coroner was pumping from a little automatic, Pat ran for the house. Too late, he recalled that his horse was in the stable, unsaddled. No time to waste attempting to get the horse. Pat made for the house. Inside, he bolted the door. Just as the sheriff's gun began throwing lead, Pat grabbed his Winchester and began firing.

He had no intention of killing or wounding the sheriff. His shots were well aimed to send both sheriff and coroner into the shelter of the bunk-house.

'Climb into yore buckboard, sheriff,' Pat called out,

56

when the two officials were inside the bunk-house, 'and take Bender's body on back to town. I don't want to shoot you, and I don't want to get shot. Just gather in your corpse and hit for town.'

But the sheriff was made of sturdy stuff.

'I'll hit for town, all right,' he roared, 'but when I go, you'll go with me, dead or alive. Surrender now or you'll be sorry.'

'Sorry, sheriff, but to-day is Friday, and it's bad luck to be arrested on a Friday. And if yo're in a sportin' mood, I'll bet you a new hat that the dead feller is no law officer nor never was. He's Charlie Jackson. Want the bet?'

'I do. And I'll collect it.'

'I'll throw in another hat for the coroner,' called Pat. 'He shore needs one. He'd look good in a brown derby.'

Pat was in a good humour, despite his troubles. He recalled Bender as being a close-mouthed, surly brute stamped with toughness. But, on the other hand, some of the big detective agencies employed just such men to do their work. And there were, among the secret operatives, some men of hard character who mingled with outlaw bands and bided their time until they could make an arrest. Some of these detectives actually took part in gang crimes, thereby gaining the confidence of the men they wanted. Perhaps the dead man, Bender, was such an operative. If so, then Pat Roper faced hanging or a long term in prison, for a crime he had not committed. Spilled milk. No use trying to gather it up again. He was into it. An hour until sunset. A brief twilight. Darkness. And he could make his escape.

During the intervening hours, Pat kept up an exchange of shots and idle banter with the trapped sheriff and coroner. He also partook of supper and did not fail to comment to the hungry sheriff regarding the excellency of the food.

Then the sheriff made a bold move that checkmated Pat's plan to steal his horse and make a get-away. It was a move that proved the sheriff brave to the point of rashness. While the coroner kept up a fusillade of shots, the sheriff made for the barn. Pat shot all around the running man, but his warning bullets could not swerve the sheriff, who gained the shelter of the barn. From there, he

57

taunted Pat with caustic remarks pertaining to the cow-puncher's bad marksmanship. Whereupon the chagrined Pat disproved the sheriff's words by putting a dozen bullets in a bucket that stood near the pump. Which silenced the sheriff's tongue but did not by any means lessen Pat Roper's plight.

'I never was much of a hand to walk,' mused Pat grimly, 'but hikin' beats jail, and I'd rather have blisters on my heels than a rope around my neck.'

Taking his Winchester and six-shooter, he softly opened a rear window of the kitchen. One leg over the sill, he hesitated. He had recalled that part of his queer visitor's letter that dealt with the habits of the horse and mule. Both animals were biscuit-eaters. Pat had turned them into the lower pasture. He now filled his pockets with biscuits and took a hackamore he had just finished repairing.

'Bareback beats walkin', if this idee works out.' He let himself out of the window, and as silently as possible made his way along a trail that led around the barn and corrals and would take him to the lower pasture, about two miles distant.

Footsore and out of wind, he plodded through the dark. The pasture was a couple of miles square. The moon was not yet up and the going was difficult. Two hours of searching failed to locate the horse and mule. He had whistled 'Turkey in the Straw' until his lips ached. Weary, discouraged to the point of despair, he halted.

'If ever any gent starts that "Turkey in the Straw" tune,' he mused bitterly, 'I'll shore do murder.'

From out of the dim light of a rising moon came the soft nicker of a horse. Pat's heart leaped. For the last time, he whistled that tune, his hands filled with cold biscuits. Two shadowy shapes came up timidly.

A few moments later the horse and mule were gingerly nibbling the biscuits. Pat slipped the hackamore on the horse, his heart pounding with renewed hope. He fed them the rest of the biscuits, then slid up on the back of the horse. As he rode away, his Winchester across his lap, the mule followed close behind. Outlawed as he now was, Pat Roper felt that he still had the top grip on his luck.

'Anyhow, the bow-legged, bald-headed little rascal

didn't lie about his biscuit-eatin' stock. And mebby he told the truth about the Bender feller. And as long as I've carried out the first of his requests, I'll gamble with him the rest of the way.'

It was sun-up when Pat Roper reached the Two Block round-up camp. The cowpunchers looked up from their breakfast in grinning surprise as Pat came up bareback, followed by a long-eared, mouse-coloured mule.

'Where's your sheep, Pat?' called his round-up boss, a lanky Texan called 'Panhandle'.

He took the joking of his men with a good-natured grin. Briefly he explained the situation, while they listened in silence.

'So it looks, boys,' Pat finished, 'like I'm due to play coyote until this Bender proposition is cleared up, one way or another. I'll have to set one of you boys afoot for a saddle. But you kin lope on down to the ranch and get mine. Fetch my horse and outfit back here, and I'll slip into camp some time tonight and change. Don't lose this horse and mule outa the remuda.

'Panhandle, I want you boys to gather five hundred head of steers. Work this end of the range where the stuff is not wild. A week oughta be plenty time.'

'Cowboys,' said Panhandle solemnly, 'you kin roll up your beds. You won't need 'em this week. Because it ain't gonna take us more than an hour or two to stay all night at the Two Block round-up camp. We gotta gather Pat a herd so's he kin sell 'em an' hit for South America where they don't annoy cowboys that gets keerless about shootin' detectives and hittin' sheriffs. Them steers will be gathered, Pat, ol' boy. And delivered to your buyer whenever you say.'

'The steers are to be delivered at the Flyin' W Ranch.'

'What? Quit joshin', Pat.'

'That's the delivery point, boys.'

'When we hired out,' complained Panhandle, 'you said we was gonna deal this Murphy cow thief a big dose of his own medicine. Now we're gonna throw in with the old cuss. You ain't sunstruck or somethin', are you?'

'Not sunstruck. Loco, mebby. I'm playin' a long shot on a hunch to win. Mebbyso I'm right, mebbyso wrong.

Mind them steers we trailed into Mexico from the lower Concho? Them Flyin' W steers? Well, these pays back what we run off.'

'Boys,' said Panhandle sadly, 'our boss has done got religion. Or mebbyso it's a girl? Bet a pinto hoss it's a girl that's got him into this state of weak-mindedness. They do tell me, Pat, that ol' Wig Murphy's daughter ain't hard atall on the eyes. Doggone, look at the sucker blush, boys!'

'If I wa'n't so laig weary,' grinned Pat, 'I'd take you an' lay you on your back, you long-geared Texas thing. And if there ain't five hundred head of steers laid down in Wig Murphy's back yard of an evenin' one week from to-day, this outfit of two-bit, bone-headed, no-account, mail-order cowboys is goin' down the wide road a-talkin' to theirse'ves. And they'll be follerin' a hearse that carries the remains of a gent they usta know called Panhandle.'

'They're your cattle,' moaned the lanky foreman, 'and we're your hired hands. And if ol' Wig Murphy asks five hundred head of prime steers for his gal, so be it, and amen. But I never seen the woman yet, black, white, or tan, blonde, brunette, or sorrel, buckskin or pinto, that I'd give more than two ponies and a few sacks of terbaccer for. Rattle your hocks, cow servants, and throw your bulls on your top hoss. We're hittin' a high lope, and we ain't pullin' up till a week from this evenin'. Our boss rides bare back an' has a mule a-follerin' him. He's got blisters on his feet an' a sheriff a-follerin' him. He's givin' off the Two Block herd to ol' Wig Murphy, an' you kin draw your own conclusions as to the why an' the whereof. But we knowed Pat Roper afore he got this a way. When he follered the cow for forty a month an' beans. When he was pore an' humble an' the seat of his overalls patched with a gunny sack. So we'll forgit his faults, cowboys. We'll weep silentlike, inside our manly breasts, but we'll foller him wherever he goes. So long, Pat, ol'timer. If we come back an' find you singin' love songs to the cook, we'll know you're practisin'.'

Pat grinned. He and Panhandle had grown up together, and Pat knew that the lanky Texan and every man in the outfit would fight to the finish for him. But he had not told all that was in that letter left on the bunk-house table. The part about returning the cattle he had kept to himself.

Just why, he could not say. He sat with his breakfast untouched as Panhandle led his cowboys away from camp. One of them, bareback, had ridden in the other direction, toward the ranch, to bring back Pat's saddle and horse, which were the only things Pat Roper felt he really owned on the Two Block Ranch.

The tinkle of horse bells. The carefree laugh of a young cowboy. Not a cloud marred the turquoise sky. Pat grinned and tackled his breakfast.

Chapter XI

Watching the shadow that he and his pony made, Sid Collins rode across the mesa. Early that morning, Sid had saddled up and had ridden away from the Flying W Ranch without his breakfast, because he wanted to get away before Tommy could talk him out of the notion. Tommy did not know what Sid had learned the night before in the bunk-house. Namely, that Pat Roper was wanted by the law for killing a detective of some kind. A cowpuncher had brought word from town that the sheriff was organizing a posse. A bench warrant had been issued for Pat Roper, dead or alive. And when it was learned that the dead man was none other than Pete Bender, one of Jim Boudry's men, the Flying W punchers spent all evening in argument and speculation. Sid had listened with both ears. Especially to every word that Wig Murphy and Billy Carter had to say on the subject.

Wig, nursing his grudge against Pat Roper, was caustic on his condemnation of the Two Block owner. The sooner Pat Roper was hunted down and shot, in Wig's opinion, the better for the cow country.

Billy Carter said little except that he doubted Bender's standing as an officer of the law. This called for a heated argument. Wig cited incidents where supposed outlaws had really been detectives seeking evidence, men of famous reputations as man hunters, men like Joe La Force and Charlie Siringo, who had ridden from Canada to Mexico with outlaw gangs.

'Just the same,' Billy Carter maintained, 'I shore wouldn't hunt far for any man that killed Pete Bender.'

There was a stranger in the Flying W bunk-house who stayed out of the conversation. A small man with bowed legs and a bald head who had hired out that evening to Billy Carter. He lay stretched out on his bunk, his eyes closed, his bald head pillowed on linked fingers. Sid took notice that one of his hands was badly maimed, two fingers being gone. The man had ridden in about suppertime on a leggy roan gelding that had the Flying W brand on its left shoulder. That roan had been missing for several months.

'I picked him up over at the edge of the Chiricahua Mountains,' explained the stranger, 'about two weeks ago. Figgered you might want him back, so I rode him here. Thought mebbyso you could use a seasoned cowhand.'

Billy Carter was tickled over the return of that roan. The horse was one of his tops and he would have put the man on, even if he had to make a job for him, out of sheer gratitude. He had taken out the little tally book in which he kept the men's time.

'What's the name, stranger?'

'Put me down as Jones. Jones or Smith.'

Billy Carter grinned. If the man didn't want his name known, that was his business. There was more than one cowpuncher in Arizona that had left his name behind him somewhere.

'I got two Joneses and a Smith or two now,' said Billy. 'I'll put you down as "Cap".'

For the fraction of a moment the stranger's eyes changed expression. 'Cap?' he questioned.

Billy, writing the name in his little book, had not noticed the stranger's eyes.

'That big roan you fetched home to me,' he explained, 'is named Captain. Cap, for short. So I'll name you after the horse.'

'That's all right with me, Carter. Cap she is.'

Sid had been standing near. Boylike he was intrigued by that scarred hand and was conjuring up pictures of knife fights and gun scrapes involving the little man with the bowed legs.

'Got a bed, Cap?' asked Billy.

'Not here. I kin sleep anywheres. The hayloft and a saddle blanket suits me.'

'No need of that, Cap. Sid, show him that extra bed in

63

the bunk-house. We're workin' out from the home ranch just now, and back every night, so that bed'll do till you get yourn.'

Sid found Cap a congenial sort. He audibly noticed Sid's boots and hat.

'My pardner give 'em to me,' explained Sid proudly. 'You ought to see the saddle and chaps he gimme. Gee, mister, you ought to meet him! He's the best guy in the world, believe me. He licked the tar outa Jim Boudry, and he ain't scared of anything that walks, crawls, or swims. I don't belong to the Flyin' W. I'm a Two Block man, just kinda reppin' over here. Pat Roper's my pardner.'

'I get you, Sid.'

'I ain't a real rep. Only, Tommy started callin' me that and now Billy and the other boys calls me "the Two Block rep." But they let me ride into the herd and cut back the Two Block stuff, just like any real hand representin' the Two Block iron. I reckon Wig Murphy wouldn't let any other Two Block man work over here. Wig don't like Pat, but Tommy says she bets that when some of the darn lies that's bin told about Pat Roper gets straightened out, Wig Murphy will eat crow meat. But I'm talkin' too much.'

'Don't let that worry you, Sid. I kin hold a secret.' Cap winked and chuckled silently.

Sid had figured on taking Cap down to the barn that evening, and showing him the saddle and chaps and spurs that Pat had given him. Then that cowpuncher had come in with his bit of startling news about Pat Roper, and Sid forgot everything save his friend's misfortune.

And at daybreak, when the horse wrangler brought in the remuda, Sid had saddled up and slipped away while the boys were at breakfast.

Now he pressed his pony for the rough hills where he knew he would find Pat Roper. Sid had guided Pat all over those hills, which he knew by heart, as a city boy knows his intimate neighbourhood. Pat would hide out at one of those remote spots that were unknown even to cowboys who had ridden the Two Block range for years.

Riding at a long lope, Sid watched his shadow as it sped across the ground. Here was adventure to stir a boy's

64

blood and quicken his imagination. Now he could be of real service to Pat.

He felt his bruised nose, which was badly swollen. When he pressed it, it ached till tears came into his eyes. Mebby it was busted. Then he'd have a crooked nose like Cap's. Only Cap's nose looked like it had bin busted a hundred times. Like a prize-fighter's nose. Sid hoped his beezer was busted. He'd look hard, then. Not like a bald-faced kid that never had bin up against it.

Looking back across his shoulder, Sid thought he could make out somebody following him. He reined the dun pony into a low swale that dropped below the skyline. He'd lose that feller behind. He followed a twisting trail that took him off a direct course. It followed down a deep arroyo that widened into a sand wash filled with brush. A mile or more of this. Then Sid swung abruptly to the left and let the little dun pony rim his way up over the ridge, keeping to the rocks and brush where the sign was hard to follow and the trail was flanked with boulders and brush.

At the top of the ridge, Sid pulled up and dismounted. He loosened the saddle cinch to let the dun catch his wind. The boy grinned as he caught a brief glimpse of a rider that followed on down the main trail.

'We sure fooled that hombre, Scorpion,' he told the pony. As if understanding, Scorpion rubbed his head against Sid's shoulder.

Several hours later, Sid Collins was squatting beside Pat Roper under a big juniper. Pat had a pair of field glasses, and from the ragged top of the mountain where Sid had found his partner they watched the sheriff's posse ride aimlessly about far below.

'They'll booger all the cattle outa the country,' said Pat. 'You stand guard, pardner, while I git me a half-hour's shut-eye.'

Tickled with this responsibility, Sid nodded solemnly. And for more than two hours the boy kept track of the riders that combed the hills below them. It was an hour past noon, by sun time, when Pat awoke.

He and Sid ate the cold lunch Pat had fetched with him from the round-up camp.

'Yo're a real white man, Sid,' he told the boy when they finished eating, 'and a sure-enough pardner.'

Sid reddened under the praise from his hero. Pat, understanding the boy's embarrassment, poked the youngster in the ribs and opened a blade of his jackknife.

For the next half-hour they played a closely contested game of mumbley-peg. Pat lost and was forced to get down and with his teeth pull the wooden peg that Sid drove into the ground.

'And now, Pardner,' said Pat, when the peg had been pulled and the two had stopped laughing, 'it's about time you slipped back down the mountain and hit for the Flying W Ranch.'

'Can't I stay here with you?' pleaded Sid.

'You kin do me more good by goin' back, pard. I have to make a ride tonight, and they ain't so apt to see one rider as two. I'm goin' over to the round-up camp for a fresh horse and some more grub. You slide out and get home before dark. Keep your eyes peeled and your ears open. If the sign is right, come back here day after tomorrow. Fetch me what news there is. And give this message to nobody but Billy Carter. Tell him that on next Friday evenin' there will be five hundred head of Two Block steers in his corral, to be vented and put in the Flyin' W iron. But for him to keep shut about it, excep' to Wig Murphy. Got that right?'

'You bet,' nodded the boy.

They took Sid's dun pony off the stake rope and the boy saddled up. Pat smiled at him oddly.

'Pardner, you never asked me if I killed Pete Bender. You just said, when you rode up, that you heard I was in a tight and you come to see what you could do. But you ain't asked me a question.'

'I'm learnin' to keep shut, Pat.'

'You shore are, son. Well, I didn't kill Bender, Sid.'

Sid caught his lower lip between his teeth. Tears sprang into his hazel eyes and his fists knotted in an effort to hold back the sob that choked him.

'Gosh—gee, Pat, I'm shore glad! Kin I tell Tommy?'

'Tell Tommy? I reckon, Sid.' Pat's face was red under the tan.

'She'll be awful glad, Pat. Because—because, you see, I up and told her about what you told me when I give you Dad's gun. It's the first time I've seen Tommy bawl since I don't know when. And then she made me tell all about how you was decent to me and how you talked to me about gettin' a school education and that it was better to grow up decent than bein' tough. And she said she reckoned that when the truth come out that you wasn't no lowdown cow thief, and that there was usually two sides to any fight, and she bet you wasn't as black as Wig Murphy made you out to be.'

'She said that, kid?'

'And some more that she made me swear I wouldn't tell. Tommy ain't as mean as she lets on to be. And she'll be frettin' to know how yo're makin' it.'

'You think so, pardner?'

'Darn right she will.'

'Give her—give her my best regards, Sid.'

'Darn right.' Sid jerked his cinch tight and stepped up on the dun pony. Pat held out his hand and shook solemnly with the boy. He hoped Sid hadn't noticed how hot his face had got when he talked about Tommy Murphy.

'So long, pardner.'

'So long, pardner.'

When he was sure that Sid had gone, Pat took from his pocket a small buckskin glove. Tommy's glove. He had picked it up from the ground where he had seen her accidentally drop it there in front of the Two Block bunkhouse. Pat smoothed out the glove and looked at it for a long time. Then he put it back in his pocket.

'I'm the biggest fool on two laigs,' he told himself. 'Wig Murphy's daughter. With a swell education and more money than I got whiskers. If this Two Block spread was really mine, that'd be a different tune. But it ain't. Pablo Guerrero owns it, and no paper kin change it. All I kin claim is them PR cattle that Pablo stole an' sold to that ol' pirate that's Tommy's father. He'd shoot me if he even thought I looked twice at her. Or I'd have to shoot him. I'm Pablo's tool here, that's a cinch. Them guns that's bein' run across the border goes to Pablo, nobody else.

Jim Boudry is his man. I'm no better than Boudry, comin' down to cases. And no matter what her dad is, that little girl is a sure enough thoroughbred.

'And when Panhandle was hoorawin' me about bein' stuck on her, he was a lot righter than he figgered. Comin' to hard facts, them cattle is goin' into the Murphy iron for no other reason than I want Tommy Murphy to think I'm somethin' besides a cheap cow thief—Pat Roper, yo're sillier than a school kid on Valentine's Day. If I had twice the brains I got, I'd be almost half-witted. But if somebody should shoot me, they'd be killin' an awful happy cowboy. Doggoned if they wouldn't, now!'

Chapter XII

The following day seemed an eternity to Pat as he sat under the big juniper. He had made his way to the camp and back without being caught. Panhandle had no news for him except bad news. The sheriff was out to get Pat Roper, dead or alive. Election was coming along in a few months and if he could make a spectacular capture, he'd be sure of a second term in office. Moreover, Panhandle passed on the news, papers found on Bender proved him to be one George Farrow, secret agent for a big detective agency whose men were employed by the banks and railroads. The agency had wired the sheriff offering a five-hundred-dollar reward for the capture, dead or alive, of the man who had killed their detective. Bender's body, on order from the detective bureau, had been shipped to Chicago for interment there. And as Panhandle bitterly stated, there were many men in that posse whose one and only thought was to claim that five hundred dollars on the dead body of Pat Roper.

Pat's mouth was a thin, grim line set in a stubble of whiskers. His puckered blue eyes held a troubled light as he watched the posse riding about, down below his lookout point. There was no trail leading to the top of the mountain. One had to lead a horse up a twisted, trackless way that seemed impossible to negotiate. Manzanita brush and cat's-claws made a perfect barrier. Had not Sid shown Pat the way, he would never have known it. No wilder spot could be found in Arizona. There were traces of old Apache sign there. Perhaps the mountain had been used by the 'Apache Kid' during his reign of terror that marks a bloody page in the history of Arizona. Not far from the big juniper were some human bones bleached white by years of sun and rain. Grass in a small park grew almost belly-deep to a horse. A small spring of clear water trickled down through granite boulders in a tiny waterfall. A hunted man could ask for no better spot than this mountain peak that rose high above the surrounding rocky hills.

Lying on his back on the blanket of thick grass, Pat Roper watched a flaky cloud driven by the wind across the sky. Drowsily, he lay there, his face losing its grimness, his eyes softening. Without the burden of guilt to weight his day-dreaming, Pat built his visions in the azure sky, while the world and all its badness, its suffering, its sham and lies, seemed remote things. Pat Roper was just a man on a mountaintop.

At dusk, he ate his cold supper and smoked until dark. His saddle blanket for cover against the night's chill, he slept.

Sunrise found him in an almost gay mood. Sid would come to pay him a visit. The boy had got into Pat's heart and he missed him. Sid would not be suspected, even if any of the posse men stopped him. But there was little likelihood of Sid's being seen. The boy knew every hidden trail between the Flying W Ranch and the mountain that was known as Big Granite.

Twice, during the long hours of the morning, the sound of shooting drifted up from below. That worried Pat, and he grew more restless as the morning hours dragged past and there was no trace of Sid. Noon. One, then two o'clock. Pat had eaten no food. The thought of eating choked him. Had something happened to Sid? Mid-afternoon found the cowpuncher's face drawn with anxiety.

Then his heart leaped quickly. Someone was coming. Somebody on foot. Pat slipped behind some boulders. It might be a man from the posse.

Now the crown of a white Stetson showed. Then the head and shoulders of—of Tommy Murphy!

Pat came from behind the big boulders. 'Where's Sid?' he asked huskily, without the formality of polite greeting.

Tommy's flushed face broke into a frank smile. 'Sid's safe. But he couldn't come. The sheriff ran into him on his way back yesterday and got suspicious. He quizzed Sid to beat the band, but you can bet that he got not one word out of that little champion. So today, we framed the law gents. I let Sid take half an hour start. He's leading those posse Hawkshaws so far that they'll be a week getting back to camp. And when the human bloodhounds were baying the trail, I cached my horse and came up on foot. I knew you'd be worried about Sid. And so I took it upon myself to act as substitute. And you don't seem at all pleased.'

'No,' said Pat bluntly, 'I'm not.'

'Thanks for putting it so courteously,' said the girl. 'You sure do know how to make a person feel right at home, don't you, Mr. Roper? After a two-hour climb up your darned mountain, you don't even say, "Sit down there on the ground, Miss Murphy, it's softer than the granite seats. And do have a piece of jerky and a drink of water." '

'It ain't that, ' said Pat, reddening. 'Gosh, I never was gladder to see anybody! But dodgin' a sheriff's posse ain't a lady's game. Supposin' one of 'em shot you?'

'Then I'd be shot, wouldn't I? I'll sit here, thanks. And I'm dead for water. But you don't put yourself out, Mr. Roper.' Her eyes mocked him as he jumped to obey. As he dipped a battered tin cup in the spring, Tommy laughed. Pat looked back over his shoulder and grinned.

Tommy took off her hat and propped her back against the trunk of the big juniper.

'Hungry?' asked Pat.

'Cowhand, I could eat an elephant raw and without salt. Any time a pilgrim thinks that dodging sheriff's don't work up an appetite, let 'em try it. Now, if Sid could only be here, we'd have the outlaw gang together. He said he'd try to make it by sun-down.'

'Sun-down?' echoed Pat. 'Gosh, you can't start back at sun-down! The trail down the mountain is tough enough by daylight. Dark'd overtake you before you got half-way down.'

71

'Exactly. That's why Sid and I decided to spend the night up here.'

Pat groaned. 'You must be joshin'?'

'Far from it. Sid and I worked it out before we left home. We've turned outlaw. I can imagine nothing more glorious than to watch the moon rise from the top of Big Granite. With the world ten million miles away; the coyotes singing; the stars so close that you can almost touch 'em; the night breeze whispering its secrets to the trees. The bigness, the glory, the beauty of it pounding your pulses and sending little shivers through you because nothing that man can create seems anything but puny by comparison to God-made night on a mountaintop.'

Pat could find no words to say to this girl who sat there on the ground, her hands clasping her drawn-up knees, her eyes soft with dreams. This girl in overalls and flannel shirt. This daughter of Wig Murphy, border pirate, who knew no law save that of his own making. Without her father's hardness, she was as gloriously lawless as her sire. And she was the most wonderful girl that Pat Roper had ever known.

Then she broke the silence with a little laugh that was like music made by silver bells. Her eyes danced impishly.

'Scared, cowboy?'

'Plumb,' admitted Pat with a quick grin.

'Sid will make a jim-dandy chaperon. I won't overpower you, honest! When do we eat?'

'Right now. And as long as you've got this thing all decided, we'll just forget that Wig Murphy will shoot me on sight and a lot of other things that will come of this business. Can't build a fire, so you'll have to like cold bread and beans and jerky and canned tomatoes.'

'I was raised on a cow ranch,' laughed Tommy, 'and that bill of fare sounds like a banquet just now. And unless Billy squeals, Dad won't know I'm here. Dad's gone to Phoenix to get robbed again by that most fascinating bandit, Pablo Guerrero. He was madder than a grizzly with a sore nose when he left. Said he was going to have the delightful Pablo hung. But he won't. Down in his cranky old heart, Dad thinks a lot of Pablo. That sounds all wrong, but it's the truth. And Pablo feels much the same way about Daddy. He told me so, one time. Both buccaneers, both lawless, both hiding their softer side under a cloak of bravado. They're like two chess players, only they use human pawns and move the pawns with six-shooters.

'And if ever a girl longed for a real thrill, she should listen to that fascinating Mexican play his guitar and warble *muy dulce* love songs beneath her window on a moonlit night. I was kid enough then to have eloped with the handsome scoundrel, but he didn't ask me. He might have, though, if Taller hadn't put in an appearance in his red-flannel undies and a double-barrelled shotgun, and run him off. Not that Taller was taking the role of protector. It was simply that Pablo's music kept him awake. Taller has absolutely no spark of romance. He was raised with a sourdough keg and has wed his life to his art of creating good food. Well, he, no doubt, kept me from a career as bandit queen of Sonora.'

'I'd like to have a talk with Pablo,' said Pat grimly.

'No chance. He's dishing up another Chili revolution. He and his Yaquis took some town the other day. He sent a messenger to the ranch with a letter to Dad and a package for me. The most marvellous Spanish shawl you ever saw. That shawl will cost Wig Murphy about ten thousand dollars. Why not? Dad can afford it, and Pablo certainly keeps him from being bored.'

Pat looked at her, puzzled. She was talking as she ate the cold food that was more filling than palatable.

'Pat Roper,' she said, making a wry face, 'as a hard-boiled rustler and partner of the dare-devil Pablo, you're turning out to be a perfect washout. I heard Billy tell Dad that you're making him a present of five hundred Two Block steers. How come? Getting cold feet? You came here to buck range with the Flying W. Now you lay 'em down as meek as Moses. And you don't look like a quitter, either.'

'You'd rather I started in stealin' cattle from Wig Murphy?' he asked, his eyes hardening.

'I think it would make you much more interesting.'

73

'I never was troubled,' said Pat stiffly, 'with any hankerin' to make myself interesting, as you call it.'

'But you and Pablo are pardners. You came here to deal the Flying W a lot of misery. Then you get religion, or fall in love, or something, and you quit. Is that treating your pardner fair?'

'So you think I'm yellow, is that it?'

'That's what I'd like to know,' she said, munching on a bit of tough jerky. 'Are you?'

'If it's yellow to be honest,' he said hotly, 'then I'm shore that colour. And if you happened to be a man instead of a girl, I'd wipe up some of this landscape with you.' He had got to his feet and stood with his back to her. Tommy looked up at his stiff back, her eyes twinkling with amusement. Then she went on eating.

'May I have another cup of water, please?' she asked in a voice that fairly dripped with sweetness.

Ignoring the brown eyes that sought his glance, he picked up her cup and went to the spring. Seething with inward wrath, he returned with the filled cup. She thanked him with a smile that made him the more angry. Darn women anyhow, with their way of makin' a man feel like two bits' worth of cat meat! He picked up her empty plate and went back to the waterfall. He was scouring it clean in the black sand when her hand on his arm made him look up.

'I'm a little bum for spoiling your afternoon, Pat. I'm sorry. I take it all back. Every mean word I said. It was just an ornery streak in me. I'm honestly sorry.'

'But you must have meant what you said?' he blurted stubbornly, avoiding her yes.

'Pat Roper, you know as much about women as I know about putting a hackamore on a dinosaur. If I figured you yellow, I wouldn't be here. Can we shake hands and be pardners?'

Pat took the hand she gave him, the hand that belonged to that little buckskin glove in his pocket. There was warmth and comradeship and generosity in her handclasp. It sent Pat's pulse pounding. Her eyes were looking up at him, holding his blue ones in their gaze. Something in her eyes gave him hope. A wild, futile, crazy hope to be sure.

74

A hope that reckoned not with that world so far below them.

'Tommy, I—'

'Tonight, Pat,' she said, in a soft voice that shook a little, 'when the moon comes up. Tell me then. When the world is a million miles away.' She withdrew her hand gently and walked away.

Pat stooped and picked up the tin plate. Tommy went back to the big juniper. So love came to a girl and a man who stood on the top of a mountain.

Chapter XIII

The shooting that Pat Roper had heard earlier in the afternoon had been caused by the discovery of some eight or ten men of Jim Boudry's gang who had been trapped in a box canyon by the posse. The outlaws had been in hiding there, waiting a shipment of guns and ammunition that was coming, by circuitous route, from the north. Boudry and his men had waited there at the head of the canyon with pack mules. And so well were they hidden that the sheriff and his men would have completely overlooked their hideaway had it not been for one of his new men who had ridden over from the Flying W Ranch to join the man-hunt that sought the capture, dead or alive, of Pat Roper.

This new member of the sheriff's posse was a small, wiry man with bald head and bowed legs, battered of feature, with keen grey eyes that missed nothing.

'I know this country fairly well, sheriff. And I figger I kin do you some good. If you'd like to grab off about half a dozen tough jaspers that has bin runnin' guns, pick some of your best men and foller me.'

'Roper's the man I want.'

'That's all right, too. When the sign is right, Pat Roper won't be hard to corral. But Boudry and his men is in hidin' close by, if you got the grit to go after 'em. These men of yourn is sashayin' around, gittin' in one another's way, or bushed up asleep, somewheres, mebby. Just as well let 'em earn the five bucks a day they're gettin' from the county.'

'I'm runnin' this show, Shorty. And yo're kinda hornin' in like you was somebody. Who are you, anyhow?'

'You'd be surprised if I told you, sheriff. If we capture Jim Boudry, you'll find out quick enough who I am. He'll say it with bullets, if he gets the chance.'

'What do you mean, little feller?'

'I'm one of Jim Boudry's gang, that's all. For certain mighty personal reasons, I quit his layout and because I know a-plenty about him and his gang, how they work and where they hide out, Jim would be just too glad for words if he could hit me between the eyes with a bullet. That's all I'm a-goin' to tell you, sheriff. Do you want Jim Boudry and his gang, or has the big son got a whizzer run on the law around here?'

'Lead us to him,' growled the sheriff. 'If this is a trick, you'll get that bullet between the horns, but it won't be from Jim Boudry's gun.'

The little man's hard grey eyes twinkled. 'That arrangement suits me, sheriff. Whenever you think I'm double-crossin' you, that'll be your pleasure and my sorrow. Get your men and I'll take 'em there.'

But something had gone wrong. Some spy of Jim Boudry's, planted in the posse, must have taken word to the outlaws. Against the little man's advice, the sheriff had broadcast the information that they were going after Jim Boudry and his men. The result of this loose information was that, while the posse, led by the sheriff and the little man with the bowed legs, moved in deployed formation up the sand-wash that led to the canyon, Boudry and his men were coming down, riding hard, shooting as they came. The posse, composed of any sort of men that could be picked up around town, were no match for the desperate outlaws that came charging down the wash. There was a swift exchange of shots, pounding hoofs. Boudry and six of his men escaped. Only three of the band were captured.

But if the sheriff had any doubts regarding the status of the wiry man with the bowed legs, those doubts were dispelled by the hard names that were flung at the little fellow by the captured bandits.

He answered their curses with a crooked, thin-lipped grin. Then he gave their names and records to the sheriff. All three men were wanted for various crimes. The sheriff, upon learning their real pedigrees, whistled soundlessly.

'Purty good day's work, at that,' he grinned. The little man shrugged disgustedly and walked away.

'The next time,' the bow-legged man told his horse as he mounted then rode away alone, 'that we have Boudry trapped, we'll hire up a bunch of Boy Scouts. Wonder what that sheriff did for a livin' before the sheepmen and town folks elected him? Bet he run a pool room, cigar store, and bureau of general information. He's a newsy party.'

Nor was the odd little man far from being right. The pompous, town bred sheriff was an example of political pull and the inability of the cowmen and their punchers to get to the polls on election day. Town politics and the miners' votes in some of the adjacent copper camps had elected a man who made a splendid town marshal but an inefficient leader on a man-hunt that led into the hills. The man was not lacking in courage. There was not enough money in the county to buy his honesty of purpose. But his forte lay in the suppression of boot-legging and gambling. And because his deputies were of the same breed, miners instead of cowpunchers, his effectiveness ended at the edge of town.

The little man with the bowed legs was not at camp when the sheriff got there with his prisoners. He had gone, as mysteriously as he had come.

'Scared, I suppose,' grinned the sheriff with a big man's easy contempt for a little man. 'He's got cold feet.'

As a matter of fact, the little man was hidden in some dense brush alongside the trackless, twisting trail that led up the scarred side of Big Granite. He was waiting for Sid to come slipping along. He had trailed him until he had made fairly sure that the boy was headed for Big Granite. That was on Sid's first trip. He had let the boy throw him off the trail. He had smiled grimly as Sid, to-day, had led half the sheriff's men off on a wild-goose chase. He knew that Sid would give them the slip, double back on this trail, and eventually climb the side of Big Granite to the hiding-place of Pat Roper. In his pocket was a brief note that he wanted the boy to take to Pat. A note warning Pat that Jim Boudry and six of his men were on the prowl, and that Boudry knew of another trail that led up the rag-

78

ged side of Big Granite. A trail that led up from the other side. And that, when darkness came, Boudry might risk the climb with those of his men that chose the dangerous ascent rather than a pitched battle with the posse. The note further advised Pat to come on down and give himself up to the blundering sheriff. Because, when the body of the supposed detective reached Chicago, a wire would come back saying that the body was not that of their operative. That it was the body of Charlie Jackson, bandit.

But Sid did not show up. Sun-down, and no sign of the boy. Dusk. The bow-legged little man began climbing. Agile as a mountain goat, he swarmed up the rocky trail on foot, scrambling, crawling, leaping across an occasional crevasse where a misstep meant death on the rocks hundreds of feet below. He burrowed through the brush, crawling and wriggling. Brush ripped his hands and face, tearing his clothes. Now and then he lay prone, gulping down great breaths of air into his tortured lungs. He was dripping wet with perspiration. His throat and lungs ached. He was fighting against the approaching darkness that would make the climb so hazardous that only a madman would take the risk.

It was his first trip up the mountain, that was certain, because he missed the trail that Sid had shown Pat Roper—a trail that was wide enough to permit a horse to climb without a rider. He was still half an hour's climb from the top when darkness overtook him. There was nothing else to do now but wait for the moon to rise. With a good moon, and by using the utmost caution, a man might make it without falling and breaking his bones on the ragged boulders far below—if he were blessed with a lot of luck.

More than an hour before the moon would rise the little man stretched out on the slanting ground and lay there until his heart stopped pounding so hard and he breathed normally. Bruised and scratched, his clothes in tatters, he took his brief rest, lying like a dead man, there on the hard, granite rocks. His eyes closed and he dozed.

A woman's screams! The sound of shots. The dozing man was on his feet, tense, a little bewildered. Then, heedless of danger, he started up the trail. And because all was quiet as death up there now, the little man moved all the faster. Inwardly he blamed himself for a fool. He had slept like a clown. The moon was up. Well for him that he had dozed, without the full light of the moon, that climb would have been suicide.

It was that ominous silence, rather than the sounds of shots, that goaded him to recklessness. That silence, and the woman's scream. For he had not seen Tommy Murphy climb the mountain. He had no way of knowing, until that scream had shattered his dozing, that a woman shared Pat Roper's danger up there on the mountain.

Chapter XIV

But Sid Collins had underestimated Jim Boudry's knowledge of the Big Granite country. So when he shook the posse, and swung his little dun pony up the back trail that would bring him to the mountaintop, he ran squarely into Boudry and his men, who had halted to rest their horses before taking the climb.

'They've put the little brat on our trail, Jim,' snarled the man who held the struggling boy. 'Gimme leave to cut his throat. I'll learn him to foller us.'

'Hold on,' Jim Boudry leered at the boy. 'Don't kill him. I got a comical idea that he wasn't follerin' us a-tall. Gimme hold of him for a few minutes. I'm gonna make the little sneak do some talkin'.'

Sid's face went white with fear. He knew Jim Boudry's way of making a person talk.

'Kindle a little fire, one of you,' grinned Boudry. 'Just big enough to heat a runnin' iron. I'll run a Two Block on him so's Roper will be able to pick him outa the herd.'

Sid's jaws clamped shut. Boudry pulled him roughly toward the little fire, where a running iron was becoming cherry red. The boy was sick with fear. He had seen samples of Jim Boudry's brutality and knew that the heat-iron was not an idle bluff. But that was not Sid's most awful fear. He was thinking of Pat Roper and Tommy, up there on the mountain, waiting. How long would he be able to hold out against the torture of that branding-iron? Could he stand the terrible pain without betraying the two people in the world who were his partners?

Boudry's big hands ripped off the boy's shirt. Two of the outlaws held Sid down on the ground, while the big leader pulled the red burning iron from the fire.

'God help me! God help me!' breathed Sid, and shut his eyes. The hot iron bit his tender skin. There was the big man's ugly face as Sid's eyes opened, wide with pain and terror. Within a few inches of his eyes, Jim Boudry's unshaven face leered at him. Into the boy's mind came the horrible picture of that same face, loose-mouthed, triumphant, bending over Tommy. Sid forgot his severe pain, forgot the icy terror that already numbed his heart.

'I'm not scared, Boudry. I'm not scared of you.'

'Where's Pat Roper?' The hot iron again touched Sid's chest.

No outcry escaped the lad's clamped lips. His hazel eyes were steady, unafraid. He tried to grin, though his chin was puckered with pain.

'Talk, you little rat! Where's Roper hidin'?'

Again that red iron seared the skin. Three sides of the Block brand showed now, vivid against the white chest of the boy. A thin little choked cry from behind Sid's clenched teeth was the only reply. A sudden mad anger flushed Boudry's face. The iron completed the block. Sid's eyes went shut. Lines of pain showed on his bloodless face. With four swift moves, the second block was made on Sid's chest. But the boy made no outcry. His body was limp. He had fainted.

'Leave the brat here,' snarled Boudry. 'We gotta make the top of Big Granite by dark. It's my guess that Roper's up there.'

'Leave the kid here to squeal?' asked one of the men.

'Knock him on the head, fool,' growled Boudry.

'Nothin' doin', Jim,' said one of the two men who had held Sid. 'This kid's dead game. He never hollered once. I won't stand for no man brainin' him.'

'No?' snarled Boudry.

'No.' There was a gun in the man's hand now and the eyes of the boy's defender were slitted.

'Jake's right,' said another man. 'The kid's had a-plenty. How about it, boys?'

'We ain't killin' kids,' agreed a third man. 'Nobody but a dirty coward would bump off a kid like that.'

'Then leave him as he is,' growled Boudry in a surly

tone. 'And if he squeals on us, and that fool posse gets us, thank your own chicken hearts for bein' ketched.'

In a black mood, Jim Boudry led the way up the mountain. The others followed in surly silence.

Some distance from the top, Boudry dismounted. 'One of you men look after the horses. Jake, that'll be your job. The rest of you peel your chaps and spurs off and foller me. We'll go the rest of the way by hand. Come on, hombres.'

Into the gathering dusk, Boudry led his men up the mountain.

Now and then a loose rock slid from under a boot heel and went crashing down below the climbers. Boudry cursed them in an undertone. They kept on up the trail, climbing toward the ragged top of Big Granite that loomed like a colossal monument against the star-filled sky.

While up on top of the mountain, Pat Roper and Tommy Murphy tried to find consolation in the thin hope that Sid, unable to shake off the posse, had gone back home. And in the long silence that held them, they stared into the darkness below, listening. Tommy's hand crept into Pat's and he sat there beside her under the juniper, miserable because he feared for Sid's safety, yet happy in the knowledge that this girl beside him trusted him and loved him, though no word of love-making had passed Pat's lips. Sid's absence, and the fact that he and Tommy were alone, had kept him from telling her that he loved her. To his cowpuncher's way of thinking, it was not playing the game to take advantage of their being alone. He knew that Tommy understood how he felt about it.

Not far down the mountainside, a rock slipped under a man's foot and bounced down into dry brush. Pat pulled the girl to her feet and into the deep shadow of some brush and boulders.

'It might be Sid,' he whispered, 'or it might be some of that posse. If it's the sheriff's men, I've half a notion to surrender. You see, Tommy, I didn't kill Bender. And I'd be a worse fool to kill any man in that posse. That would make me a sure-enough outlaw. So I'll try to compromise with 'em.'

'Good head work, partner.' Her whispered laugh was shaky. 'I'd hate to quit Dad and be a real she-outlaw with you.' She smiled up into his face, swaying toward him. Pat kissed her awkwardly and went weak-kneed as her arms crept around his neck. He could feel his heart pounding in his throat. Again their lips met, then she pushed him gently away. Pat, still in a queer sort of daze from the spell of her love, left the brush patch and crossed the open park. He had almost reached the shelter of some big boulders when something moved, there on the trail. Pat dropped prone, just as a gun spewed flame, not fifty feet distant. Other guns added their staccato cracks, filling the night. Tommy, thinking Pat had been shot, screamed and ran toward where he lay.

A man's harsh laugh. Boudry's ugly voice. 'We got him, boys! And look who's keepin' him company!'

Pat's gun spat a red streak of flame. Boudry ducked back with a startled oath, one hand clapped to an ear that Pat's bullet had nicked. Pat pulled Tommy into the shelter of the rocks.

'Come and get it, you skunks!' He flung the words at the outlaws.

From where he crouched, he could cover the trail. A man grunted with pain as one of Pat's .30-40 slugs tore through his shoulder. They scrambled for shelter as the cowpuncher's Winchester pumped stinging lead into the shadows that held them.

'Why don't you come on, you rats? Step up and I'll be glad to accommodate you.'

'Don't shoot, boys,' snarled Boudry in an undertone. 'I don't want any bullet holes in that Murphy girl's purty hide. She's my daisy.'

Aloud he called to Pat. 'Better give up the girl, Roper, before us boys commence smokin' you both up. Give her up, and we'll let you go free.'

'Do you know any more good jokes, Boudry?'

'There's enough of us to come and get you, Roper.'

'Then come ahead. While yo're gittin' a meal, I'll get a few bites. And from now on, big feller, I'll shoot for the heart. You can't rush me without losing plenty of men.

And you'll be the first one to drop, mister. Why don't you come?'

But neither Jim Boudry nor any of his pack seemed to have any immediate craving to test Pat Roper's marksmanship. Pat, well barricaded, could drop them as they came across the intervening open space.

'We'll have to drop back, boys, and flank him,' said Boudry in a voice that carried to the trapped cowpuncher.

Pat looked at Tommy. She crouched there, a .38 Colt in her hand.

'Scared, Tommy?' he whispered.

'Not too scared, cowboy. Not too scared to fight some.'

There was a lot of old Wig Murphy's grit in the girl's make-up. She had been raised on the Flying W Ranch and had seen some rough times there. Whatever fear was in her heart now, she hid courageously behind a straight little smile that won Pat Roper's admiration.

Minutes of sinister silence, unbroken save by the soft scuffing sounds of moving men. Pat's eyes strained to catch sight of any man who might attempt the dangerous business of flanking them.

Now a sound came from behind them. Pat's gun swung around. His finger was on the trigger of his cocked Winchester. Only the fear that it might be Sid stayed his trigger pull. Then a cautious voice from that creeping shadow that had come up the other trail.

'You there, Roper?' called a husky voice.

'I shore am. And I got you covered.'

'Hold your fire, son. Keep your shirt on.'

'Who are you?'

For reply, there came a thin whistle that followed the tune of 'Turkey in the Straw.' In spite of the threatening danger, Pat grinned.

'Come on, old-timer,' Pat called, 'but keep to the shelter. Boudry and his coyotes are behind yonder brush on the other trail.'

Dodging, running, crawling, the bow-legged little man wormed his way to the boulder patch. The bullets whined around the rocks, ricocheted off into the night, or flattened against the hard granite.

'Bless me for a sinner,' he gasped, 'if it ain't Miss Murphy! Where's the Sid young un?'

'I'd give a lot to know,' said Pat huskily.

'He led a bunch of them sheepheaded posse gents way down the country. Mebby he didn't have time to make 'er back.' The little man saw the look of deep concern on the girl's face and lied like a gentleman. 'I thought the boy would do just that. That's why I come on up here to tell you Boudry and his wolves was on the prowl. Lucky I come, too. With two of us here, they can't win much.'

'Three of us,' Tommy corrected him.

'Lady,' said the little man, 'I beg your pardon. The correct number of guns that'll stand off them snakes is three. Mind if I make a little speech to the Boudry layout?'

'Have at it, mister.' Pat was trying to figure out this amiable little killer.

'Are you there, Jim Boudry?' called the bow-legged man.

A long moment of silence, then Boudry's voice cut through like a cross-cut saw.

'I'm here, you banty-shanked little traitor.'

The little man chuckled. 'Then take an old-timer's advice and get on back down the hill as fast as you kin make it. And when you meet the sheriff, surrender to him, because there's a ranger who knowed Tim Collins that's killin' you where he finds you, regardless. He knows that you was the bushwacker that killed ol' Tom. And if I was in your fix, I'd shore surrender to the sheriff before that ranger got a chance to line his sights on you. You shore signed your own death-warrant, Boudry, the night you got drunk there on the Concho and bragged about killin' Tim Collins.'

'You yellow traitor!' snarled Boudry, his voice shaking with fury. 'You sold me out, did you?'

'That's what I did, Boudry. And bless me, now, if I know just where you kin go and not get the dose of lead you got comin'. Pablo Guerrero is waitin' for you in Mexico. The rangers is follerin' close on your sign here in Arizona. Looks like you'll have to dig a deep hole, crawl into 'er, and pull the hole in after you. Anyway you look at it, Boudry, you're licked. The sheriff's posse will be swarmin' all over this hill about daybreak. You won't have a rabbit's chance. Nor will your yellow gang. You got just one chance, and that is to get down the mountain before daylight.'

'I'll get you and Roper before I go.'

'I wouldn't lay no big bets on that, Boudry. Whenever I'm up against a big overgrowed cuss that makes a target that even a kid couldn't miss, I shore feel proud that I'm a runt and hard to hit. Pete Bender was a quicker shot and a better shot than you ever was. You know what happened to him. And what almost happened to you when you quit him like a coyote that night at the Two Block. The light was bad or I'd 'a' had you. But tonight I kin shoot you dead centre between the eyes, Boudry. Whenever you feel like you got luck, come on over and we'll have a lot of fun.' The little man chuckled throatily.

'Jim Boudry, you savvy,' said the little man in conversational tone that must have carried to the waiting outlaws, 'is about at the end of his rope. He killed Tim Collins because Tim ketched him smuggling opium. Then he double-crossed Pablo, or tried to, by sellin' guns to a rebel feller down there that Pablo didn't like. That shuts Boudry outa Mexico. About all he kin do is cut his suspenders an' go straight up. And he's most likely to be hauled up at the end of a stout rope. Ladies and gents, this outlaw life don't pan out. I found that out, a long time ago. Mighty few of 'em get away with it. And what becomes of them few? They're holed up in some God-forsaken country, sleepin' uneasy every night, never knowin' when the long arm of old Jawn Law is gonna reach out and grab 'em. It's a coyote life, at the best. You got a little taste of it, up here, Pat. And I bet you'll be glad when you ride down the hill, able to tell that cigar-stand proprietor wearin' a sheriff's star that he's bin about as silly as a brayin' burro.

'When I pulled out that night, I didn't have any idee that I was lettin' you in for all this dodgin'. I had a deal on that needed 'tendin' to. I'd give my word to Pablo Guerrero that I'd meet him at a certain place at a certain time. And I always try to keep a promise like that. Lucky I did, too. Because he cleared up a point or two I wasn't sure about. And when I was done with Pablo, I come back across the border and landed at the Flyin' W. And it was there I finds out that our town-bred sheriff is out after you, thinkin' you've killed a detective that's bin dead and buried for two months. Bender killed the detective and then has the supreme gall to ride into town and make that cigar-peddlin', pool-playin' sheriff think he's a law officer. He takes the dead feller's name. Shows the sheriff the detective's badges and papers. Pulls the wool over the big law-man's eyes, and the general result is that here you are up here on top of Big Granite, and down yonder is half a hundred men stealin' the country's good money.

'It shore is comical. And he's gonna feel awful cheap when he learns what a mistake he made. The only thing he kin do to save hisself from bein' hoorawed outa the country is to ketch Jim Boudry. But he'll have to work fast, or ol' Seth Harker, the ranger captain, is gonna beat him to it. Cap'n Seth Harker was a mighty close friend of Tim Collins. So he come plumb here from San Antone to get a line on the gang that did for his friend Tim. Seth is a good friend of Pablo Guerrero's. Pablo give him the right tip on who to go after. Seth took the tip. Ever hear of Seth Harker, Pat?'

'Ever since I was knee-high to a hop toad.'

'Seth belongs to the old-time rangers that figgered that bullets cost less money than these long-drawn-out jury trials. Some claim he's too quick on the trigger. But he saved Texas an almighty lot of money by shootin' first and askin' his questions after the smoke had cleared the end of his gun barrel. And he never yet killed a man that didn't need killin'. He made sure his man was guilty, then he went after him. And in the end, he got him. Just like he's gonna get Jim Boudry. The same way he got Pete Bender, alias Charlie Jackson.'

'Are you Seth Harker, sir?' gasped Pat Roper.

'That's my name,' chuckled the little bow-legged man.

From the brush and rocks that hid Boudry and his men, there came the low mutter of voices, followed by the un-mistakable sounds of the outlaws beating a hasty retreat. Because the name of Seth Harker was one that chilled the courage of border renegades. The veteran ranger was a

88

man of courage whose praises were sung in rangeland ballad. He struck with the swift ferocity of a puma. Yet he had never shot a man in the back. He always gave a hunted man his final chance to die with a smoking gun in his hand. There were some ugly scars on Seth Harker's tough hide that gave mute proof of narrow escapes from death. His name was linked with swift gun-play and manhunts that led from Mexico City to Canada.

'They've pulled out,' said Pat Roper. 'Boudry and his men have gone.'

The little old captain of the rangers smiled grimly. 'We'll now be able to enjoy the moonlight, son. You, and the young lady, and me. The sign ain't quite right gatherin' in Jim Boudry. Besides, there is a lady present, and somehow ladies hate to see blood spilled. Might I borrow the loan of a smoke?'

Chapter XV

Little Sid Collins moaned and opened his eyes. A man was holding a canteen to his dry lips. It was the man Boudry had called Jake.

'Take it easy, boy. They've gone. You needn't be scared, button. Jake Quinn never harmed a kid yet. I should've killed Boudry for hurtin' you, but I was afraid one of his men'd get me and you too, so I held back. Directly you get to feelin' better, we'll go on to the sheriff's camp.'

'Did Boudry go up the hill, Jake?' asked Sid.

'They did, kid. Boudry and his gang is all gone.'

'Pat's up there. Pat and Tommy, too.'

'That's tough lines, but there's nothin' we kin do about it. We'll never get up that trail in time to help any. Gotta chance it that Roper will hear 'em comin' and hold 'em back. They're shootin' right now.'

For a long time, the boy and man waited there. Jake had put a cooling mud poultice on Sid's burned chest. He made the youngster lie quietly.

After a wait that seemed endless, they heard Boudry and his men coming back down the trail. Jake and Sid hid in the brush until the men passed. And they caught enough of the passing conversation to know that Tommy and Pat were unhurt, and that Captain Seth Harker of the rangers was up there with them. When the outlaws had gone on, Sid grinned gamely.

'We missed that show, didn't we?'

'Seems that a-way, button. Think you kin set that pony of yourn?'

'You bet I can, Jake.'

90

'Then we'll go on to camp. I got somethin' to say to that clumsy sheriff.'

But before they reached the sheriff's camp, they were halted by that confused and excited officer and his men.

'Surrender, Roper!' barked the leader of the posse. 'We got you dead to rights.'

'Hold your fire, sheriff,' replied Jake wearily. 'Neither me nor Sid Collins happens to be Pat Roper. If Roper is wanted by the law, then he's already caught.'

'How's that again?'

'Up on top of Big Granite is Pat Roper. With him is none other than Captain Seth Harker of the rangers. Did you ever hear tell of Seth Harker?'

'This ain't the time for crackin' jokes. Who are you, anyhow?'

'My name is Jake Quinn. I come from San Angelo, Texas, where I was born about thirty years ago, the youngest of three children. My dad was named Mike Quinn, and he was a Texas ranger. I'm a cowpuncher that old Wig Murphy hired to ride with the Boudry outfit to keep tally on how many cattle Boudry stole from him so that Wig could steal that many back. I earned all the wages Wig has bin payin' me here at the Two Block. When Roper gets hold of the outfit, I stay on with Boudry for personal reasons. But tonight I quit, and here I am. And that's about all there is to it except that I kinda played in with Seth Harker when he joined up with Jim Boudry's layout. If you want any more information, you'll have to wait till we meet up with Cap'n Harker.'

'Hmmm! A likely story. What are you doin' with that kid that's bin leadin' my men off on false trails?'

'I was fetchin' Sid to your camp. The lad's hurt. Look here at his li'l ol' chest. Boudry did that. And if you had the sense of a fool hen, you'd be on Boudry's trail right now. Not that you'll ever find him, but it might furnish you with some exercise that'd take off that overweight yo're totin' around.'

'That'll be all I want to hear outa you. You're under arrest. So is the kid.'

'That suits us,' grinned the Texan. 'Sid needs attention. We both kin use up some grub. Better send along fifty or sixty men to see we don't rabbit on you. You may be some

91

pun'kins around town, big un, but you're shore harmless out here. Come on, Sid, let's drag it.'

The sheriff sent two deputies along with them. Jake ignored them. He talked to Sid, joking with the boy until he almost forgot the painful burns on his chest. At camp, they found Billy Carter and several Flying W cowpunchers.

'Where's Tommy?' Billy asked Sid. Sid grinned and pointed to the top of Big Granite.

'She's up yonder.'

'With Roper?'

'I reckon so, Billy. Gosh, you look mad!'

'I reckon it's up to me to kill Roper,' said the Flying W boss, his face a little pale and his eyes blazing. 'If I don't, Wig Murphy will.'

'No, you won't. Neither will Wig Murphy.' Sid's voice was shrill with anger. 'If either of you touch Pat, I'll tell who killed my daddy. Wig Murphy killed him, and you know it.'

Little Sid had gone through an ordeal that would have shattered the nerves of a grown man. He had not meant to blurt out that black secret that, because of his loyalty to Tommy, he had vowed to keep hidden always. Billy Carter was staring hard at the boy, a hurt look in his eyes.

'Hush, button,' said Jake Quinn gently. 'You got your wires all tangled up. Wig has his faults, but he ain't a bushwhacker. Wig never killed Tim Collins, even if folks do claim that he did. Jim Boudry did that dirty job, and it was him that planted evidence to make it look like Wig was guilty.'

'How do you know?' asked Billy Carter tensely. For Wig had never denied that black charge against his honour, not even to Billy Carter.

'I heard Jim Boudry brag about it, Carter, one night when he was drunk. I looked for Seth Harker to kill Jim then and there, but he didn't. The sign wasn't right, just then.'

'You mean Seth Harker, captain of the rangers. is in this country?'

'He shore is. And he's up on Big Granite right now, probably with his back propped against a boulder, spinnin' yarns to Pat Roper and Tommy Murphy. Didn't a little

92

feller with bow legs and a battered-lookin' face ride a big roan over to the Flyin' W Ranch, here recent?'

'You mean that bald-headed little gent is Seth Harker?' gasped Billy excitedly.

'That's Cap'n Seth Harker, and I don't mean mebby. The fightin'est hu-human that ever spit in Old Nick's eye. And he's just about tied up the worst gang of badmen in this section. Between Tim and Pablo Guerrero, they're gonna clean up the Two Block range and make the border tighter than a cement wall fifty-foot high.'

'Harker and Guerrero?' Billy Carter smiled his disbelief. 'Pablo's the crookedest snake in Mexico.'

'I wouldn't go that far, Carter. Mexico has some awful slick gents. Pablo is a slippery article, no foolin'. But he'd have to be awful crooked to beat old Wig Murphy, the old rascal that pays you and me. And, on the other hand, I wouldn't want a better friend than either of 'em.'

'Wig Murphy is a mighty big man,' said Billy Carter.

'So is Pablo Guerrero,' said Jake Quinn, with a queer smile. 'And he's the one human that has give old Wig as good as he sent out. But all this is between you and me and the Sid button. The big clean-up ain't started yet. But it won't be long, now. A few days more and she'll pop. And I wouldn't miss it for a million dollars. Jim Boudry and his gang is pushin' hard for the border right now, to join up with the rest of the smuggler spread. There's a big gang of 'em, and what I mean, Carter, they're plenty tough. And they'll be all the tougher when they find that it's their last stand and they've got their backs crowded to the wall.'

'I wouldn't mind bein' in on it,' mused Billy Carter aloud.

'Don't fret, cowhand, you'll be there. So will Wig Murphy and some more of the Flyin' W. So will Pat Roper and his boys. Along with Seth Harker and his rangers. And down across the border will be none other than Pablo Guerrero and his Yaquis. And because word has gone out to the different border gangs, there'll be a good-sized army of men like Jim Boudry. And it will be any man's fight till it's finished.'

'How about me?' asked Sid, who had been listening in wide-eyed silence.

'I'll see to it, personal, button, that you get a ringside

seat. Carter, this kid is about the gamest young un I ever met. Take a look at his chest.' Jake unbuttoned the boy's shirt and gently lifted the poultice.

Billy Carter's lips were a bloodless slit. 'Who did it?'

'Jim Boudry.'

'Now,' said Billy Carter, 'I know for sure that I'll be there at the big clean-up. Sid, old-timer, we'll make that big buzzard pay.'

The sheriff and his men were now returning. Jake and Billy traded amused looks.

'He means well,' said Jake, 'but he's all lost out here. Come to think of it, Sid, you and me are under arrest, ain't we? I plumb forgot.'

Chapter XVI

Up on top of Big Granite, a camp fire blazed. Tommy Murphy sat beside Pat Roper, covertly holding hands, while Captain Seth Harker of the rangers talked on about many things. He had an uncanny knowledge of Wig Murphy's dealings in 'wet' cattle and spoke bluntly on the subject, watching Tommy's face the while. He neither condemned nor excused the old border pirate. He swung to the interesting subject of Pablo Guerrero, dabbler in revolutions and high ransoms. And after he had related a dozen colourful episodes in the career of this versatile Mexican bandit, Seth Harker said that the ultimate aims of Pablo Guerrero rather justified the means he used toward gaining them. He described the swaggering, soft-spoken, hot-blooded Pablo as a true patriot of Mexico. The money he wrested from such men as Wig Murphy, he used not for personal gain, but to keep his beloved Yaquis and their families in food and clothing. And contrary to many opinions, Pablo and his Yaquis fought only on the side that shared the fiery rebel's views on that heart-breaking, stupendous task of saving the border States of Mexico from the greed, and avarice, and unscrupulous hands of Americans who preyed upon the Mexican people. Such men as Wig Murphy, who bought stolen cattle and made slaves of the poor peons who worked in his mines.

'It has always been a battle of wits between your father,' Cap Harker told Tommy, 'and Pablo. No holds barred, either. Neither of 'em ever hollered.'

'Pablo give me the Two Block outfit,' said Pat Roper. 'Why?'

'You saved his life once, so he told me. On the other

hand, he wanted an honest man here. He wanted a man who would wipe out Jim Boudry and his smugglers. And he wanted a man who wasn't scared of Wig Murphy. A man that Wig Murphy could neither buy nor bluff out. Boudry had gotten plumb outa Pablo's control. He and the others like him has bin smugglin' guns to anybody down there that'd pay for 'em. And they was bringin' back opium and other drugs. And Boudry was stealin' plenty of Two Block cattle. Not knowin' that Pablo owned the layout, he makes Pablo an offer to supply his Yaqui army with Two Block and Flyin' W beef. And while Pablo don't have no objection to buyin' Murphy beef, he draws the line at payin' out good money for cattle that's already his. He decides it's time to cut down Jim Boudry. But he can't do her without help from this side. So he turns over the Two Block to you. And he gets word to me that it's Pat Roper that's took over the ranch, and asks me to look you over and see if yo're on the level. So I cut my string loose from Boudry's layout. He and Bender foller me, thinkin' I'm yaller and aim to tell the law about how they're workin' and about Bender murderin' a detective. You seen the result of that, Pat.

'Knowin' this sheriff ain't any too bright, I don't dast risk that coroner's inquest. I leave Pat holdin' the muddy end of the stick while I ride down to have her out with Pablo. Bettin' that you'll take the rap fer killin' Bender, and likewise bettin' that you'll pay back them five hundred head of steers you run off the lower Concho, I tells Pablo that Pat Roper is more on the level than he figgered. That you aim to wipe your slate clean. And that I'm backin' your play.

'I expected Pablo to blow up. Not so. He smiles like he is pleased. "It is very good, Señor Cap," says he, "to know that here is an honest Americano in the cow business. Even if it should cost Pablo Guerrero much money, and gives the Señor Wig Murphy the big laugh on me, I am very glad to find the honest man. I feel like that Señor Diogenes who went about with a lantern, seeking for himself one honest hombre. I have often wondered, Señor Cap," says Pablo, smilin' wider, "if that hombre Diogenes was, like me, a rebel who wished to find the honest hombre to put in for governor, perhaps, or for El Presidente. I bet you something that thees Señor Diogenes has something up the sleeve, no?"

'So,' finished Captain Harker, 'when I find how Pablo feels, I ride back to have a medicine talk with Wig Murphy and Pat Roper. With the help of the Two Block men, and Murphy's men, I kin round up the Jim Boudry outfit and the others that are holed up on the border. Then this town sheriff goes hawg wild, and here we are.

'Here we are, up on top of Big Granite. And because we got a hard lot of work tomorrow and for the next several days, I'm turnin' in. You young folks kin set here and count the stars.' The old ranger got to his feet a little stiffly. He smiled at Tommy and Pat.

'In case the subject comes up some way,' he said, before he moved away, 'don't think that you ain't 'titled to the full ownership of the Two Block spread. Pablo ain't any Injun giver. He meant it. And by the time you help me clean up this smugglin' gang, you'll have earned it, son. With you ownin' the lay, and your men ridin' the line, cooperatin' with the border officials, the border patrol will be able to take their first easy breath in several years. This Two Block spread is worth money. If I was your age, and fixed like you are, and found the right kind of a girl, I'd marry her just as fast as I could find a preacher. Well, good night, young uns.'

And Captain Seth Harker of the rangers took great pains to make sufficient noise so that the man and the girl beside the fire would know that he had bedded down far beyond earshot.

Pat Roper broke a long silence. 'What do you think, Tommy, about what Cap'n Seth Harker said?'

'He has a lot of good, hard sense, hasn't he? I think he's just splendid, Pat. Where is the nearest preacher, do you suppose?'

'You mean, Tommy, that you'd marry a bone-headed cowpuncher?'

'Do you think for one part of a minute, Pat Roper, that I would marry any other kind of a man? This is my country, my kind of a life. I belong here, not in a city. My dad's a cowman. My husband will be a cowman.'

'But you've bin away to school, and you'd be ashamed of me.'

97

'Do you think an education can change the fact that my mother was a waitress in a restaurant when Dad found her and married her? Do you think, Pat Roper, that skimming through a few school books would ever make me forget that I was born and raised on a cow ranch? The same ranch where Wig Murphy punched cows and his wife cooked for a crew of men. The same ranch where I learned to ride, and rope, and cook, and mend Dad's socks. Gosh, Pat, if I married some city dude, Dad would kick us both out! And it would bust his old pirate's heart to think I'd quit the Flying W for the best city in the world. Anyhow, I haven't been at that trick school where he sent me. I got expelled for being a rowdy. So I went into training at a big hospital where I scrubbed floors and worked harder than I ever again expect to labour. And Dad was actually tickled when he found out that it was a nurse's diploma, not the fancy pigskin from that la-de-da finishing school, that I lugged home from the East. I'm just a little roughneck. Just an unvarnished splinter off the unpolished Wig Murphy block. And now that I've done most of the proposing, I'll play my string out. Will you marry me, Pat Roper?'

'Will I? Gosh!' And that, as Tommy whispered softly, some minutes later, settled that question.

Chapter XVII

Five hundred head of Two Block steers passed through the wide gateway that separated the Two Block range from the Flying W domain. One side of the gate sat a dust-covered girl in cowpuncher clothes. Her black horse was sweat-streaked, and his sleek coat powdered white with dust. As the big steers crowded through the gate, she tallied them. For each count of a hundred, she tied a knot in her bridle reins, until the last steer had passed through and a fifth knot was added.

'Five hundred!' she sang out.

'Five hundred!' checked Sid Collins, who sat his dun pony on the opposite side of the gate.

Panhandle rode up, grinning. 'Where's Wig Murphy and Billy Carter?' he asked. 'They was to be here to receive these steers.'

'And Pat Roper was to deliver them,' said Tommy gravely, 'but he didn't show up. But I'm the Flying W rep, and my pardner Sid Collins represents the Two Block outfit, so if you'll take our tally and checked tally, I reckon everybody will be happy. Are you Panhandle?'

'You read my brand correct, ma'am. And I'm plumb satisfied to take your tally. And I'd like to say that two old hands couldn't've done a neater job of tallyin'. Them steers is boogery and if you hadn't stayed back a-ways as we poured 'em through that gate, them leaders would've turned back and we'd've had to fight 'em half a day. You and Sid has real cow sense.'

'We should know something by now about cattle,' smiled Tommy. 'But where is Pat Roper?'

'I wish I knowed, lady. He stopped at camp night before last, him and a little bow-legged gent. They stayed about long enough to change horses, swaller their grub whole, and then they drug it, headed southward. Mysterious as two Injuns plottin' agin' the whites.'

'Did Pat leave orders for you to drift south with your boys?' asked Tommy.

'He did. Said to meet him at the drift fence gate on the lower Concho, soon as I'd tallied over these cattle to Wig Murphy. And we was to wear our fightin' clothes. Mebbyso Pat's gone loco.'

'Dad pulled out at daybreak,' frowned Tommy, 'with a Winchester across his saddle. He fired poor Billy Carter last night. And he wouldn't say where he was going this morning. But from the way he lit into me at supper last night, I'd make a guess that he's started out to kill Pat Roper.'

'He's laid out a hard job for hisself, ma'am. Pat is hard to kill. What put Wig on the prod, anyhow?'

'I told him that I was going to marry Pat.'

'Howlin' hyenas! You don't say!'

'He fired Billy for taking my part. I don't know when I've seen Dad so ringy. He was in a bad humour when he got back from Phoenix. And when I broke it to him that Pat Roper and I were going to get married, he pawed dirt for sure. And if he'd stayed half an hour longer, I know he'd have thrown a big fit. Because some good judges of horseflesh cut the horse pasture fence in a dozen places and stole the remuda.'

'You ain't got a thing on us, lady,' said Panhandle grimly. 'Our Mex horse jingler that's night hawkin' the horse cavvy didn't show up this mornin'. Neither did the cavvy. The Two Block outfit is plumb afoot except for what horses we're forkin'. And Pat expects us to be there to meet him by sun-down. We'll be lucky to make it by tomorrow at daybreak on these leg weary mounts. I've just about come to the odd conclusion, ma'am, that our Mex night-hawk ain't honest. And if us boys expect to make it at all, we better be startin'. *Adios,* lady.'

Tommy read the bitter chagrin behind Panhandle's banter. And she felt alarmed at this wholesale horse rustling. The horse thieves could not hope to sell the Two Block and Flying W remudas. It had been a bold move on the part of Jim Boudry's outfit to set the Two Block and

Flying W men afoot so that they could not reach the border in time to aid the handful of men who hoped to wipe out the border smugglers. Captain Seth Harker, Pat Roper, Jake Quinn, Billy Carter, and a few men of the border patrol would be easy pickings for the Jim Boudry killers.

Tommy's voice halted Panhandle. 'Wait! Wait a minute!'

She caught up with the Two Block riders. 'My horse is fresh, Panhandle. And so is that tough little horse of Sid's. You and one of your lighter men take our horses. And perhaps you'll get there in time to fight Jim Boudry's outlaws.'

'You know what's up, then?' asked Panhandle, swinging to the ground and unsaddling.

'Of course. Captain Seth Harker told me himself.' Tommy pulled the saddle from her beautiful black gelding.

'Miss Murphy, yo're a real guy!' grinned Panhandle. A small man with a scar across one cheek was changing horses with Sid. Sid tried to grin gamely as he now gave up his chance to see that fight on the border.

Panhandle mounted, and the little man was already on Sid's dun.

'Ride 'em like you owned 'em!' called Tommy bravely.

And when the girl and the boy were alone, Tommy put her arm around Sid's shoulder.

'It's hard lines, little pardner. But we're doing more good this way, aren't we, old-timer?'

Sid nodded. He and Tommy had planned to slip away from the ranch and watch the fight. Dejectedly, they saddled the weary-legged horses left them.

Then they rode slowly back to the ranch that was vacated except for Taller, the cook. Below the horse pasture, at the Two Block round-up camp, a crowd of long-faced cowboys swore at the bad luck that had sent them afoot. And there is nothing so comically pathetic as a cowpuncher without a horse to ride.

Suddenly one of them gave a shout. A large group of horsemen were coming from over toward Big Granite. The last of the sheriff's posse, heading for town.

'Here,' said the Flying W cowpuncher who had taken Billy Carter's job as boss, 'is where we set somebody afoot. Either gently, or some other way, we'll take ourselves some good, stout, fresh grain-fed horses. We'll ask 'em to eat. Them posse gents is always hungry when they get out here in the wide-open spaces. Pick your ponies, boys, and I'll fire the man that cain't get a horse. Cowboys, don't tell me this ain't Christmas!'

The sheriff and his men rode up to the round-up camp. The law officer eagerly sniffed the air, which was flavoured with savoury odours of good beef and fresh bread and strong coffee.

'My mess wagon has gone on ahead,' he told the boss, 'and we're almighty hungry.'

'Light,' invited the Flying W round-up boss, 'and look at your saddles. The cook will take the wrinkles outa yore bellies.'

The possemen followed their leader into the spacious mess tent. Their own chuck wagon had gone ahead yesterday, and they had no breakfast except cold bread and bacon. The Flying W cook whistled loudly as he clattered tin dishes in the dishpan. The members of the posse filed past the stove, heaping their plates with good grub, filling pint cups to the brim with steaming black round-up coffee. The odour of food put them in a festive mood, and the tent was filled with their chatter.

Some ten or fifteen minutes later the sheriff emerged from the tent. A cry of dismay broke from him. The horses they had ridden were gone. Gone also were the Flying W cowpunchers.

Only two or three horses remained outside the tent. The sheriff, his face suffused with rage, mounted in clumsy haste and started out. The rest of the posse, after a first burst of profanity, finished their breakfast and lighted up their tobacco.

'Our pay runs on,' grinned one of the crowd, 'till we get back to town. Boys, we'll never earn our money any easier than this.'

In half an hour or so, the irate sheriff caught up with the Flying W cowboys.

'Halt, you horse thieves! Turn back from here with them stolen animals!'

'Boys,' said the round-up boss, cupping a hand to his ear, 'did I hear a whiffletree bird a-callin'?'

'I think you heard a sidehill gouger whinin',' said

another cowboy, as they all completely ignored the presence of the wrathy sheriff in their midst.

'Me, I'd've swore it was a pup wowser huntin' its mammy.'

'Yo're all wrong, Bob, this ain't the season for young wowsers. I'll bet a hat it was a spade-tailed mucket, lost. Them spade-tailed muckets go blind for two weeks durin' this season of the year, and they roam about makin' odd noises. You heard a mucket, that's what you heard.'

'Looky here, you men,' blurted the sheriff, 'a joke's a joke, but this has gone far enough. Fetch back them horses and I won't prefer no charges!'

'That wa'n't no spade-tailed mucket,' chirped a cowboy. 'This is too far south for muckets. Boys, that's nothin' less than a specimen of the rare and shy-mannered, red-eyed, nickerin' wumble. A wumble is a cross between a vinegaroan and a Argentine goadafrow. They run backward up all the hills and make strange sounds by scrapin' their hocks together. What you heard was none other than a cowhocked wumble. Noisy when they're cuttin' their tusks, but plumb harmless and gentle as a baby. When they want somethin' that they can't have, they nicker.'

'Do you reckon it'll foller us plumb to the border? It might get hit by a stray bullet when we jump out Jim Boudry's gang.'

'We might be able to swap it off to a Mexican for a bottle of tequila. Don't drive it back, boys. Humour the pore thing. It never had no daddy nor no mammy. Let it foller along. Now, if we only had some of them five-cent election seegars to feed it, it would be plumb content. It plays pool and seven-up for its amusement, eats at lunch counters, and exterminates blind pigs. Thrives good in pool halls and card rooms, but is apt to go kinda queer if it gets exposed to the sun.'

It had been a bitter week for the town-bred sheriff. Captain Seth Harker had, in a few short sentences, humbled the blundering officer. There would be a caustic letter from the big detective agency awaiting his return to town. Now these reckless, carefree cowboys were openly taunting him. They had set his men afoot, and now they ignored him and his badge of office. It was humiliating. It was a bitter dose to swallow. He forced a sickly grin.

'You win, boys! This is a horse on me. Have all the fun you want, but I'm comin' along. Try to stop me, and somebody will get hurt.'

'When the cow-hocked wumble nickers, boys, it's a sign of winter comin' on. Shall we let it foller us?'

'Why not? We need a mascot. Them Two Block gents will shore be jealous when they see what we picked up. And in case we get Jim Boudry alive, we'll neck the two of 'em together. And some time before New Years, the wumble will come trailin' into town, sniffin' the air to ketch the scent of moonshine likker, his ears pricked up to ketch the click of pool balls bein' racked up. An necked to him will be Boudry. There's times when a well-trained wumble is shore worth his keep. Hit a lope, you under-paid cow servants. We got a hen on a-settin'.'

Chapter XVIII

Growling to himself, Wig Murphy rode hard for the lower
Concho. Between his teeth was clenched a black pipe that
had been cold for two hours.

'Pablo calls for the big pay-off, does he?' Wig mused in
a muttered undertone, as he recalled a most unsatisfactory
hour in the office of Señor Arturo Gonzales, attorney-at-
law, in Phoenix. The smooth-tongued lawyer had named a
sum of money, a certain place where that money was to be
paid, and the name of the man who was to receive that
money.

'I would suggest twenty-five thousand dollars, Señor
Murphy. To be paid in currency at the gate in the drift
fence on the lower Concho. My client, Señor Pablo Guerrero, will be there in person to receive the money. This
money is payment for the delivery of five hundred head of
Flying W steers that strayed across the border into Mexico,
some time ago. My client informs me that revolutionary
activities are at a standstill. There being a lull, he and his
men have done you the favour of gathering those strayed
beef cattle and will deliver them on the lower Concho. Fifty dollars per head is a reasonable price. They are easily
worth a hundred dollars per head at present market
values. As my client explains, he might easily sell them
elsewhere for a hundred dollars per head. But because of
old ties of friendship between you and himself, he would
rather take a twenty-five-thousand-dollar loss on the cattle
to do his old friend Wig Murphy a good turn. A generous
man, Pablo Guerrero.'

'A rascal and a thief, you mean. This is blackmail, Gonzales.'

The Señor Arturo Gonzales shrugged and smiled. 'An ugly name, Señor Murphy. And a poor attitude for you to assume in the matter. You need not accept the cattle. There is nothing compulsory about it. Mexico offers some ready markets for those same cattle. Shall I get word to my client that he need not make the delivery?'

'Do nothing of the kind, you oily crook. I want them steers. I'll be there to accept delivery on 'em. And I'll be prepared to pay off Pablo Guerrero in full.'

'Splendid, señor. You are a man of discriminating judgement.' Señor Arturo Gonzales rose and bowed formally. Wig turned and stalked to the door. His hand on the polished brass door-knob, he turned.

'What about them five hundred head of Two Block steers that Pablo's slick pardner, Pat Roper, is deliverin' to me. I'd like to know what's the price on them?'

'That,' smiled the attorney, 'is for the Señor Pat Roper to decide. Pablo has nothing to do with the Two Block herd.'

'Horse radish!' snorted Wig Murphy.

'As you wish señor.' He bowed again. '*Adios,* Señor Murphy.'

Again Wig Murphy snorted. The door banged behind him. There came a tinkling of glass as the frosted upper half of the door, neatly lettered in gold leaf, shattered from the impact. Without a backward glance, the old cattleman strode on down the hall, glaring straight ahead.

Inside his ornate office that carried the faint, yet pungent odour of jasmine, Señor Arturo Gonzales leaned back in his beautiful red-leather chair. He pressed a button on his mahogany desk, and a rather frightened-looking Mexican youth, followed by a frightened-looking but very beautiful Mexican stenographer, entered.

'Manuel, order a new glass for the door and send the bill to Señor Wig Murphy at the Flying W Rancho. But first bring a sliced lemon, some salt, and a bottle of cooled tequila and put the tray in the inside office. Also a box of Corona cigars and a box of the perfumed cigarettes favoured by the señorita.

106

'And you, my *muy chiquita* Señorita Rosita, wipe the fright from your eyes. The barbarian has gone. You will take a letter and then we shall declare a holiday.'

The very beautiful señorita followed her smiling employer into the inner office. The tray with the tequila was placed on the desk there. When the Señor Arturo Gonzales had tossed off a generous drink, followed by a pinch of salt, and a bite of sliced lemon, and when his cigar was going, and after the dark-eyed secretary had lit her perfumed cigarette, he brushed an imaginary speck of ash from his Bond Street tailored coat, inspected his highly manicured fingernails, and nodded.

'The letter is to Señor Pablo Guerrero, and is to be put into code as usual. Say to our dear friend Pablo that the gringo barbarian has called. Say that he will be there at the gate on the lower Concho to receive the cattle and pay for them the sum of twenty-five thousand dollars.'

Señor Arturo Gonzales paused, blowing a smoke ring, smiling softly as he watched it drift upward.

The beautiful secretary paused, pencil poised above her pad.

'That is all señor?'

'That is all, *si*. That is all for the Señor Pablo Guerrero.' He took one of her hands in both his rather plump and soft-looking ones. His eyes glittered brightly and his thick lips smiled silkily.

'That is all for our war-making *amigo*. And unless I judged our big barbarian wrongly, it will be the total and very final end of our troublesome rebel. But for you, *chiquita,* and me, it marks the beginning of glorious adventure. In the bank, not to the credit of Pablos Guerrero, but in the name of Arturo Gonzales, is half a million dollars. Would it not be a crime, *chiquita,* to waste that lovely money buying guns and bullets for unwashed Yaquis to kill our countrymen? Would it not be a more Christian thing to take that money and spend it on beautiful clothes and ocean trips to Paris and Vienna? Hah, my pretty one, you and I are not of the restless blood that thickens on revolutions. Me, I have no desire to face the Mexican firing squad or be shut up in a gringo prison. Tonight, *chiquita,* you and I leave on a late train that carries us to New York. I have arranged for a lovely cabin on the finest steamer. You and I shall put behind us such sordid things as revolutions and gringo barbarians who break doors. Tonight, you and I leave, no?'

'But your wife, señor?'

'Is fat and ugly and loves me no longer except for the money I give her. But you, *chiquita,* you are beautiful as a dream. In Paris I get the quick divorce, no? And you and I shall be married and live on the caviare and the champagne of the world. No more revolutions. No more tequila. And no more Pablo Guerrero. I drink to our honeymoon, *chiquita. Salud!*'

The very beautiful secretary's dark eyes promised much as she slowly withdrew her hand from his lips.

'I will need to pack, Señor Arturo.'

'Get the letter off to Pablo by messenger, first. Then go to your home and pack the few things you need until we can buy you the most beautiful clothes in New York. And till tonight, my *chiquita, adios.*'

Señorita Rosita de la Vaca smiled back at him as she closed the door behind her. She hastily put the letter in code, sealed it, and gave it to Manuel to deliver into the hands of a waiting messenger. Then she put on her chic little hat, slipped into a fragile but beautifully made jacket, and left the office of the Señor Arturo Gonzales for the last time.

On the street, she hailed a taxi and gave the driver an address on the edge of town. 'Make haste, please. Much haste!'

The taxi-driver grinned as she thrust a five-dollar tip into his hand. 'Hang on tight, lady! Because we're about to do some travellin'.'

Ten minutes later she dismissed the taxi at a modest little cottage surrounded by tall trees. When he had gone, the girl went up the cement walk to the front door. In answer to her ring, a middle-aged woman opened the door, beaming and murmuring extravagant compliments.

'Is any one home, Margarita?'

'*Si, señorita.* In the back room.'

'All friends, Margarita?'

'All friends of our Pablo, *chiquita.*'

'Ugh! Do not call me *"chiquita"* again ever! Take me to

the room where those friends sit, quick, as you love our patron, our Pablo, the brave one.'

The woman servant led her to a room that was heavy
with tobacco smoke. Five men stood up, bowing and
smiling.

'What news, señorita?'

'It is as I have warned you. Arturo Gonzales is a
traitor. He plans to run away, the coward. He will take the
money that belongs to Pablo. Pah! The oily pig would also
take me along instead of the good wife who has grown too
heavy to suit his delicate taste. But worse than that. He
sends our Pablo a letter that lies. The big gringo Murphy
plans to pay for his cattle, not with money, but in bullets.'

'*Diablo!* A trap, no?'

"*Si señors,* a trap. Set By Arturo Gonzales.'

'Arturo Gonzales does not suspect that you have come
here?'

'*Dios,* no! The vain pig thinks I love him. He offers me
fine clothes and champagne and caviare. Aye, even marriage. *Valgame Dios,* I prefer to wear rags and follow
Pablo Guerrero until death overtakes us both!'

'*Viva! Viva Rosita!*'

'And now, señors, I must find Pablo quickly. Have I
not earned the right to go to him I love? Have I not done
my work here until it is finished?'

'You wish to go to Pablo, señorita?'

'Even as I wish someday to find heaven, *si, señors!*'

'Then you shall go, little patriot. By the fastest
automobile in Arizona. Then, by the fastest horse.'

'What of Arturo Gonzales, señors? Does he escape
punishment?'

'Arturo Gonzales shall be attended to, comrade.'

' '*Sta bueno, señors.* I thank you.'

A tall, white-haired man of military bearing filled the
empty glasses.

'Drink, compadres,' he said, in the crisp voice of a man
accustomed to giving commands, 'drink to the Señorita
Rosita de la Vaca! Empty your glasses to a true daughter
of old Mexico. *Salud!*'

'*Salud y pesetas!*' Heath and money, the toast meant.
'*Salud!*'

109

'*Y amor,*' added a younger patriot. For what are health and money without love?

'*Y amor!*' came the chorus of men's voices, and they drained their glasses.

Chapter XIX

Even as Wig Murphy alighted from the Phoenix train, and started for the Flying W ranch, Señor Arturo Gonzales lay sprawled in his red-leather chair, the hilt of a knife protruding from his ribs. And Rosita de la Vaca was racing toward the Mexican border to warn Pablo Guerrero against his gringo enemy.

When Tommy told her father that she planned to marry Pat Roper, the old border buccaneer was stunned for a moment. Then, with words more forceful than wise, the grim-lipped old cowman denounced Pat Roper in no uncertain terms. This happened at supper-time, as Tommy, Billy Carter, and old Wig were finishing their meal.

'Gonna marry Pat Roper, huh? Not while I kin line a pair of rifle sights, you won't marry that dirty thief. Think I'm gonna let my own daughter make me the laughin'-stock of Arizona? Think I'm gonna let that *paisano* lover slip over a trick like that! Roper don't give two hoots for you. He's fooled you with his good-lookin' face and his slick talk. He's after my money and the Flyin' W Ranch. And he's bin bought by Pablo Guerrero, body and soul. Pablo put him over on the Two Block in order to smash me. The low lived coward hits at me through my daughter. I'll kill Pat Roper on sight. I'll shoot him down where I find him. The same as I'm killin' Pablo Guerrero.'

'You got your shirt on backward, Wig,' said Billy Carter. 'I had a talk with Captin Seth Harker about Pat Roper. Seth Harker says—'

'So that's it, huh?' Wig shook his fist at Billy. 'You had a talk with Seth Harker, did you? Why, you spineless, brainless young coot, don't you know that Harker's the man that swore he'd break me of handlin' wet cattle? Are

111

you so blind that you can't see Seth Harker's game? You bone-head! You sheep-brained bone-head! You yellow dog! Get! Right now! Get off my ranch, or I'll run you off! I'll take the doubled end of a hard twist rope and I'll whip you plumb outa the country! Get!'

White-lipped, shaking with suppressed rage, Billy Carter pushed back his chair.

'I'm a-goin', Wig. And I ain't ever comin' back. I've worked for you, lied for you, stole for you, and took your abuse. But I'm through now. Only for Tommy, I'd see who was the best man. On her account, I let you call me a yellow dog and get away with it. So long, Tommy! I hope you and Pat will shore be happy. Whenever you need me, holler.'

'Thanks, Billy. You're a brick.'

'Yeah,' snorted Wig Murphy, 'a brick. Yellow mud makes the best kind of bricks. Drag it, Carter!'

When Billy had gone, Tommy faced her irate father. She was a little pale, her nerves taut as fiddle-strings, her heart pounding with anger.

'You've fired the best man that ever drew wages here, Dad. You fired him without giving him a chance to explain anything. But you can't fire me. And you can't bluff me, either. I will marry Pat Roper, and you can't stop me.'

'Go to your room, young lady. And stay there, understand? I'll tend to you when I settle with Pablo Guerrero and his gringo pardner. And if Seth Harker horns into the game, I'll settle with him.'

Old Wig Murphy walked the floor until dawn. Then he saddled up and pulled out. A grim-mouthed, bitter, old bull of a man, rumbling profane challenge to any and all men who sought to humble him; alone, unafraid, dangerous, and a little pathetic, with a Winchester across his saddle and a glint of battle flickering in his eyes, seeking trouble at the end of a smoking gun. A king whose crown was a battered Stetson, a despot whose sceptre was a blue-barrelled .45. Without a single man to follow him, he rode alone, carrying the fight to his enemies. Unbeaten by disaster, a splendid old pirate on horseback, he rode to battle.

Old Wig Murphy's head lifted. A shaggy, white-maned head. His eyes swept the hills and mesas. As far as the eye

112

could see, the land belonged to him. The thousands of cattle that grazed there were his. He had come here with a good horse, a stout rope, and a running iron. What he owned, the land and cattle that stocked the range, all were his by the right of conquest. He laid no claim to virtue or honesty. Let men say of Wig Murphy that he was a cow thief, a trader in stolen cattle, a ruthless buccaneer. But no man could call him coward or weakling.

A grim smile crept across his lips. Pride lighted the smouldering sparks in his eyes that looked from under shaggy brows. Let the enemies of Wig Murphy beware! No man could steal his cattle and his daughter and escape punishment.

Tommy! The pride of his lawless life. She had never before deserted him. Right or wrong, she had stayed by him, staunch, loyal, unquestioning. Would she quit him now? When he had killed Pat Roper, would this daughter of his own fighting blood turn away from him? That would be the only thing this side of death that could break the old cattleman. And now, as he rode into the sunrise, he told himself that his enemies were using her as a weapon to smash him. Pablo, the cunning fox, was striking at him through his daughter.

Wig rode down into a dry wash. On either side were huge boulders and patches of brush. Beyond, to the southeast, was the lower Concho.

The crash of a rifle filled the dry wash with the confused echoes. Old Wig swayed drunkenly in his saddle as his horse reared, leaped sideways, then lunged forward. The old cowman toppled sideways, fell heavily to the rocky ground, and lay in an awkward heap, motionless as the rocks that cradled his still form.

A man high up on the hillside jerked the lever of his Winchester, ejecting a smoking .30-40 shell. He stood up, trying to locate Wig Murphy's body among the rocks below. But the granite boulders blocked the view. A leering grin spread across the face of the bushwhacker. 'That pays you off in full, Wig.' And Jim Boudry knocked the ashes from his pipe. He mounted his horse and rode off, pushing hard for the rough hills beyond the drift fence, there to join his men.

Boudry skirted the spot where Pat Roper, Seth Harker,

and Jake Quinn were camped on the lower Concho. Nor did the bushwhacker make his presence known to Billy Carter, who sat his horse on a ridge that overlooked the ranger camp, his anxious eyes watching for the coming of the Flying W cowboys.

'You make a sweet target, you,' snarled Boudry, 'and I've a mind to knock you over! But them others would hear the sound of the shot. Look at the dummy, waitin' for his cowboys to come! And them afoot back on their own range, the same as them Two Block waddies! You'll all get your fill of fightin' this evenin', gents. So *adios* till then, hombres.'

Spurring his horse to a lope, Jim Boudry shoved on toward the hills that jutted against the blue sky.

Chapter XX

It was some hours later when the Flying W men, riding single file down the dry wash, found old Wig Murphy, sitting in a crumpled heap, swearing slowly as he made crude attempts to stop the flow of red that came from a smashed collar bone.

'Who done it, Wig?' asked the new boss, as he began bandaging the ugly wound.

'How do I know?' growled old Wig. 'Git her tied up, then fetch me my hoss! And I'll make out to settle with that bushwhackin' hombre. His shot jarred me loose from my saddle. Musta hit my head on a rock. Jerk that bandage tight! Then see where my Winchester fell! I'm gonna need it before dark.'

'Where'd the shot come from, Wig?'

'Up yonder in them rocks.'

One of the cowpunchers rode up there. He came back down as Wig mounted painfully. 'Whoever he was, he smokes a pipe and runs his boot heels over. And he uses a .30-40 gun,' the puncher reported.

'Smokes a pipe, huh?'

'Pipe ashes up there. And his boot tracks shows plain.'

'Then it wa'n't Pat Roper.' Wig's tone was tinged with disappointment as he stared up at the rocks. 'Was them tracks big uns?'

'They shore was, Wig.'

'Jim Boudry has big feet. His boots is run over at the heels. And he smokes a pipe. And his gun is a box magazine .30-40 carbine that he bought off Billy Carter last year.' Old Wig started off at a trot that jarred his injured collar bone and made him grit his teeth.

'Say,' he growled, 'what fetched you boys down here, anyhow? And where did you git them hosses?'

'Billy stopped at camp last night and left orders for us to meet him at that gate on the lower Concho.'

'He did. Well, he had a nerve! Billy Carter is fired. What did he want you here for? To receive them cattle, I suppose?'

'He never said. Just told us to fetch our saddle guns and plenty ammunition. And to get an early start. But somebody run off the remuda durin' the night. We borrowed these geldin's from the sheriff. Say, what's become of our John Law, anyhow?'

'He stopped back yonder to fix his saddle blanket. Here he comes.'

The sheriff, his face red and dripping with perspiration, came up.

'Murphy,' he exploded, 'your men stole these horses from my posse. Make 'em return what they stole, or there'll be trouble.'

'What was your posse a-doin' while my men was taking their hossflesh?'

'They was at breakfast at your round-up camp. I demand the return of these mounts.'

'Yeh?' A faint grin spread across old Wig's tight lips. His men were grinning widely.

'I represent the law, don't forget it, Murphy!'

'What law?' asked old Wig.

'Arizona law, of course. I'm sheriff of this county.'

'Come to think back on it, you are the sheriff, ain't you? I was thinkin' that you still run the Smoke House pool hall and seegar store. I recollect now, the miners elected you while we was all out on the round-up. You busted up old Pinal Jones' whisky still. He made the best corn likker in the country. The stuff I get now ain't near as potent. See them ridges on all sides of us, sheriff? As far as you kin see with a naked eye? Well, that is my boundaries. This is my land. The laws we go by here on the Flyin' W range is all made and enforced by ol' Wig Murphy. See me about these hosses some time next week. This is my busy day. Come on, boys!'

'Shall we let this John Law trail with us, Wig?'

'Shore thing, if he's a mind to, and if he won't get in the

116

way. But he comes at his own risk. This ain't any whiskey-still raidin' party.'

'What is it, then?' snapped the sheriff in an irritated tone.

'It's a war. A war that'll make the Pleasant Valley fracas look like a Sunday-school picnic. Foller me, you Flyin' W cowboys! Foller old Wig Murphy, the daddy of all the he-wolves of the Mexican border! Foller me, you jerky-eatin', likker-drinkin', fun-th'owin' sons!'

'We're right at yore back, Wig, Lead us to it!' And with a wild whoop they followed the daddy of all the he-wolves of the border. Not knowing what dangers lay over the ridge. Not caring. Where Wig Murphy had the courage to go, they did not lack the nerve to follow. For such were the hand-picked crew that drew Flying W wages. Reckless, careless, danger-loving sons of the border country. Making up in courage and loyalty what they lacked in honesty and discretion. Rough of habit, careless of tongue, hard riding, fast shooting, uncomplaining. Hard men with love of adventure in their hearts that never grew old. Asking no compromise, no favours. Snatching at fun from their saddles; grinning into the black eyes of death, riding their way at a gallop; eager where other men might have cause to be timid, with the word of their boss their only law. Men of a vanishing breed. Cowpunchers.

Such was the crew that rode with old Wig Murphy to the drift-fence gate on the lower Concho.

Cattle, gaunt-flanked and showing signs of the long trail out of Mexico, grazed hungrily on the green banks of the lower Concho. The two or three Mexican or Yaqui vaqueros on day herd sat their horses lazily, dark faces shaded by huge sombreros, shabby leather chaps and jumpers looking the shabbier for the gay-coloured serapes flung across the riders' shoulders. Flat-horned, silver-crusted saddles, rawhide reatas, huge-rowelled spurs that chimed like bells.

One of the Mexicans, his weight in one wide, wooden stirrup, strummed a guitar that was slung across his straight shoulders by a faded, red ribbon. His rich voice sang a plantive love song:

'Adios, adios, amores! Adios, porque me ausento—'

117

Singing of love on the evening before death might come, riding lazily around the grazing cattle; a guitar in his slim hands, guns slung to his wide belts; putting off death until tomorrow, dreaming of love in the sunset!

'Where's your patron, hombre?' inquired Wig Murphy. 'Where is Pablo Guerrero?'

The Mexican waved his cigarette toward a sycamore grove down the river. 'At the camp, señor.'

'Come on, boys.' Wig rode ahead of them. He expected to be halted by Pablo's Yaquis. Instead, he found Pablo squatting on his spurred boot heels, picking a guitar and singing softly to a very beautiful señorita dressed in riding clothes. He laid aside the guitar and got to his feet, sweeping off his silver-crusted sombrero with a magnificent gesture.

'Señor Murphy! Caballeros!' His white teeth flashed a quick smile.

Wig Murphy's six-shooter was in his hand. He scowled at Pablo, ignoring the girl, even as Pablo chose to ignore the cowman's drawn weapon.

'I was expect' you, señor. Please to get down and rest. There ees a red bandage on the shoulder. You are hurt, no?'

'I kin still use a gun, Pablo,' said the cattleman significantly.

'Si, señor. To be sure. And weeth you, you breeng the firing squad, no? And even the sheriff of the United States law ees also present.' He tuined to the girl, whose dark eyes were wide with fear.

'Do I not say to you, my bonita, that the Señor Murphy ees a smart man? That only thees muy maldito Arturo Gonzales ees fool them weeth evil lies, no? That Arturo Gonzales ees jealous because the Señor Murphy and your own Pablo are the good friends. Muy simpatico.'

'Friends, huh?' growled old Wig Murphy. 'What kind of sucker do you think I am, anyhow? You rob me, then expect me to smile all over and say I like it. Muy simpatico, huh? You've blackmailed me for the last time, Pablo. Pull your gun!'

With a quick cry, Rosita was between them, her slim form shielding the man she loved. Pablo smiled over her shoulder at the scowling cowman.

'You see, señor, how eet ees. Besides, I am unarm'. Always, when I sing the love songs, I remove the gons— Permit me, señor, to present the Señorita Rosita de la Vaca who, by the kind generosity of the *Señor Dios,* shall be the wife of Pablo Guerrero. *Bonito mio,* this is my old amigo, Señor Murphy.'

Whatever reply Wig was about to make died unspoken behind his grim lips. From the distance came the sound of rifle shots. Every man there stiffened in his saddle. Pablo stepped to the limb of a nearby sycamore where his two wide cartridge belts hung, with their white-handled guns.

'Your friends, Señor Murphy, and my friends, are in danger. That *maldito* hombre, Jeem Boudry, has begun the attack. Four, perhaps, five of our brave compadres are defending themselves against a hundred of the thrice-cursed Boudry's wolves. Pronto, señor. Make haste.'

Pablo turned to the girl. 'My Yaquis who are in camp across the border will offer you their protection, *querida.* Wait there for me. If I do not come, this is *adios.*' Gravely, he bent and kissed her hand. Rosita's dark eyes brimmed with tears as she threw her arms about him and kissed his mouth fiercely.

'May the *Señor Dios* protect you, my own Pablo. May our Lady of Sorrows intercede for me, and send you back to me. *Adios,* my brave one.'

'Hold on, Pablo,' said Wig suspiciously. 'What kind of game is this, anyhow?'

'My friend,' said Pablo dramatically, 'I play no trick. By the soul of my sainted mother, I swear it. Today, tonight, and perhaps tomorrow, you and I shall fight side by side. If you doubt me, señor, take this gun and kill me now!' He handed the cowman one of his white-handled weapons.

'You're a convincin' sort of cuss, Pablo. I know I'm a fool, but I believe you. If it's Jim Boudry we're fightin', let's go.'

With a gay laugh, Pablo was in his silver-crusted saddle. He waved his sombrero to the girl who watched.

'*Adios, querida!*' he called.

Side by side, Wig Murphy and Pablo Guerrero rode in the last slanting yellow of the setting sun.

'Who's the greaser?' asked the sheriff.

'That's no greaser, mister,' said the Flying W wagon boss, 'that's the bravest caballero in all Mexico. And when you've bin on this border as I have, you'll use the word "greaser" mighty careful.'

'He's got a slick-lookin' sweetheart, anyhow.'

'Which is nobody's business but Pablo's,' the cow-puncher rebuked him stiffly. 'It's bad luck to make personal cracks about a caballero's girl. They don't like it, any more than you'd like some Mexican to sound off about your wife or sister. Do you get the idea?'

'You ride down there and steal Mexican cattle,' said the sheriff, 'and do a lot of plain and fancy shootin', I don't see where you got any call to get huffy because I say that dame is good-lookin'.'

'Mister, if one of us boys was to insult a Mexican girl in any way, old Wig Murphy would just nacherally wipe up the corral with us. You wouldn't understand, even if I had time to explain it. You're just like these pick-swingin' bohunks and pool-room dudes that elected you. You don't know what it's all about. But you may learn a few things on this *pasear,* if a hard bullet don't stop you.

'Before you hit Arizona, this was cow country, and us boys was raised mighty careless along some lines. When we was kids, there wasn't much law, and what there was, was made by our dads who was cowmen. We ain't used to town laws, and there's times when town folks think we're a mighty hard lot. But you never yet had call to arrest a cowboy—a real cowboy—for insultin' a woman, kickin' a kid or a dog, or talkin' mean to old folks. We might steal a loose maverick or borrow a horse if we was afoot, but we never rolled a drunk man or grabbed a woman's purse. There's some cowboys that's doin' time for train robbin', but there ain't a one that's in the pen for takin' a widder woman's savin's by sellin' her worthless stocks and bonds.

'That's the way we was raised, mister. And we'll never learn them town tricks. When the towns begin to crowd us, we move on. We eat jerky instead of fried chicken. We get our water from the same water-holes where our horses drink, instead of turnin' on a brass faucet. Wrap a white collar around our neck and we look like a mule a-lookin' over a whitewashed fence. We don't belong in town, no more than you belong out here in the hills. Let us alone and we'll work out our troubles. Prod us with law poles and we're apt to show fight—'

And the sheriff scowled thoughtfully as he followed behind the crowd of joshing, grinning cowboys whose blued-steel guns belied their easy tolerance. Perhaps, in time, he would understand these sons of the cow ranges. But most likely he never would. Few strangers have ever been able to understand the heart of a cowpuncher. Because the cowboy hides a lot beneath that hard, rough exterior. And only those who really are given the gift of a rare insight can ever know.

Back from the crowd drifted the clear, soft voice of a cowboy singing a song. It was one of those plaintive, wistful, sad ballads, so dear to the cowboy's heart. The tune and the words came out of the gathering twilight:

'It was once in the saddle I used to go dashing,
    It was once in my saddle I used to be gay,
But first to drinking and then to card playing;
    Got shot in the breast, and I'm dying to-day.
Then swing your rope slowly and rattle yore spurs lowly,
    And give a wild whoop as you bear me along;
And in the grave throw me, and roll the sod o'er me,
    For I'm a wild cowboy, and I know I done wrong.'

Chapter XXI

Hemmed in a nest of boulders, four men were fighting desperately for their lives. Pat Roper and Seth Harker held one side of the natural granite fortress, while Billy Carter and Jake Quinn manned the other side. And from the brush and boulders on either side, a hundred rifles spattered soft-nosed bullets against the boulders.

'Wonder what's a-keepin' the Two Block boys,' said Pat, shoving cartridges into the magazine of his Winchester.

'Mebby they got into a poker game,' Billy flung back across his shoulder.

'And mebby them Flyin' W things you call cowboys has bogged down in their mess tent. They say you got a good cook, Billy. Now me, I never hire a cook that's too good. Them Texans of mine like good grub and if I was to feed 'em anything but beans and jerky and Dutch-oven bread, they'd get foundered. It don't take my hands long to eat dinner.'

'Best and fastest work I ever seen a bunch of cowhands do,' put in Cap Harker, 'was down in Chihuahua. We was gatherin' beef stuff in the Palomas country. That Terrasses herd. Rebels cleaned us outa grub. Pancho Villa's outfit, I reckon it was. Left us one sack of salt. We lived on mesquite beans an' beef straight. Had to wind up the work before the salt give out. And, cowboys, did we ride hard and far? Did we, Jake?'

'I'll tell a man we did, Seth! Stand any one of them cowboys agin' a strong light, and you could see plumb through him, end of that first week. Take a swaller of water and you could hear her splash in your stomach. That's why the mesquite tree ain't my favourite bush.

122

Rebel bullets went plumb through us without drawin' blood, we was that ga'nted up an' bloodless. Gittin' kinda bad light for linin' sights, ain't it?'

'Them Boudry snakes can't see no better than we kin, that's one consolation,' chuckled Cap Harker. 'See that hat a-stickin' up? Watch me knock the dust out of her.' His gun cracked and the hat vanished abruptly.

'Ol' Jim Boudry is a ornery soul,' sang Jake, 'send him to heaven with my ol' smoke pole.'

'Heaven, Jake?'

'Well, not exactly heaven, Pat, but somewhere beyond the Big River.'

Further talk was suspended as a crowd of dodging, shooting men charged the rocks. The four defenders drove them back in confusion. Cool-headed, making their shots tell, they scattered Boudry's men and sent them to cover. Jake Quinn yelled his defiance, taunting them. A steel-jacket bullet had sprayed his face with splinters that made his leathery face bleed in half a dozen places.

'I bet there's men among you yaller coyotes that'd hit a old man wearin' specs. Don't you know better'n to go shootin' keerless that a way? I'll have you all arrested for not packin' a huntin' licence. And unless you bone-headed dudes wanta get blowed up, shy away from Boudry. Cap Harker's got a bullet with Boudry's name on it. And Boudry's so full of bad booze that he'll explode shore, when he's hit. Come again, you coyotes, when you get over bein' so scairt. We'll git chilled, settin' here doin' nothing'. If we had a lantern, we'd start a game of seven-up, or old maid, or coon-can.'

Jake made up several uncomplimentary verses to his song about Jim Boudry and sang them in a loud, nasal tenor.

'There's no way of stoppin' that wild hombre,' grinned Seth. 'He's like that when he's fightin'. Some cusses, some prays, but Jake runs off at the head like a magpie.'

Darkness added to the danger. They dreaded that hour or two until moonrise. When a blot moved in the shadow, their guns spat orange flame. Boudry's circle of men were slowly closing on them. One concentrated rush, a few minutes of desperate, close battling and then—the four trapped men would die fighting.

123

Boudry had called to them that his men had run off the two remudas. He took great delight in telling how he had killed Wig Murphy. The others had to hold Billy Carter back. Billy, mad with grief, was for charging Boudry.

'Which is just what Boudry would like, son,' said old Seth Harker. 'And anyhow, he's probably lyin'.' But Boudry's ugly, triumphant voice had the tone of truth.

Now, beyond that closing circle of outlaws, came sounds of men on horseback. A big, bellowing voice hailed the trapped men from the darkness.

'Are you there, Billy Carter?' Wig Murphy alone could bellow so loudly.

'Here, Wig!' yelled Billy. A cheer went up from the four trapped men.

'*Vai, amigos!*' shouted Pablo Guerrero. '*Caballeros! Viva el combate! Cuidado malditos! Aviso, gringos!* Look out for Pablo Guerrero!'

With a wild, cowboy cheer, they charged the Boudry circle, scattering the outlaws, driving them to the shelter of higher ground, Wig Murphy loudly shouting orders to ride down the Boudry coyotes.

But Jim Boudry's men had not finished fighting. They ran, dodging up the sides of the barranca where horses could not follow. Their guns bit red streaks in the darkness. But in that blackness, no man could see. Jim Boudry called grim orders. His was an organized crew well schooled in bush fighting. It was a sniping game now, shooting at gun flashes. The night was filled with the echoes of gunfire, the screeching of ricocheting bullets. The shouts of men. Shouts of triumph, screams of pain. Every man for himself. To win or lose. To live or die. Kill or be killed.

It was too dark to tell friend from enemy. Two of Boudry's men, in the confusion, had shot one another down before they found out their mistake. To call out one's identity would be foolhardy. Nor could Wig Murphy, and Pablo, and the Flying W men, reach the boulders that barricaded the four men who were shooting only when they were positive that the bullet would not hit a friend. Between the rock barricade and Wig Murphy's men, Boudry had thrown the bulk of his warriors. Already drunk, they kept on drinking from the bottles each one car-

124

ried. There were some of the Boudry crew that preferred the Mexican drug called *marijuana* to whisky. Their crazy shouts marked them in the darkness. Their senses blurred, these drugged men would fight to the death.

Jim Boudry moved cautiously among his men. A slap on the back, a few whispered words of encouragement; a pint of whisky to one, a package of *marijuana* mixed with tobacco to another. And to a picked few, he whispered a brief order that was met with grinning, cunning nods. He moved on. And had some of his men been more sober and more sane, they might have taken alarm at the fact that, here and there along the line, a man slipped away into the darkness. These men were not drunk, nor were they drugged with the brain-maddening *marijuana*. They were fairly sober, cold-brained and cunning—cautious where their fellows were reckless. And they were the men favoured by Boudry with that brief order.

'Slip back to where we left the horses,' Jim Boudry had told these picked men. 'Wait for me there. Let these drunken fools fight till they drop. While they're swappin' bullets with the smart-minded sons that think they kin wipe us out, us boys will be travellin' yonderly.'

'Mexico, Jim?' asked one of the picked crew.

'With them Yaquis a-waitin'? Naw. We'll slip back up the Concho, cut acrost through the Flyin' W home ranch, where we'll start us a bonfire made outa Murphy's house, then cross over into New Mexico. These fools here won't miss us till daylight. With a twelve-hour start, they'll never ketch us. Them that gets in our way will get hurt. Now, slip back to where the horses are. I'll be there directly, when I get the rest of these hop-heads supplied so they'll do our fightin'.'

A keen observer might have rightly guessed that Jim Boudry had long ago figured out his way of retreat in case the fight went badly. Also, that the big outlaw leader had a definite object in choosing a route that led past the Flying W Ranch, where Tommy Murphy might be found unprotected but for an aged cook and Sid Collins.

It had been the booming voice of old Wig Murphy that broke Jim Boudry's nerve. Old Wig, who should be lying dead back on the trail! Boudry would have sworn that his bullet had finished the old pirate. He took Wig's ap-

125

pearance as an evil omen. Then there was Pablo Guerrero, who should be down in Mexico fighting a revolution. What was the wily Pablo doing here? Another bad omen. And the sudden arrival of the Flying W cowboys was queer. They should be back at their camp, without horses to ride. Jim Boudry was quick to smell disaster. He and a handful of picked men would slip away into the night. And when they reached the Flying W Ranch, he would take his revenge.

Boudry slipped along the line of drunken fighters. 'We're whippin' 'em, boys. Fight, you curly wolves! There ain't enough men in Arizona to make us quit. Smoke 'em outa their rocks, you tough gun-throwers. Sock it to 'em. There's plenty money a-waitin' when we win. And plenty *marijuana* and booze enough to go around to everyone when we slip into old Mexico. Fight, you hombres!'

And when the drug-crazed renegades were fighting with a recklesss insanity, Boudry joined the half-dozen picked gun fighters that awaited him. Saddle cinches were jerked tight. Single file, they rode into the night. Silent, thumbing the hammers of their guns, deserting their companions who fought on in the darkness.

Chapter XXII

Forking the finest horse in all Arizona, Panhandle, close
followed by the little Texan who had Sid's dun pony, rode
at a fast trot that ate up the long miles. They heard the firing of rifles in the distance and knew that the battle with
the outlaws was on with a vengeance. But the darkness
slowed them up and they were still some distance from the
scene of the fight when Panhandle suddenly pulled the
sweating black gelding to a halt.

'Somebody's comin',' he called to his companion in a
low tone. 'We'd better duck into the brush till we find out
who it is. By the sound they're a-makin', they're in a
hurry.'

Dismounting, they led their horses into the brush. They
were hardly hidden when Jim Boudry and his men came up
the trail. Boudry's rasping voice revealed his identity.

'We'll make the Flyin' W before daylight, boys. We'll
make that old pot-rassler git us a ham-and-egg breakfast,
and the Murphy girl will wait table. Old Wig has a keg of
good corn likker, too. From now on, you curly wolves, we
lead the life of Riley. And the best in the land ain't too
good—'

When they had ridden on, Panhandle and the Two
Block cowboy talked over the situation in low whispers.

'That little girl is in a tight place,' said Panhandle, 'and
here we are on leg-weary horses. While the chances are
good, Boudry and his men fork fresh horses. Our only bet
is this: You go down to where all this shootin' is goin' on.
I'll foller Boudry and his men. You get word to Wig Murphy, or Pat, or somebody, what's goin' on. Tell 'em to
come a-foggin'. And unless the black horse dies under me,
I'll keep them skunks worried till help comes, savvy? I

never throwed a leg over a better piece of horse meat than this black of Tommy Murphy's, and if I don't take it back to the Murphy ranch, it won't be because this black geldin' ain't game. Mebbyso it'll kill him, or if he does live, he may be plumb useless from this night on. But we gotta make it tough for Boudry and them drunk brutes that ride with him. There's a chance that our boys may run into Boudry, but it ain't likely, as they're comin' the other way on the chance of findin' our remuda and gittin' fresh mounts. But tell Pat that I'll hold 'em off as long as I kin pull a trigger. Now drag it, pardner. Good luck.'

'Good luck, Panhandle. You'll need a lot of it.'

Panhandle grinned in the dark and patted the black's neck. He swung into the saddle and rode after Boudry and his renegades. The splendid black horse swung his head impatiently. He would travel without the touch of a spur until his game heart quit beating. And he would give his rider nothing less than the best that was in him. Behind his sire and the race mare that was his mother was a heritage that had never been marred by a faulty ancestor. Carefully bred to attain the utmost in speed and endurance, this superb specimen of desert-bred horse would carry a man far and fast. But it would call upon every atom of strength and every fibre of gameness to out-travel the stout, fresh horses of the outlaws.

Black Arab seemed to know that he would have to give much, perhaps all, to win this desperate race. His sleek, hard muscles knotted and flexed. Eagerly, the black gelding took the challenge. Panhandle talked to him in a low voice that was soft with admiration and love.

The trail climbed to a wide mesa. Here was Panhandle's chance to swing around and pass the outlaws. Out and around. By way of a twisting cattle trail. Out and around the hard-riding outlaws at a swinging lope. Adding a few more miles because of the circuit he must make to pass.

There was a faint light now as the moon pushed up over the skyline. The black gelding was giving his best and Panhandle had to ride with a tight rein. Suddenly, the tall Texan gave a sharp exclamation. He had not swerved far enough from the main trail. There, not fifty yards to one side, rode Boudry and his men. Panhandle swung abruptly to one side. Rifles cracked. Bullets snarled and

128

whined. Panhandle gave Black Arab free rein and flattened himself along the horse's neck. Seconds of agonizing fear. Seconds that seemed eternity. The bullets were going wild now, missing by a wide margin. Ten minutes later, Panhandle breathed more freely. Black Arab had left the other horses behind. Now for a gruelling pace that would let horse and man hold that lead. For Boudry would ride hard to overtake him.

Panhandle was using every bit of his horseman's skill to save the Black Arab, using every little trick he knew to lighten his burden. Tired as he was, he rode up with his horse, so that there was not a pound of dead weight to increase the burden of his weight. No jockey ever rode a finer race. Chancing that there would be guns at the ranch, Panhandle threw away his carbine and most of his ammunition, thus lightening the burden. A few miles farther on, he discarded his heavy saddle and rode bareback. He slipped off the heavy bridle and rode with a hackamore. Even his boots and chaps and hat were discarded. Like many another cowboy, Panhandle had ridden through his first youthful years without benefit of saddle. He knew how to ride, that lean Texan, with the skill of an Indian.

Hour after hour at a steady trot. Black Arab had his second wind now. And when they forded a creek, the wise horse knew better than to touch the water.

No sounds of pursuit. Perhaps Boudry did not suspect his purpose. Perhaps the renegade discounted the ability of one man to hurt his plans. Panhandle eased the black horse down to a quieter gait.

Dawn was cracking the skyline when Panhandle rode into the Flying W Ranch a scant mile ahead of the Boudry gang. Old Taller, the Flying W cook, was already up. He stepped to the kitchen door, rifle in hand.

'Save your bullets for the Boudry layout,' called Panhandle. 'Wake Miss Murphy and the kid. Get the doors barred and locate me a Winchester and lots of shells. I'm gonna take care of this horse, then we'll learn Jim Boudry some tricks. Make 'em fast, old-timer, they're only about a mile behind.'

'Who are you, anyhow?' growled old Taller suspiciously.

'He's Pat Roper's ramrod,' chirped Sid's voice as the

boy appeared half dressed. 'He's all right, Taller.'

Panhandle was already at the barn, rubbing down the loyal-hearted Black Arab. He let the black horse drink a little, then opened the gate that led to the pasture. 'You'll be safer there than in the barn, old boy. You sure are a horse. The best horse in the world, old man. Now trot down there outa sight, take a good healthy roll, and go to grazin'. They're crowdin' me too doggoned close, you understand, to let me take care of you as I'd like to. But I'll shore tell the little girl all about you.'

Black Arab rolled luxuriously, then trotted off, head and tail up, gamely hiding the weariness of that hard trip. Boudry and his men were in sight as Panhandle ran to the house. Taller thrust a Winchester into his hands. The old cook was likewise armed. Tommy and Sid each had small calibred rifles.

It was Taller's impatience that warned Boudry. The old fellow had cocked his rifle in a moment of excitement. The rifle had a sensitive trigger. And just as Panhandle was telling them to be quiet and let the outlaws come up within range. Taller's gun accidentally went off.

With a quick oath, Boudry jumped his horse into the shelter of some calf sheds, his men at his heels.

'Take a club,' groaned Taller, 'and whip me over the head.'

'It's done,' said Panhandle ruefully, 'and knockin' you over the head won't help none. I never seen but one cook that had gun sense, and he was the worst cook in ten counties. He swelled up and died one day and the coroner decided his own cookin' had poisoned him. See that jasper's foot a-stickin' out around the corner of the shed? Well, watch ol' kid Panhandle trip his corns.'

The Texan's rifle cracked and the man jerked back his foot with a sharp cry. Panhandle grinned. 'That's a good joke on that feller, ain't it? It may plumb ruin him for dancin' and such. Taller, when you get time, could you rassle me a cup of java and mebby a biscuit? I'm behind on my grazin'. Seems like I ain't et for a month.'

'I'll get the grub,' said Tommy.

'Just any old thing,' said Panhandle. He kept up a steady flow of careless chatter, telling her what little he knew of the fight on the lower Concho.

130

'Stands to reason, ma'am, that Boudry was gittin' licked, and that's how come he tried to run for it. We kin be lookin' for Pat, and your daddy almost any time, now.'

Now came Boudry's hard voice, thick with anger. 'We'll give you five minutes to open them doors and come out, peaceful and quiet. Surrender now and nobody will get hurt. But if you don't throw away them guns and come out in five minutes, we'll set fire to the ranch. We'll smoke you out and treat you rough. What do you say to that?'

'I can't say it, Boudry. There's a lady present.'

'If they set them haystacks afire,' growled Taller, 'and the breeze a-pullin' in this direction, we'll be broiled alive.'

'Ain't you the cheerful thing!' Panhandle hid his fears with a wink and a grin at Tommy and Sid. Sid's shirt had come unbuttoned, and Panhandle saw the ugly red welts of the Two Block brand which Boudry had burned there. There was a queer glint in the boy's eyes, and his hands gripped the .22 high-power rifle. Beside the boy stood Tommy Murphy. In her overalls, high-heeled boots, and flannel shirt, she looked like a boy. If she was afraid, she hid her fear well.

'Givin' ourselves up won't help the situation none,' said the tall Texan. 'Boudry's word ain't worth a plugged dime. He's aimin' to set fire to the haystacks and burn us out. We got five minutes to do somethin'. And I got a scheme that's just about wild enough to pan out.

'Taller, I want you to take Sid and go into that front room. From there, you kin throw lead enough to keep Boudry and his men behind the sheds. Throw enough bullets there and they'll be a-scared to show a nose. And while you're keepin' 'em under cover, I'll slip acrost to that cowshed where they left their horses. At the same time, lady, you hit for the barn. That horse I swapped you for that black is rested enough to stand a ride. And while I keep the Boudry outfit cut off from their horses, you ride for the Flyin' W round-up camp. They won't shoot a woman, I don't reckon. And once you're gone, and I explain to Mister Boudry how Pat, and Wig Murphy, and Seth Harker is ridin' this way, and let Boudry and his skunks get their horses, they'll ride hard for New Mexico.'

'I won't run off and leave you three boys,' said Tommy stoutly.

131

'But you gotta do it, ma'am. It's you that Jim Boudry is after. And it's a cinch that his men ain't pleased with the idee of losin' time here over a woman. Taller, you and Sid rattle your hocks now. Pepper them shed corners with bullets. Once I get to that cowshed, I'll have the drop on 'em, and it'll be my turn to talk turkey.'

'Good headwork,' chuckled old Taller. 'Come on, Sid.'

A moment later, the boy and the old cook were keeping the Boudry faction behind cover. Panhandle opened the kitchen door.

'You wait here till I holler for you to go, lady. Then get that horse and ride like you had a date with a million dollars and was ten minutes late in startin'. No argument, now. So long.'

Panhandle leaped from the open doorway, his long legs covering the ground in great strides. From somewhere a rifle cracked. Panhandle staggered a little, swerving in his stride, then sped on. He dodged in among the frightened horses. His gun cracked. And the man who had taken a snapshot at Panhandle, crumpled.

'Stand your hands, you polecats!' barked Panhandle's voice. 'I got Boudry covered and I'm rearin' to shoot. Stand your hands. Fust man that moves, I'll drop Jim Boudry.'

Boudry and his men, crouched against the log wall, saw a carbine barrel poked through the chinking between the logs of the cowshed.

'Now listen, you snakes!' continued Panhandle. 'I just killed one of your gang. I got the drop on the rest of you. So don't get funny. Boudry come here to bother Wig Murphy's daughter. And the rest of you tinhorn sports follered along, wastin' time that you shore need if you're aimin' to quit the country. Listen to Boudry and you'll all hang. Do as I tell you, and bimeby you kin hit the trail for New Mexico. And gents, you better ride hard and fast, because my pardner has got word to Pat Roper and Wig Murphy and the others that you boys is bent on travellin'. We was hid in the brush while you passed up the trail outa the lower Concho. I come here and the cowboy with me took word to Roper and Murphy. That's the lay of the land. Boudry's delayin' your game, because he's stuck on Wig Murphy's daughter, you poor bone-heads!'

Panhandle raised his voice to a jubilant shout. 'I got 'em in the sack, lady. Do your stuff. I'll drop the first one of these coyotes that makes a move.'

Panhandle saw Tommy run to the barn. A few moments later, she rode away at a run. Panhandle grinned mirthlessly. Blood was flowing from a bullet hole that, by some miracle, had missed his heart. The steel-jacketed bullet had smashed a rib and torn a hole in his shoulder muscle. Each breath he took stabbed like a dull knife. A dangerous wound. Unless it had proper care, he would bleed to death.

'Stand your hands, you curly wolves,' he flung the warning through set teeth, 'or I'll begin the slaughter.'

Panhandle's brain was still clear, in spite of the dizziness and nausea from pain. He knew that it was only his keyed up nerves that kept his brain from reeling. It was now a question of how long he could hold out. No use in taking these men prisoners. Old Taller and Sid could never hold them. And it would be only half an hour or so until pain and loss of blood would render him unconscious. Better to let the girl get a fifteen-minute start, then let these border renegades ride on their way.

'Supposin',' he called to the helpless, raging men, 'that I decided not to kill you? Which way would you ride?'

'Not after the woman, bet on that!' growled one of Boudry's men.

'I'm givin' the little lady a long start, boys. Then I'll let you travel along. I got nothin' agin' you personal. It's jest part of my job. I'm even lettin' Boudry go. I gave my promise to Seth Harker that I'd save Boudry for him. Seth'd be awful put out if I was to weaken to temptation and put a bullet in Boudry. Seth'll be along after a while. So I'm savin' Boudry for the last. After you boys has pulled out, I'll let Jim Boudry go. He'll be forkin' the sorriest horse, and he won't be able to ketch up if you boys travel fast which you'd better do if you don't want to be ketched.'

With a string of curses, Jim Boudry stood up from his crouching posture. Panhandle's carbine roared twice, and Boudry ducked back behind his men. There were two holes in his high-crowned hat.

'Stay down, Boudry, or I'll plant the next one square

between your eyes and save Seth Harker the trouble. Now, boys, come up one at a time. But leave your guns behind. The last man, exceptin' Boudry, who follers the drag end, will fetch along your artillery, providin' you all act nice. I'm givin' you fellers your chance. If you're wise, you'll do like I say.'

'That goes with us, mister.'

One by one, they got their horses and rode away, glad of the chance to get beyond range of the tall Texan's carbine. The last man rode off, loaded down with guns. Only Jim Boudry remained behind.

Perhaps the big renegade, with fatalistic vision, pictured the rope and scaffold that would be his deserts if captured alive. It may be that he dreaded that inevitable meeting with Captain Seth Harker. Or it might have been that the man was, after all, courageous.

At any rate, he swaggered forward, crouched a little from the waist, shooting with two six-shooters at the cowboy inside the shed. He could not hope to hit the man who crouched behind the thick logs. Yet he emptied both guns. A dazed look crept into his eyes when Panhandle did not return his fire. His guns empty, his bravado seemed to wilt. He stood there, his guns empty in his hand, horror stamped on his face, waiting for Panhandle to kill him.

For a long minute Jim Boudry stood there, waiting for death. Then, reeling like a drunken man, he made his way to the two horses that stood snorting, their hackamore ropes in the stiffening hand of the dead man. He mounted one of the horses and rode away, hanging to the saddle horn, like one on his way to meet death.

But Panhandle did not see him leave. The tall Texan had not even heard the roar of the big outlaw's guns. Because he lay in a huddled heap, as a dead man lies, the blood oozing sluggishly from the wound in his chest, his still form in the log manger. Panhandle had passed out. He had endured all that any man could endure. Pain and exhaustion had drained his endurance to its final drop.

So Taller and Sid found Panhandle and carried him back to the house.

'Is he dead, Taller?' asked Sid.

'Nope. I've seen worse. These Texas cowhands is tough. Fetch me a sheet from Tommy's room, while I cut off his shirt. Then locate me a bottle of Wig's corn whisky while I get some warm water and a drop or two of carbolic. We'll have this cowboy patched up in no time.'

Panhandle opened his eyes. 'Are they gone, Taller?'

'Boudry was the last to high-tail it, son. And he shore looked sick. Now, lay quiet till I get this hole in you patched up.'

'If your doctorin' is as good as your cookin',' Panhandle grinned, 'I'll get well. Has Pat Roper or Wig Murphy showed up yet?'

'Not yet.'

'Then I reckon somethin' must 'a' happened to that cowboy. They never got my message.'

Nor was Panhandle far from wrong. A chance bullet had killed the Two Block cowboy just before he joined the Flying W men. Death had struck out the message.

Chapter XXIII

Dawn found the battle on the lower Concho ended. Boudry's men laid down their guns. Except for a few wounded and one dead outlaw, there were no further casualties. The Two Block cowpunchers had arrived shortly before dawn, and against these big odds the outlaws lost their false courage. And when they discovered that Boudry and his lieutenants had deserted, their denunciation was indeed bitter.

Two leaders on the other side were also missing. There was no trace of Pablo Guerrero or Captain Seth Harker. They, also, had vanished some time during the night.

'I told Pablo I aimed to have a showdown,' growled Wig Murphy, as Billy Carter patched up the cowman's shoulder. 'I reckon I scared him off.'

'I wouldn't gamble too much on Pablo scarin',' said Billy.

'Nobody asked your opinion. Dang it, you're fired anyhow!'

'Which,' grinned Billy, 'gives me the right to say what I doggone please on any subject that pops into my head.' And he grinned the wider when Wig swore lustily.

Pat Roper rode up. 'I hear you made the crack you was goin' to kill me when you found me, Murphy?'

'I did. And I'll do so, quick as this shoulder is fixed. Git a move on, Billy.'

'Ain't you kinda goin' off half-cocked?' asked Pat Roper.

'Don't go givin' me advice, you young cow thief. I know enough to see through your game. You think you kin marry my daughter and kinda edge into the Flyin' W. I know your game. You and Pablo make a good team. He got cold feet and run off.'

'If Pablo ran off, he'll come back,' put in Billy Carter, 'because he don't scare worth a darn, Wig, and you know it.'

'Quit hornin' in, Billy Carter! You get your men together and head for the home ranch.'

'Gather your own men. You fired me, and that goes as it lays. I've hired out to the Two Block.'

'You'd quit me when I'm in a tight, after all I've done for you?'

'When I'm fired, I stay fired,' grinned Billy. 'I've hired out to Pat Roper of the Two Block. We're startin' in, tomorrow, gatherin' them PR cattle.'

'Tomorrow,' said Wig Murphy savagely, 'you'll be attendin' Pat Roper's funeral— Where's my gun? Billy, did you—'

'Did I see your guns? I did, for a fact, Wig. When you got kinda faintish a while ago, I lifted your guns. You're as harmless as a rattler with his fangs pulled.'

'You—you—' Wig purpled with anger. Billy and Pat grinned.

'We got him a-stutterin', Pat. Too bad Tommy ain't here. You may figger you're lucky, pardner, but I wouldn't have Wig Murphy for a daddy-in-law for all the cattle in Arizona.'

'I'll have to take some grief along with the good breaks, Billy. I give Tommy my word I wouldn't get into a jangle with her dad. Just like I promised Seth Harker I'd give Pablo a chance to explain about them PR cattle.'

'Do you know where Pablo and Seth went, Pat?' asked Billy.

'Do you, Billy?'

'I'll make a guess that they're a-trailin' Jim Boudry. Seth would like to take Boudry alive. So would Pablo. Mebby they will, but most mebby they'll have to kill him— Wig, there's a lady waitin' to see you about them cattle Pablo fetched up.'

'A lady?' gasped Wig. 'You mean Tommy?'

'She says her name is Rosita de la Vaca and she wants the wide world to know that she's gonna marry Pablo Guerrero. And that if a big barbarian named Wig Murphy

137

has killed Pablo, she'll come back here with a bunch of Yaquis and mop up the range around here. What I mean to say, Wig, that lady is on the prod.'

'Send her on her way, Billy. I never could talk with a woman.'

But Rosita de la Vaca was not to be easily got rid of. She came up now, accompanied by two embarrassed-looking cowpunchers. She faced Wig with blazing eyes.

'You have killed my Pablo, you beeg barbarian?' she snapped the accusation at the bewildered cowman.

'Young lady, I don't know where your Pablo is. Trot along and don't bother me. And when you meet your Pablo, tell him I'll pay them five hundred head of cattle the next time we have snow in July at Yuma.'

'*Dios,* do you never think except in terms of cattle? A Señor Pat Roper ess steal five hundred cattle from you. My Pablo, because he ees the honest man, return those same cattle. Ees that not so, Señor Roper?'

'How you knowed my name, or how you get the idea that Pablo's so gosh-darned honest, I don't know,' grinned Pat, 'but I shore did swipe them cattle, and Pablo Guerrero shore fetched 'em back.'

'You stole them cattle?' roared Wig. 'You admit it?'

'Why not? I wouldn't dispute this lady's word for anything. You got your cattle back, what's your holler about?'

'Pablo's askin' only twenty-five thousand dollars for them cattle. That's what I'm hollerin' about. But I'm through payin' that slick hombre any more money.'

'Did Pablo ask you for that money, señor?' asked the girl.

'Ain't you the young woman that works in Arturo Gonzales' office?' barked the harrassed cowman. 'You shore are. And you was probably listenin' at the keyhole when that oily snake put me the propositon.'

'I do not listen at keyholes, señor. That is w'at you call the old stuff. I have the dictaphone made in the wall. I hear very plainly what Arturo Gonzales say and what you reply. And you break the glass in the door when you leave. If you are so brave, why did you not break the neck of Arturo Gonzales?'

'Huh?' gasped Wig.

'Because Arturo is the very smooth article, señor. He is

138

a very expert liar. And because you are so stupid, you believe that liar. Arturo Gonzales will not lie any more. He is, by now, very, very dead. And for the sake of hees wife, who ees no longer beautiful, I am glad. On the life insurance hees widow collects, she may live in comfort.'

'I ain't interested in widder woman,' growled Wig. "Billy, get rid of this woman before she pulls a knife or somethin'.'

'Seems like she's worried about Pablo, Wig. And so if you know where he is, you better come clean.'

'Ask Roper,' suggested Wig. 'He's Pablo's pardner.'

Rosita stamped her booted foot. 'If my Pablo ees gone on a little trip, then I do not worry. But Señor Murphy, if you have keel Pablo, I tell you now that before tomorrow you also die.'

'Lady,' said Pat Roper, 'Pablo rode away some time durin' the night with Captain Seth Harker of the rangers. I think they set out to find a gringo named Jim Boudry.'

'*Gracias,* Señor Roper. You make me very happy. Then my Pablo weel return to me. Because Pablo say you are a man of honour, I believe you. But thees beeg barbarian, he ees the double-cross'. He even pay much money when he theenks Pablo ees get kill' by the firing squad. And still my Pablo, who ees like the trustful boy, he say he has the great admiration for Señor Murphy. Pablo calls heem the very amusing enemy. But for these five hundred cattle, he asks of Señor Murphy not one single peso. They are the wedding present to the Señorita Murphy when she marries Pablo's very good friend, Pat Roper.

'Pablo explain to me like thees: *"Querida,"* he say to me, "thees Señorita Murphy ees very wonderful girl. My friend Pat Roper ees a man of honour, a true caballero. Would it be nice, then, for Pablo to bleed the pesos from the father-in-law of my good friend Pat Roper and the papa of the bride? No, *querida,* and it makes me very sad to lose such an amusing enemy like Señor Murphy. But such ees the case. I must look elsewhere for the pesos to maintain my brave Yaquis." And my Pablo swears the solemn oath to never again take the pesos from Señor Murphy.'

'The sentimental idiot,' growled Wig Murphy. 'I suppose

139

he'll get married now and go to raisin' sheep. The lovesick chump.' His hard eyes twinkled brightly under their bushy brows.

'Miss Rosita, no man or woman ever called ol' Wig Murphy a bad loser. You've stole my pet enemy off me. You've shore licked me. Let me know when you get married so I kin send you a little somethin'. You're gettin' the biggest rascal unhung, barrin' Wig Murphy. And since him and me can't go on bein' enemies, I hope we kin be good friends. If ever you need me, holler. Good luck to you both.' And he flushed crimson as the impulsive Rosita, with a choked little cry, threw her arms about his neck and kissed him quickly.

'There, señor. Now we can never be enemies again. You have make me very happy—my friend. And now, señors, *adios!*'

When Rosita de la Vaca had gone, old Wig Murphy scowled at Billy Carter and Pat Roper.

'Billy,' he growled, 'you got plenty of faults, but I never knowed you to make a mistake in sizin' up a man. What's your honest opinion of Pat Roper, here?'

'Pat's a white man, Wig. About the whitest man I ever met.'

'You're willin' he should take Tommy away from us?'

'I'd hate to see her pick any other man, Wig.'

'Then I reckon that settles it. I'd always kinda hoped you and Tommy would hit it off together, Billy. You'd growed up together like a brother and sister. But if you say Pat Roper is right, then he shore must be a winner. To tell the truth, I bin of that same opinion from the start. Shake, son.'

Chapter XXIV

Now, Jim Boudry rode alone. Ahead showed the blue peaks that meant a goal of safety. Another night and he would be drinking and boasting among the scurvy crowd of renegades that made their home in the fastness of those mountains. Under his leadership, those furtive outlaws would become bold. He would feed them on *marijuana* and tequila and lead them forth to pillage and murder honest ranchers.

His trail led through a deep arroyo, clogged with brush and boulders.

'Reach for the blue sky, Boudry!' Captain Seth Harker stepped out on to the trail, a long-barrelled six-shooter in his hand.

'Pronto, Señor Boudry!' And Pablo appeared from the brush.

'Take him, Pablo. Step off, Boudry, and tell Pablo the truth when he questions you.'

'Thank you, my frien',' smiled Pablo. 'You will give to me, Boudry, the names of those men who pay you to run guns across the line.'

'They'd kill me, if I told.'

'You are mistake,' smiled the Mexican. 'Those *muy maldito* hombres are not killing anybody. They are dead. Arturo Gonzales no longer lives. He is the chief, no?'

'He hired me,' admitted Boudry, 'Pancho Cordova and Aurelio Lopez received the guns.'

'And paid you, not een money, but een opium, and morphine, and cocaine?'

'Yes.'

Pablo nodded and smiled at Seth Harker. 'Did I not say that I made no mistake when I lined up those two hombres and let them die before the firing squad? And so put Sonora to the trouble of finding new customs officers. That ees all, Boudry.'

'I kin go?'

'Directly, Boudry,' said Seth Harker bluntly, and ignoring the outlaw, held out his hand to Pablo.

'So long, pardner. And good luck! Give my regards to Miss Rosita and tell her I'll be there for the wedding if I'm not in my grave.'

'*Adios,* my frien'.'

Pablo Guerrero mounted his horse and rode away. Seth Harker walked into a brush path and mounted. Jim Boudry watched the ranger's movements with a puzzled scowl.

'Well, Boudry,' said the wiry little captain of the rangers, 'this'll be the last time I'll ever see you alive, I reckon, unless I kin get time off to attend your hangin'. They're gonna hang you for the murder of Tim Collins. No matter which way you ride from here, Boudry, you'll run into my men. They got orders to fetch you in dead or alive. Your game's finished.' He grinned crookedly. 'So long, Jim Boudry!'

Seth Harker turned to ride away. With a snarl, Jim Boudry jerked his gun. As flame streaked from the outlaw's gun-barrel, Seth Harker quit his saddle with the agility of a startled cat. It seemed that his six-shooter cracked even before he lit on the ground. Boudry's knees buckled, and he dropped, an ugly black hole between his eyes.

Seth Harker smiled queerly. There was a bullet hole through his cheek. He fished a clean handkerchief from his pocket and held it to his wounded face. He glanced from the dead outlaw to the long-barrelled gun in his hand.

'Well, Tim, old pardner,' he said aloud, 'I got 'im! Got 'im with your old gun. He aimed to get me like he got you, Tim, but that was what I figgered he'd do. So I got him. He took his chance, Tim. And saved hangin' expenses.'

Captain Seth Harker mounted and rode toward town without even a backward glance at the dead outlaw.

'I bet I'll lose a couple of teeth,' he mused. 'But it was worth it—Tim's gun that I swiped from Pat Roper's

142

cabin. Same gun he took from li'l ol' Sid—I hope that fool coroner an' two-bit sheriff don't claim that Boudry is Bob Pinkerton or Burns— Hope this face of mine will get healed in time for Pablo's weddin'. Lucky I had my fool mouth open or I'd lost my upper store teeth— Get along, pony! We gotta ketch that El Paso train. That vacation of mine is up tomorrow —Tim, old pardner, you was right when you claimed this six-gun never missed an—'

It was near midnight that night. Camp fires burned where the Two Block and Flying W round-ups camped on the river bank just below the Flying W home ranch. The horse bells of the recovered remudas tinkled in the moonlight.

Inside the house, old Wig Murphy, Billy Carter, and Panhandle played seven-up. The sheriff had taken his posse and his prisoners to town, a wiser, more humble sheriff than the one who had tried to arrest Pat Roper.

In a corner of the room, Sid Collins dozed over a thrilling detective yarn. Sid was the official Two Block rep. His dun pony was down in the pasture with Tommy's Black Arab and Pat's big bay. Near them grazed a small mule and a horse that awaited the return of Seth Harker, who had left word that he would be back soon.

Under a giant sycamore tree sat Tommy and Pat Roper, sometimes talking in low tones, sometimes silent as they dreamed out their future.

'Listen, honey,' whispered Pat Roper.

Filtering through the moonlight came a Mexican love song. A very old love song, 'Love is a Butterfly':

'Es el amor maiposa, Caque a la salido del sol—'

Pablo, heading south on the winding trail that would take him to where love awaited him. Nor would he pull rein until he found his Rosita. For that is the way of a caballero in love.

A little sad, a little wistful, that song. For who, save the *Señor Dios,* could know how long Pablo was fated to ride his reckless way? Pablo, who had paused to gaze at many flowers in the garden and had at last chosen the most beautiful of the red roses of Mexico. As a rider might lean from his saddle to snatch at a rose, so Pablo had taken the

143

love of Rosita de la Vaca. At some adobe-walled mission there waited a brown-cowled padre. A white-haired padre who was father to a people whose hearts never grow old. Ministering, understanding, baptizing, marrying, comforting, burying with a final prayer. Such as the hard-riding, gay-hearted Pablo, and the fiery, loyal Rosita, were the children he most loved. For such as they more sorely needed his blessings. For them he knelt before his altar, with its onyx baptismal font, its images of saints, its candles, wearing threadbare that brown robe that cushioned his aged knees on hand-hewn, wooden kneeling benches. For them he counted his wooden rosary, worn thin by prayers. Those were his children. Gay and sad, fierce in their hatreds, generous in their love. So waited that white-haired, brown-robed man of God to sanction the love of Rosita de la Vaca and Pablo Guerrero. There behind the white-washed wall of his patio garden.

Beyond there, somewhere beyond, was another adobe wall, its whitewash pocked by bullet scars.

Some day, some early morning, Pablo Guerrero would stand with his straight back against that wall, a last cigarette between lips that would not tremble. His slender brown hands would bare his chest. His level gaze would not falter. His voice would come from bravely smiling lips:

'Shoot well, *hombrecitos*.'

For this is the way of a caballero.

And at sunset a black-garbed woman would kneel with a brown-cowled padre beside the fresh earth of a grave.

'Es el amor maiposa—'

The song of Pablo Guerrero was lost in the distance.

PONY SOLDIERS

They were a dirty, undisciplined rabble, but they were the only chance a thousand settlers had to see another sunrise. Killing was their profession and they took pride in their work—they were too fierce to live, too damn mean to die.

_____ 2620-1   #5: SIOUX SHOWDOWN
                        $2.75 US/$3.75 CAN

_____ 2598-1   #4: CHEYENNE BLOOD STORM
                        $2.75US/$3.75CAN

_____ 2565-5   #3: COMANCHE MOON
                        $2.75US/$3.75CAN

_____ 2541-8   #2: COMANCHE MASSACRE
                        $2.75US/$3.75CAN

_____ 2518-3   #1: SLAUGHTER AT BUFFALO
                       CREEK $2.75US/$3.75CAN

LEISURE BOOKS
ATTN: Customer Service Dept.
276 5th Avenue, New York, NY 10001

Please send me the book(s) checked above. I have enclosed $_____
Add $1.25 for shipping and handling for the first book; $ .30 for each book thereafter. No cash, stamps, or C.O.D.s. All orders shipped within 6 weeks. Canadian orders please add $1.00 extra postage.

Name _____

Address _____

City_____State_____Zip_____

Canadian orders must be paid in U.S. dollars payable through a New York banking facility.   ☐ Please send a free catalogue.